MIKKI AND ME AND THE OUT-OF-TUNE TREE

MARION ROBERTS
MIKKI AND ME AND THE OUT-OF-TUNE TREE

ALLEN&UNWIN
SYDNEY·MELBOURNE·AUCKLAND·LONDON

First published by Allen & Unwin in 2022

Copyright © Marion Roberts 2022

All rights reserved. No part of this book may be reproduced or transmitted in any form or by any means, electronic or mechanical, including photocopying, recording or by any information storage and retrieval system, without prior permission in writing from the publisher. The Australian *Copyright Act 1968* (the Act) allows a maximum of one chapter or ten per cent of this book, whichever is the greater, to be photocopied by any educational institution for its educational purposes provided that the educational institution (or body that administers it) has given a remuneration notice to the Copyright Agency (Australia) under the Act.

Allen & Unwin
83 Alexander Street
Crows Nest NSW 2065
Australia
Phone: (61 2) 8425 0100
Email: info@allenandunwin.com
Web: www.allenandunwin.com

A catalogue record for this book is available from the National Library of Australia

ISBN 978 1 76052 679 5

For teaching resources, explore www.allenandunwin.com/resources/for-teachers

Cover and text design by Debra Billson
Cover illustrations by Shutterstock: sky by one AND only; trees by Cat_arch_angel; galah by Daiquiri; boy by NotionPic; bicycle by alphabe; girl by coffee hop; and notes by 123Done.
Internal illustrations by Shutterstock: emojis by Carboxylase; kanji by Alexandra Leikina; and trees by jenny on the moon.

The quote on page 287 is taken from page 28 of Diana Beresford-Kroeger's *The Global Forest: 40 Ways Trees Can Save Us*, published by Particular Books an imprint of Penguin Books in 2011.

Set in 11/16 pt ITC New Baskerville by Midland Typesetters, Australia
Printed in February 2022 in Australia by McPherson's Printing Group

10 9 8 7 6 5 4 3 2 1

The paper in this book is FSC® certified. FSC® promotes environmentally responsible, socially beneficial and economically viable management of the world's forests.

For Otis and Maggie

CHAPTER 1

So, not only is my mother the current world expert on table manners and social etiquette (her book has sold literally millions of copies), but today Mum found out she's been invited to do a TED Talk in Sydney. That's why we were meant to be celebrating, even if I still couldn't believe anyone would want to read a book or listen to a talk about table manners. As if the whole tidying-up frenzy a few years back wasn't enough! Can you imagine what mealtimes are like at our place since *Tammy Bracken's Guide to Modern Manners* hit the Amazon Best Sellers list? Sascha has even stopped begging for treats under the table, and that's saying a lot considering Labradors are famous for overeating.

Clementine and I had made fish tacos. Clementine's my younger sister and if I was being a complete liar I'd pretend she wasn't annoying. If only! In our house, Clementine is a constant cause of chaos. Especially when she's around Mum, which isn't even that much these days considering Mum's always locked in her den.

Mum has a strict closed-door policy when it comes to her den. She says, *How else am I supposed to get any work done?* Clementine and I are hardly allowed to make a peep. Summer break has only just started. We should be the ones saying, *How are we expected to have any fun?*

According to *Tammy Bracken's Guide to Modern Manners*, tacos are one of the few meals that are acceptable to eat with your hands, which is why Clementine had wanted to make them.

> **Tammy's Tips**
> #1 EATING WITH ONE'S HANDS
> *Meals should be eaten with a knife and a fork — not with fingers and hands. The only exceptions to this rule are when eating pizza, corn on the cob, French fries, sandwiches, and tacos or other wraps where fillings may fall out.*

If Clementine had it her way she'd eat every meal with her hands, even soup. Clementine had already set the table. No cutlery at all, a sure-fire trigger for one of Mum's manners rants. Would it have killed Clementine to put down the odd fork? I just wasn't in the mood for any of Clementine's antics. I was feeling gloomy about Sylvie, who up until then I'd thought was my best friend.

There was absolutely no denying that ever since school had broken up, when Sylvie had 'accidentally' left me off the socials group for the beach gathering, she'd been acting super weird. I was slowly starting to put all the puzzle pieces together. Sylvie didn't invite me back to her place after the silent disco in the school hall either, then pretended it was just another mistake. Did she think I wouldn't notice? In a small town like Kingfisher Bay everyone notices everything, believe me! Especially now that there are hardly any tourists. Not since the sewerage spill in the front beach car park, which is way too disgusting to think about when you're about to eat a fish taco.

Anyway, that afternoon at the back beach, it was official – Sylvie was acting weird. We had been bobbing out on the waves on our boogie boards when Sylvie started talking all cryptic about my parents.

'So how does your mum even still talk to him?' Sylvie asked, literally out of the blue.

'To who?' I asked.

'Your dad!' she scoffed.

Why would Sylvie know the first little thing about my dad? Who even cared about other people's parents anyway?

Sylvie and I never finished the conversation. Before I could ask what she meant she was paddling like a machine, kicking her feet and lining herself up to take the next wave. But it was obvious that Sylvie knew something. And whatever it was, it wasn't good and it was about my dad, which made me want to stick up for him. Everyone knows you're the only one who's allowed to actually bag out your own parent.

Dad took a big bite of his fish taco. 'Mmm!' he said. 'Delicious salsa, girls, love the fresh coriander!'

'Thanks, Dad!' said Clementine, licking her fingers.

'Clementine!' Mum scolded. 'I accept that this is an eat-with-your-hands situation but that doesn't mean you can eat like a barbarian. Use your napkin, please!'

Clementine put the half-eaten taco back on her plate, licked her fingers again then wiped her face with her napkin.

'And, Alberta,' Mum snapped, 'how many times do I have to tell you to disconnect your elbows from the table?'

It was going to be one of those dinners for sure. I gave Dad my best basset hound eyes. *Do something!* I silently pleaded.

Tammy's Tips

#2 ELBOWS

There should be no elbows on the table! In my opinion a 'no elbows on the table' rule demonstrates good manners and proper table etiquette.

'How's the TED Talk coming along, love?' Dad asked cheerfully, passing Mum the platter of fish.

'Fine,' said Mum in a capital letter FINE kind of way, which everyone knows means, *I'm not at all fine.* As I watched Mum struggling to fit two chunks of fish plus some avocado and tomato salsa into her tortilla, I couldn't help thinking of what Sylvie had said that afternoon in the water again. That's when most of Mum's taco filling spilled out onto her plate.

'Damn it! How on earth are you meant to eat these things?'

'I'll show you,' Clementine said eagerly. She positioned her half-eaten taco, tomato juice dripping down her wrists, and shoved the whole thing into her mouth. 'Nike dis!' she muffled.

Mum pulled her lips into a tight thin line and clenched her teeth. The muscles in her jaw bulged. She was on the verge of a total table manners meltdown. Dad lowered his head, bracing himself for the oncoming explosion. Somebody had to come up with a distraction!

'Dad?' I asked. 'What's happening with that cottage? The one in the middle of the Bunnings car park. Anyone bought it yet?'

My dad worked at Kingfisher Bay Real Estate and asking him about the properties he had listed was *the* best defence against Mum's manners rants. Dad looked relieved.

'Funny you should ask, Alberta.'

'Hilarious!' Clementine said sarcastically, still chewing.

'I had to go there today as a matter of fact,' Dad said. 'Unfortunately there hasn't been much interest on account of the—'

'Poo?' Clementine asked. A cube of diced tomato shot from her mouth onto the table. Mum's face turned a similar shade of tomato red.

'That's it!' she yelled. 'Clementine, if you are going to make a complete mockery of proper table etiquette then you can jolly well skip dinner and go to your room!'

Clementine's chair scraped the floor.

'Fine!' she said, swallowing hard. She picked up her plate and stomped into the kitchen, clanged it into the sink and stomped down the hall to her room. Dad was just about to resume his story when she slammed her bedroom door. The three of us sat in silence, as if to recover. Then Clementine opened her bedroom door again and at the top of her voice screamed down the hall, 'Daaaaaaaad! Can I use your iPad?' Mum shot Dad a stern look.

'Surely you're not going to reward this terrible behaviour?' Mum whisper-hissed.

But we all knew that while giving into Clementine might not be the best strategy for her personal growth, it did mean we'd get to finish dinner in peace.

'Only if you calm down!' Dad yelled. Clementine stomped into the kitchen and took Dad's iPad from its charger. We all held our breath until we heard her bedroom door slam again.

I sighed 'So...why is there a cottage in the middle of the Bunnings car park anyway?'

'Well, apparently,' Dad said, 'when Bunnings was built they knocked down two whole streets of old miner's cottages to make the car park.'

'Typical,' said Mum. 'People these days have absolutely no respect for history or tradition.'

'But there was one old lady who just refused to sell,' Dad continued.

'That'd be me,' I said, reaching for another tortilla. Mum smacked my hand and swept the plate out of reach.

'Don't stretch across the table like that, Alberta! Ask for the plate to be passed to you!'

'But Bunnings didn't think for a minute that an old lady just might have all the money in the world to fight it out in court,' Dad went on.

'Love her!' I said.

'And would you believe, she won?'

'Well, isn't that glaringly obvious, Roger?' Mum said. 'The cottage is still there.'

'That'll show 'em!' I said.

'Still, that the poor old lady had to live out the rest of her days surrounded by a miserable car park!' Mum pointed out.

> ### ❦ Tammy's Tips ❦
> #### #3 REACHING
> *Don't lean past the person sitting next to you. If a share plate is present it should be passed around the table. Each diner should hold it for the person next to him or her to serve themselves, using only the serving utensils provided.*

Just then Clementine was stomping back down the hall with Dad's iPad, her face lit up by the screen in the dark hallway. What was it this time?

'Dad, who is Ursula Hoffman and why is she messaging you about some dream she had?'

CHAPTER 2

I woke up to the smell of burnt toast and the sound of Mum tapping on her computer in the den. You could always tell what sort of a mood Mum was in by how fast and loud she tapped. Today was one of her faster, louder, more furious sounding tapping days. Dad would already be at work, Clementine would be outside doing her circus training drills and Sascha would no doubt be lying in the morning sun, stretched out on the lounge room floor. Summer holidays at Kingfisher Bay used to feel as predictable as the ocean. Each day swelled up beneath us and just like a wave eventually delivered us to night.

But that summer was different. Ever since the poo incident the whole town had been cloaked in an eerie summer silence. In fact, most tourists had cancelled their holidays at Kingfisher Bay. And all because of some excavators who had dug too deep while working in the front beach car park in November. Their digger had struck an underground sewage pipe and the council had to close all the beaches due to high levels of poo seeping into the water. So bad! You could still smell poo in some parts of town. You could hardly blame the tourists for cancelling their holidays at Kingfisher Bay. As if anyone wants to be swimming with actual poo! Luckily, the back beach was fine. The only pollution out there was a bunch of local surf grommets who called themselves 'Kingfisher Krew'.

Each morning there'd be a group chat on socials. Usually between Sylvie, Bella, Georgette, Harrison, Pip and me. We'd chat about how big the waves were going to be that day, and what the tide would be doing and what time we'd all meet up at the beach. But that morning there was nothing from them at all. Could Sylvie's weirdness have infected our whole friendship group too? It was enough to make me decide to ask Clementine to come to the beach with me. That's how desperate I felt.

Sascha was waiting outside my bedroom door and thumping his tail on the floor. He was getting so old. He rolled onto his back, curled his front paws in the air like a dead bird and closed his eyes in anticipation of a tummy rub.

'Aw, Sash,' I said, 'you're a good ol' boy but who burnt the toast, huh?'

In the empty kitchen, breakfast-radio banter filled the room. I turned the radio off and opened the window above the sink to clear the burnt-toast smell. Clementine was outside, jumping up and down on the pogo stick Uncle Gus had given her for Christmas. He'd given me a boring notebook. Clementine had one hand held fast to the handle. In her other hand, a piece of blackened toast smothered with strawberry jam. I seriously don't know how Clementine managed to jump and eat at the same time but she would do absolutely anything to defy Mum's rules about table etiquette and proper eating. Last week she'd insisted on having breakfast on the garage roof.

I stood on my tippy-toes and leaned out the window. 'Hey, Clemmy!' I yelled. 'Want to come to the beach? It's going to be a stinker.' But I already knew what her answer would be. Clementine never wanted to go to the beach and not because of the poo incident either. Clementine did the same thing every day of the holidays – a strict training routine for a non-existent circus.

'Nah,' she said, taking a bite of toast. 'I need to finish training before it's too hot, then I'm going to the library.'

Oh, I forgot to mention the other thing Clementine does apart from creating eternal conflict with Mum and training for her non-existent circus: Clementine volunteers at the library, covering books. I'm not complaining or anything, just saying that when it comes to having a sibling and the potential for any kind of fun...or the potential to have them come to the beach with me and make up for the weirdness of a whole gang of friends... I may as well have been an only child. Instead, while I was at the beach trying to avoid the Kingfisher Krew, Clementine would be stilt walking, hooping, juggling, standing on her hands, doing the splits or playing sevensies with a tennis ball against the garage wall until someone (usually Mum) told her to stop.

I checked my phone again for messages. Nothing! Clementine stepped down from the pogo stick, wiped her jammy, sweaty palms on her shorts and set about jotting down her pogo repetitions in her training diary.

'Can't you skip training just this once?' I pleaded. 'We all know there's never going to be a circus at Kingfisher Bay.'

Clementine threw herself into a forward bend, her plaited hair brushing against the bricks. When she stood up again her face was puce red.

'You'll see,' she said. 'At least when they come I'll be ready, unlike you, Birdy! Besides, you know I hate the beach!' (If you're wondering why Clementine calls me 'Birdy' it's because she couldn't pronounce 'Alberta' or 'Bertie' when she was two, so she called me 'Birdy' instead... and it stuck!)

'Fine!' I said, and closed the window with a thud.

'Fine!' Clementine parroted back.

※

I gathered everything I'd need for the beach into my backpack and got my bike and boogie board out of the garage. Checked my messages. Still nothing. Not about the three-metre swell coming with high tide by noon, nothing about the expected top temperature of forty-one degrees. Nothing about the southerly coming through later in the day, nothing about where we'd all meet to avoid Seth Cromby and the other loser surf grommets of the Kingfisher Krew, nothing about whose house we might all go back to after. Nothing. Nothing. Nothing. I started pedalling down Waratah Street towards the highway. Mr Henderson was out watering his front garden. Soon he'd be shuttered inside like most of the other oldies in Kingfisher Bay with the aircon up full blast. He waved as I rode past, but I couldn't wave back on account of holding my boogie board under one arm. I just gave a nod and even that made me go into a complete wobble.

'You be careful, Alberta!' he hollered. He was probably wondering why Mum wasn't giving me a lift to the beach, and to be honest so was I. But that morning I hadn't even said goodbye. I could hear she was on an important call, probably to some big-wig publisher in England or America because it seemed the whole world was going nuts about *Tammy Bracken's Guide to Modern Manners*, and I could tell by the tone of her voice that interrupting her would be a huge mistake.

The highway was heaving with freight trucks heading north to Sydney and locals buzzing in and out of Kingfisher Bay for their shopping before it got too hot. I got off my bike and waited for a break in the traffic. There was a bike path on the other side, then it was an easy roll down the hill to the ocean. I tried not to think about Sylvie and the others. Instead I saw myself out in the waves where everything was okay.

Just then I heard someone approaching from behind and steered myself to the left of the bike path so they could pass me. I managed to flick a quick glance over my shoulder. To my horror it was Seth Cromby, pedalling as fast as he could towards me. Seth! Why? He absolutely never rides to the beach. Seth Cromby is usually running around while everyone's still asleep, doing footy training or rock climbing or working out at the gym to make his muscles bulge. I guess Seth thinks having bulgy muscles makes up for what he clearly lacks in the brain department. After all, it was Seth who'd come up with the tragic name of Kingfisher Krew and Seth and his gang of grommets who made it their business to be first at the beach to convince themselves, and anyone who crossed their path, that they own it. Krew own all the waves too. Obviously!

For a few hideous moments Seth Cromby's hairy gym thighs were pumping right next to me. He was doing his best to get in front. Naturally, my first impulse was to speed up to make it harder for him, but this thought was quickly overpowered by another voice inside, a voice that told me to slow down and make it easier for him to pass. This was what Dad might call 'the path of least resistance' which, in this case, translated to 'don't waste your energy on a ferret like Seth Cromby'. Let's face it, I had already been given a way-too-close-up-view of his sweaty pockmarked face, his venom-yellow teeth and clumpy blond hair, which was stuck to his face under his helmet.

But even worse, I'd noticed Dylan Mortimer approaching. Dylan was also Krew, and if there's one thing a girl knows for sure, it's that when a ferret like Seth is around other mean boys his meanness is going to get a whole lot worse. Next thing I knew, Dylan was right beside me too.

'Hey, Dylan, you wanna join the Hate Alberta Club?' Seth taunted.

With that, I pulled my brakes and stopped, hoping Seth and Dylan would keep going. But they both stopped too. When Seth looked at me it was like his eyes drilled actual holes through me and even though he was talking to Dylan he kept staring right at me.

'You should join too, Alberta,' Seth said. 'The Hate Alberta Club's growing more and more each day!'

Dylan laughed. 'I'll join. I'd love to hate Alberta!'

'Yeah, right!' I said. I could never think of the perfect insult on the spot.

I could feel my heart beating in my chest. All I could do was hold my ground and wait for them to get bored with me and leave. Eventually they did, but not before Seth threw a little more hate my way. He looked back over his shoulder as he started riding off. 'You'd better keep off our waves today, Alberta. They hate you too!'

'Yeah, Birdy,' yelled Dylan. 'Or there's trouble, you hear?'

CHAPTER 3

At the beach there was an old wooden shelter down the back of the car park where everyone locked their bikes. Years of sun and salt-drenched wild ocean winds had bleached it a ghostly grey. There wasn't a single cloud in the sky and the sun, still low, stung the back of my neck as I dropped my backpack and leaned my boogie board against the outside wall. A seagull paced hopefully on the roof above. All I could think about was getting into the water, even though I knew it would involve encountering Seth and Dylan again, and whoever else was here from the Kingfisher Krew. Inside the shelter Sylvie's and Georgette's bikes were locked to one another. Pip's and Harrison's bikes were both there too. At the other end of the shed I saw Seth's and Dylan's bikes in a tangle on the ground with a bunch of others. Seth's words hung heavily in my mind. *The Hate Alberta Club.* Could Sylvie and Georgette be in on this too, without even telling me what I'd done wrong?

I stood at the top of the stairs winding down to the beach. From there I could see the whole of Kingfisher Bay, carved between the two forest headlands of the national park, turquoise waves rolling into the shore in neat sets. Coloured beach shades were scattered across the sand like confetti, families bunched up close between the flags. I could hear the faint squeals of children as the frothy white water swept over them. I peeled off my sandals and padded down the stairs. I recognised Sylvie's boogie board straight away. And there she was, lying on her back with a T-shirt over her face. There were beach towels spread either side of her – Georgette's, Pip's and Bella's. They must have all been in the water. The sand was burning hot. I ran as fast as I could towards Sylvie, spread my towel out next to the others and stood on it to relieve my feet. Sylvie peeked out from under her T-shirt and did nothing to hide the disappointment on her face when she saw it was me, rather than one of the others.

'Did you bring my top?' she snapped.

'What top?' I asked.

'Serious? My netball top. Get real, Birdy. You've had it since the last day of school.'

Sylvie was right, of course. I had borrowed her netball top for the interschools but it wasn't like she didn't have spares. Sylvie's family actually owned Kingfisher Sports in town. The whole store! I remembered Sylvie's netball top on my desk, all washed and neatly folded Marie Kondo style. Mum was huge on returning borrowed items. Huge.

She had even made it one of Tammy Bracken's 'Golden Rules' in her book.

> **Tammy's Tips**
> #4 BORROWED ITEMS
> *Borrowed items should be returned in a timely manner and with the same level of enthusiasm with which you borrowed them. Never put a person (kind enough to lend you something in the first place) in the awkward position of needing to ask to get something back.*

'Sorry, Sylvie!' I said. 'I just forgot.'

'Birdy! I need it for tonight!'

I rummaged through my backpack for my phone.

'Don't worry. Mum can drop it at your place.' I was hoping like anything Sylvie would say no because I knew Mum would be furious if I actually did ask her to run an errand for me while she was working. Sylvie bunched her lips into a pout. I really didn't understand what the huge deal was.

Just then, Georgette appeared, dripping wet and breathing hard from the surf.

'Hey!' I said, welcoming the distraction.

'How's it going, Birdy?' she said, peeling off her rash vest. Underneath, her bronze skin was all goosebumpy.

It did feel like Georgette's hello was a little cold but she might have just been puffed out. She lay the vest on her boogie board to dry. I was itching to get into the water myself, but I had to sort out the problem with Sylvie's shirt and the sooner I did, the sooner everything could go back to normal.

'I'm texting Mum now,' I said, thumbing my phone.

Sylvie, now sitting cross-legged on her towel, exchanged a look with Georgette. A look I could only interpret as *we both know something that you don't know.* Then Sylvie said, 'Um... don't worry about it, Birdy. Just remember it next time, okay?'

I couldn't help thinking about how if the netball top was *so* important to Sylvie then she could have messaged to remind me. None of it made any sense.

Sylvie and Georgette exchanged more looks. I was starting to get annoyed.

'Do you want to tell me why you're both acting so weird?' I asked.

Sylvie and Georgette eyeballed one another again. I could feel their words bouncing between them like a silent game of ping-pong. *You tell her. No, you tell her. You. No, you.*

It was Georgette who eventually spoke. 'Look... I just don't get how... Don't ask us... Like, for real, Birdy, the whole town knows!'

I was seriously confused and I couldn't understand why they were being such cows. It sure felt like what

Seth and Dylan had said that morning was true. It really did feel like there was a Hate Alberta Club.

'Fine.' I said, Mum-style, meaning, things were *not* fine at all. I wanted to bundle up my things and go find some other people to hang out with. Complete strangers would do. But I decided to immerse myself in the ocean instead, out where it was honest and pure and where there was no need to interpret what the waves or the tide or the wind was actually saying. In the distance, out past the breakers, I saw Bella sitting up on her board. In that moment, Bella was the closest thing to normal I had.

Bella used to be a boogie boarder too, but she'd taken up surfing last summer. So had Harrison. But that didn't mean Bella was part of the Kingfisher Krew. Somehow Bella managed to belong to both worlds. She was a free agent – she'd earned the respect of the Krew (Bella was seriously good and would probably compete in the Junior State Surf Titles), so they laid off hassling her or thinking they could bully her off their waves. Bella didn't behave like Krew and didn't even want to belong to their gang. It wasn't like that for Harrison though. He had fallen to the dark side. In fact, these days Harrison was so totally Krew that he denies ever boogie boarding at all.

I kicked my fins hard to get out past the white water where Bella was waiting for the next set of waves to emerge. What had looked like dots from the beach grew into real people as I got closer. Seth and a bunch of other Krew grommets were scattered about, some sitting up on their boards, some paddling about trying to find a patch of sea to themselves. But none of them mattered to me. I wasn't scared of Krew with Bella around. As I anchored myself to the back of Bella's board I noticed she was shivering. She must have been in the water for ages.

'Hey, Bells!' I said.

'Hey, Berts,' she replied. But I could see she was distracted, looking past me and out to sea where a neat set of waves was swelling up and rolling towards us.

'I think I'll take this next one in,' she said. I let go of Bella's board and she dropped to her stomach, got into position, and straightened herself up. Then she started paddling hard. The Krew, further out back, had all done the same, making sure they were in the right position and had gathered enough speed to catch the wave. But I decided to sit that first wave out. That way I'd have the next one all to myself.

I felt Bella's wave swell beneath me, gently lifting me up then dropping me into a gully so deep it made the wave behind it look like an actual wall approaching. I saw Bella scoop herself up and into a low squat as she took off, then she turned herself to surf the face of the wave. I straightened up, tightened the muscles in my butt and worked my fins hard. I felt a huge surge forwards as the wave gathered me up, rocketing me towards its crest. For a millisecond, just before it broke, I felt airborne, accompanied by a familiar rush of terror as the wave thundered and broke.

I'd learnt that when it comes to the surf you have to completely surrender. You never know what the waves have in store for you. Any scenario had to be okay. You just had to accept it, relax, ride it out and hope. The ocean made me realise it was the same with Sylvie. I just had to accept her weirdness and what was happening to our friendship. Just had to wait it out and hope. If I could.

※

On my way home that afternoon I felt a strange case of deja vu. There Seth Cromby was, powering up behind me on the bike track. But this time he pulled into a skid right in front of me, forcing me to brake to avoid a crash.

'Thought I told you to stay off our waves?' Seth sneered. He had totally gross white balls of saliva at both corners of his mouth.

I stepped off my bike and steered it around him as if Seth was nothing more than a brick obstructing my path, or perhaps a dead wombat, although he was worse than that because I do love wombats, even dead ones. On the scale of disgusting dead things Seth would be more like a dead cane toad. I got back on by bike and rode off, ignoring him completely even though every little piece of me wanted to say, *Get out of my way, you ferret!*

But, within seconds Seth was riding alongside me again.

'You just don't get it, do you?' he puffed.

'Oh, I get it all right,' I said sarcastically.

'Yeah? Well, get *this*!'

That was when everything changed to slow motion. Seth's foot lifting off the peddle and a sharp kick landing in the spokes of my back wheel. I came down hard onto the concrete, my arm, still clutching my boogie board, took the full force of the fall. I heard an actual crack, like something snapping, like my actual arm. Pain like nothing I'd ever known before, as I hit the ground and watched Seth disappear. I screamed after him as loud as I could, '*Ferret!*'

CHAPTER 4

Mum knelt beside me, my bike, backpack and boogie board in a heap at the edge of the bike path. Every time I moved the pain soared. Calling Mum was all I had managed before collapsing back down to where I had landed.

'Darling, you're as white as a sheet!' All I could think about was getting myself into the safety of the car, along with all my stuff. Mum tried to help me up, at first hooking one arm under my neck and the other under my knees like she was carrying a baby, but she soon realised there was no way she was going to be able to lift me.

'Mum, ouch!' I shrieked. 'You'll drop me!'

Next she pulled me into a sitting position. Then I used my right hand to cradle the elbow of my injured arm. Surely it had been broken. There never used to be a bend in the middle of my forearm. I could see something trying to poke through the skin and felt like vomiting when I realised it must have been a bone.

'Oh God!' Mum said when she saw it. She opened the passenger door and helped me up. Once I was buckled in the tears finally came. It was like all the bravery I had mustered while waiting for Mum evaporated the moment I heard the click of the seatbelt. The pain intensified with every small movement. The only positive, if there could possibly be a positive in that grim scenario, was that Mum was being extra nice for a change, although it was torture watching her struggle to fit my bike into the back seat.

'That Seth Cromby!' Mum cursed. 'Fancy just leaving you there. How rude!'

Rude? Purposefully breaking my arm sure felt a little more serious than rude to me, but it wasn't the time to argue with Mum about words. I was feeling dizzy and like I might vomit. What if I did? I wouldn't even be able to open the car window. I'd end up throwing up on myself.

'Just leave the bike, Mum! Get Dad to pick it up!'

'Fat chance of that!' Mum growled.

Finally, we got going, the handlebars of my bike hanging out the back window.

Kingfisher Medical Centre was only five minutes down the road, but when we got to the highway, Mum turned in the opposite direction.

'I think we'd better go to the Regional Base Hospital instead,' Mum said.

'But why?' I moaned. 'It's miles away.'

'Kingfisher Medical can be so...it's always so...Oh, never mind, Alberta, just let me handle this my way.'

I couldn't believe that at a time like this Mum was going to put some gripe she had with the local medical centre above me. I bet it was some tiny detail that only she would notice, like the waiting room magazines being out of date or some doctor not remembering her name. But all my argue power had been knocked out of me. I was defeated.

'Fine,' I said. 'Whatever.'

I fixed my eyes on the horizon as we headed out of town, at the parched brown wheat fields, the rows of wind turbines along Copperhead Bay. Road signs flashed past warning of high fire danger, low levels of water in the reservoir, road works ahead. As Mum slowed down her phone sounded and Dad's name came up on the car display. I wanted to talk to him so badly. Would he be meeting us at the hospital? What about Clementine? Did either of them even know what had happened?

But Mum didn't pick up, just made a huffy sound, and drove a little faster as she let Dad's call go to voicemail.

'Hello!' I screeched. 'What if I wanted to talk to him?'

'Not now, Alberta!' Mum snapped. 'Please!' Not at all how you'd expect the world expert on modern manners and social etiquette to speak to a child with a broken wing.

***

The Kingfisher Regional Base Hospital had a huge pharmacy in the foyer and a florist full of carnations in plastic tubes and helium *Get Well Soon* balloons. Sitting behind a glass screen at reception was a woman with an

ID badge that said, *Hello, my name is Nurse Margaret*. Nurse Margaret asked us about a million questions. Finally, she pointed to a row of seats by a drink vending machine.

'Just wait over there,' she said. 'Doctor shouldn't be too long.'

'Thank you sooo much,' said Mum. 'But I was hoping to get something for Alberta's pain while we're waiting. Her arm does appear to be badly broken, poor thing... some Nurofen perhaps?'

I'd seen it all before. Next Mum would say something over-the-top fake-nice, hoping to charm Nurse Margaret into giving us better treatment. 'Oh, what a lovely pendant you're wearing,' Mum said.

See? Just so transparent.

Nurse Margaret pointed behind us. 'Pharmacy's over there,' she said.

'Thank you sooo much,' faked Mum.

Sitting in the waiting area, the Nurofen did start to kick in and soon the pain in my arm had dulled to a manageable throb. I imagined Sylvie and Georgette, still at the beach and completely unaware of what had happened. My impulse was to send Sylvie a photo of me in the hospital waiting room with my mangled arm. Maybe she'd snap out of her weirdness if she knew what Seth had done. Maybe her hatred of Seth Cromby would outweigh the meanness she suddenly had for me, for absolutely no reason. But my phone was in the car and it had died anyway. Plus, if I did send Sylvie a pic and she didn't message me back... well, it would pretty much prove that she wasn't just being weird but that she'd actually ghosted me, and I wasn't sure I was up for that kind of proof right then. Where was the hope in that?

I had no idea how many people were in front of me or how long I had to wait before it was my turn. So, to fill in time, I studied all the people in the waiting room one by one, trying to figure out what might be wrong with them. And because nearly all of them were glued to their phones none of them noticed me staring. Mum flicked through a tattered *New Idea* then started reading some story about Prince Harry and Meghan Markle. She was only halfway through the article when her phone rang. I couldn't help seeing Mum's screen. It was Dad again.

'Oh, what now!' Mum said, loud enough for everyone to hear. Nurse Margaret made a *tsk-tsk* noise from reception.

Tammy's Tips
#5 WAITING ROOM ETIQUETTE

While in a waiting room phone calls should not be taken. They can be annoying for others and can also be heard by those providing professional care. Personal calls should not be taken, unless absolutely urgent, in which case one should speak as quietly as possible.

Nurse Margaret pointed to a sign near the vending machine saying mobile phones should be switched off or turned to silent while in the hospital.

But Mum had already answered.

'Can I talk to—'

'Just stay here please, Alberta!' she whisper-hissed, heading for the glass doors.

It was like watching a silent movie, Mum outside, head down, face all screwed up and angry. Veins bulged at the side of her neck. But when she came back she was as calm and composed as anything, apart from her eyes, which were glassy from either the pressure of whisper-yelling, or from actual tears. She smiled fake-politely at Nurse Margaret, sat back down next to me and let out a long, slow, controlled exhale as she picked up the magazine and started reading where she'd left off.

Soon, a middle-aged man with glasses and a clipboard appeared in the doorway. I hoped like anything he was a doctor. He scanned the room with anticipation, like he was trying to match an actual person with the name on his list.

'Alberta Bracken?' he called.

'That's me,' I said, getting up.

Mum put the magazine back on the pile and smoothed down her skirt.

'Oh, good,' he said. 'Would you like to follow me, please?'

He took us to a small room with a desk in one corner next to a sink and a metal cabinet. He pointed to a big chair with wide padded armrests.

'Alberta, if you could sit there please,' he said. I winced at the thought of putting my arm up there, and someone actually touching it, but I knew I had to.

'I'm Dr Melendez,' he said, carefully supporting my elbow as he arranged my forearm onto the armrest. 'Now, let's take a good look at that arm.'

A large bruise had already formed around the swollen bone-poking-through part.

'Hmm,' he said. 'Must have been quite a fall. We'll need to take some images to see exactly what we're dealing with.'

We followed Dr Melendez to the X-ray department and he introduced us to a woman wearing an ID badge that said, *Hello, my name is Celeste.*

'Celeste is our radiographer,' Dr Melendez explained. 'Once you're done here, I'll meet you back in the examination room. It won't be long.'

To be honest, I wouldn't have minded if it was long... it was only when we were back in that small room with Dr Melendez and that big chair that I was hit with the full brunt of the bad news. It was like falling from my bike all over again. Dr Melendez clipped the X-ray images onto a light box over the metal cabinet and switched on the light to illuminate it. There was my arm, ghostlike and hollow on the screen. Dr Melendez pointed at one of the bones in my forearm. 'See here?' he said. 'This one's called the radius and this one's your ulna. Both have suffered from the impact.' He indicated two very obvious areas where the bones had been broken. 'This arm is going to have to be completely immobilised,' Dr Melendez explained.

'You mean, like in plaster?' I asked.

'Like that, yes. But thankfully there's been a lot of improvements since the old plaster of Paris days.' He switched off the light box and rummaged through the drawer in the metal cabinet.

'We use fibreglass now,' he explained. 'So you'll be able to get it wet at least. No more putting your arm in a plastic bag to bathe, thank goodness!' He laughed.

Mum fake-laughed along with him but I didn't find it funny one bit. It felt like they were both laughing *at* me.

'So I can swim then?' I asked hopefully.

'Alberta, being able to bathe is quite different from going swimming!' Mum said sternly. 'You heard Dr Melendez. Your arm needs to be *completely* immobilised.' Mum looked to Dr Melendez for validation like the worst kind of a teacher's pet at school.

'I'm afraid your mother is right,' said Dr Melendez. (Cringe.) 'It is a complex fracture and the whole arm will need to be braced so that it can adequately heal.'

'What? Like for how long?'

'Alberta, don't say "what" like that, darling. It sounds very rude.'

Was she serious? I was *not* in the mood for a Tammy Bracken manners rant.

'So—'

Mum cut me off before she even knew what I was going to say. 'Use the doctor's name, Alberta. There's no excuse not to. It's right there on his badge.'

Dr Melendez cut in. He had probably seen it all when it came to helicopter parents. 'It's okay Mrs—'

'Mrs Bracken,' said Mum. 'But please... call me Tammy.'

'Very well then, Tammy,' said Dr Melendez. 'As I was saying—'

That's when Mum started crying. God knows why? She's not the one who had to have her arm completely immobilised.

Dr Melendez put on a concerned face.

'Mrs Bracken, please be assured that young Alberta *will* make a full recovery.'

He offered Mum a box of tissues. Mum plucked out two.

'I'm sorry, Dr Melendez.' Mum sniffled. 'Just a few things happening at home right now, that's all.'

Oh God, Mum. Even I knew not to say things like that to a doctor. Next thing he's going to think I'm a victim of domestic violence. Dr Melendez cocked his head to one side, looking appropriately concerned.

'Mrs Bracken... Tammy... I—'

'Oh no, it's nothing like that, Doctor. Don't worry!' Mum laughed awkwardly. Dr Melendez joined in at first, but soon put his serious face back on and leaned in. 'I can refer you to people who can help,' he said. 'It would be completely confidential.'

'No, no, really, Dr Melendez,' said Mum, drying her eyes. 'I don't know what's got into me... the shock of seeing Alberta so hurt, I suppose.' Seriously, how had Mum managed to make this all about her?

Finally, Dr Melendez focused on me again, and the question I'd tried to ask earlier. I was already dreading the answer.

'Sorry, Alberta,' Dr Melendez said. 'You had a question?'

'Dr Melendez, how long will it be before I can swim in the surf and go boogie boarding?'

That's when Dr Melendez gave it to me straight. 'To be honest with you, Alberta... a complex fracture like this... you're looking at a minimum of six weeks.'

CHAPTER 5

The whole drive home I felt dazed, like I was in some kind of trance. It was the worst day of my life. Definitely the worst. My arm was still throbbing, now inside a hard blue cast and strapped against my chest in a sling. It was immobilised all right. I felt like my arm didn't even belong to me anymore. And all the while Mum just wouldn't stop ranting, which made me feel like I'd done something wrong, like Seth Cromby breaking my arm was my fault.

'That Seth Cromby,' Mum hissed. 'I should go round there right now and talk to his parents!'

'Mum, please don't!' I cried. 'I just want to go home.'

'We should be going to the police – that's what we should be doing.'

'Six weeks!' I yelled. 'What am I supposed to do for the rest of the holidays? God! School will have started again before I get this thing off!'

'Hush, Alberta! Please!' Mum scolded. 'You're lucky you only broke your arm and didn't wind up with a broken neck! Look on the bright side...You'll have done all your reading for the school year ahead.'

'Oh yeah?' My eyes welled up with tears. 'I won't even be able to turn the pages!'

Dr Melendez said I had to resist using the hand of my broken arm too, even though it still functioned perfectly as a hand. I tried unzipping my backpack using my one good hand. Hopeless! How was I supposed to get dressed, or worse, how was I supposed to go to the loo? Would Mum have to help me like she helped Granny when she came to stay? I'd seriously rather die!

Just then Mum's phone rang. It was Dad again, but she didn't pick up.

'Mum, *what* is going on?' I demanded. But she ignored me and just kept ranting about going to the police.

'That ghastly bully should have to suffer some consequences for what he's done. I've got a good mind to—'

'Where's Dad?' I asked. 'Have you even told him what's happened?'

'Of course, Alberta. I spoke to him at the hospital,' Mum said.

'Well, did you consider for one moment that I might want to talk to him too?' I shrieked.

'Oh, Alberta! Now, you're just being hysterical!'

The cool night air from the open rear window was giving me goosebumps at the back of my neck. A feeling of gloom had settled over me. The whole thing just felt so unfair. Mum was right. Seth should have to suffer some consequences. I was the one being punished. I was the one with the six-week prison sentence. All while Seth Cromby got off scot-free. Where was the justice? My tummy rumbled. The only food I'd eaten all day was a Snack n Go and a bag of jelly beans from the vending machine at the hospital.

'What are we doing for dinner?' I asked. 'Is Dad cooking?'

'Shh!' said Mum. 'We need to collect Clementine. She's over at Chelsea's where no doubt she'll be learning more bad manners. It might be best if you go in and get her, Alberta.'

Tammy Bracken's Guide to Modern Manners had a whole chapter on the etiquette of play dates, including pointers for parents picking up and dropping off their kids. Usually, Mum had a real beef about parents texting their kids to let them know they were waiting outside in the car.

Tammy's Tips
#6 PICKING UP CHILDREN FROM PLAY DATES

When picking up children from play dates parents should knock at the door but make it clear they won't be coming inside. The pick-up should be a short interaction where the picking-up parent ensures their child expresses sufficient appreciation to both their friend and the parent(s).

Nowhere in the book does Tammy Bracken recommend sending an older sibling in to collect a child while the parent waits outside blocking calls from their father. Especially not an injured sibling fresh from hospital and starving hungry, who will definitely ignore proper manners. But that's exactly what Mum did. As she sat brooding in the car with the engine running, I had to go in for Clementine.

When we got home there was a veritable mountain of clothes piled up on the front lawn. Had Mum had gone overboard with letting go of things that didn't spark joy? But when Clementine and I got out of the car and looked closer at the pile, it soon became clear that none of the clothes were Mum's or mine or Clementine's. Everything belonged to Dad – which could only mean one thing. Either Dad had spent the day doing some pretty frantic clutter-clearing (highly unlikely) or...just like in the movies... Mum and Dad had had a mighty huge argument.

Where was Dad? More importantly, where were the cooking smells? Instead, the house was in complete darkness and there was an undeniable sense of no one being at home. Clementine and I stood by the edge of the clothes pile, which seemed to contain absolutely everything Dad owned, including his electric toothbrush and the back scratcher in the shape of a monkey. We were transfixed, like staring into a cold bonfire.

'Does your arm hurt?' Clementine asked.

'A little bit,' I said.

'Did you cry?' Clementine asked.

'A little bit,' I said.

'It's all my fault,' Clementine said.

'What are you talking about?' I asked.

'I told Mum about the message on Dad's iPad. That's why she made me go play at Chelsea's and threw all Dad's things on the lawn.'

My heart quickened. Everything was starting to make sense: Mum not taking Dad's calls, her crying at the hospital, the comment to Dr Melendez about things *happening* at home. Then I remembered Georgette's comment that afternoon at the beach... *Like, for real, Birdy, the whole town knows!*

'I've actually known for days,' said Clementine.

※

Inside, Mum ushered us into the front room, the one we only use on special occasions, with all the good furniture. Usually, we were completely banned from the good couch. Ever since Clementine was caught eating toast and Vegemite on it and got grounded for a week. But I guess this was a special occasion because it's not every day you get your arm broken and come home to find all your Dad's things piled up on the grass. Now Mum was telling us to sit on the good couch.

Mum took one of the good dining chairs from the good dining table that we also never used and positioned it in front of the couch. She leaned in. This was never a good sign.

'Girls, this isn't easy, but I'm going to be completely straight with you.'

'Finally!' I said.

'Alberta, please!'

'Well, whatever it is it sure seems like half of my friends already know!'

The pain in my arm intensified again. Everyone knows there's nothing worse than being the last person to find out about something. The whole thing (especially on an empty stomach) just made me feel angry.

Mum took a deep breath. 'I wanted to speak with you both at once,' Mum explained calmly.

'Clementine said she's known for days!'

With that, Clementine started crying. 'It's all my fault,' she said.

Mum reached for Clementine's hand.

'No, darling Clementine. It's not your fault, at all. Everything...absolutely everything is your father's fault. He and that—'

'It *is* my fault. I know it is.' Clementine wept.

'Could someone *please* just tell me what's going on!' I shrieked.

Mum double-clapped her hands, exactly like Mrs Heggy did at school when the class was out of control.

'Stop it!' she scolded. 'Both of you. Just let me speak.'

Clementine and I were shocked into silence.

Mum took another deep breath, and exhaled slowly.

'It has come to my attention,' she said. 'That your father has been—'

Clementine started sobbing again. I pressed my leg firmly against hers but she was inconsolable.

'Hush, Clementine!' Mum snapped. Then, looking a little guilty said, 'Believe me, this is as hard for me as it is for you, but as I was saying... It has come to my attention that your father has been carrying on with that... that... receptionist from the medical centre... that—'

'Ursula Hoffman?' Clementine blurted out.

'Yes, that Ursula Hoffman! It seems she and your father have been having a... a... *thing*!' Mum's voice trailed into thinness. Shrill, like a tiny bird.

'A thing!' exclaimed Clementine.

'Yes, darling. A thing,' Mum confirmed. 'Consequently, and I didn't make this decision lightly, mind you... but I do believe there should be consequences for wrongdoing... I had no choice other than to ask your father to leave.'

'Leave?' Clementine's face crumpled. 'You mean for the whole night?'

Mum looked defeated. 'More than one night I'm afraid,' she said. 'I'm very sorry but it's the only option I had if I'm to retain even a morsel of self-respect.'

'No!' Clementine sobbed. 'Noooooo!'

Mum left the room. We heard her putting the light on in the den and the door closing with a hollow thud. Soon she'd be on the phone, downloading the events of the day to Aunt Robina.

'So that's why Mum refused to take me to Kingfisher Medical,' I said. 'She didn't want to bump into Ursula Hoffman!'

Suddenly Clementine stopped sobbing. The room was flooded by car headlights as someone pulled into the drive. We made a dash for the window, hid behind the bunched-up curtains and peeked out.

'It's Dad!' Clementine squealed. I held her close with my good hand to stop her from running outside. Together we watched as Dad gathered his things and piled them into the boot of his car. I couldn't believe he wasn't coming inside, cheery like always when he got home. I couldn't believe what he'd done. I squeezed Clementine's hand.

'Birdy?' she whispered.

'Yes, Clemmy,' I said.

'Birdy, what's a *thing*?'

CHAPTER 6

I desperately wanted to message Sylvie and tell her what had happened. Not about the hoo-ha with my parents (seemed she already knew about that), but about Seth Cromby and how he had broken my arm. But she sure hadn't felt like my friend that day on the beach, and she was way grumpier than she should have been about me not returning her dumb netball top. Especially when she was always boasting about how she could just go get any old thing she liked from Kingfisher Sports. Then I remembered Sylvie would actually be playing netball right then so what would be the point of messaging her anyway? I wasn't going to get a reply. And I knew I should have been more concerned about how Mum had thrown Dad out of the house, but the throbbing pain in my arm wouldn't let me concentrate on anything else. How was I going to cope with not going to the beach for the rest of the holidays? Why couldn't I have broken my arm in the winter? At least I could have still gone out on the whale-watching boat with Dad like we had most weekends.

Still in the front room, Clementine had wrapped herself up in the curtains like a caterpillar. We used to both do it when we were younger, pretending we were in cocoons. But Mum would always catch us and make us unroll way before we had reached the butterfly stage. I could hear Clementine snivelling. The last thing we needed was for Mum to go nuts about Clementine's snot all over the good curtains! I gently unravelled her.

'Clementine, come out. I need your help.' It was true. I actually *needed* my little sister for the very first time in my life. It was a total shock to her too.

'What? How?' she asked, wiping her nose with her sleeve.

'Come with me, and promise you'll stop being upset,' I said. Clementine followed me down the hall.

'Shut up, Birdy. It's not every day you lose your dad!'

'Hmph! He's hardly lost, Clementine. I bet he's all goo-goo eyed on Ursula Hoffman's couch, sipping champagne. I bet he soon forgets about us completely.'

'Don't say that!' cried Clementine.

The throb in my arm had taken on a life of its own. Like my arm had its own heartbeat. Dr Melendez had given Mum a box of tablets and said that when it came to pain the trick was to stop it before it started. Mum had left the box on my desk for me. The instructions said to take two tablets every four hours with meals. Fat chance! I thought. Dinner was nowhere in sight. I passed the box of tablets to Clementine.

'Here, I need you to get two tablets out,' I said. 'Oh, can you get my phone out of my backpack and put it on the charger too? And I need a glass of water.'

Clementine hesitated, like it had just dawned on her the exact nature of the help I'd be needing. But I gave her my best wounded-bird eyes, and it seemed to work a treat. I was still all salty from the beach. My hair hung in stringy clumps but the thought of having a shower seemed all too much and I sure didn't want Mum to help me. I managed to pull on my pyjama bottoms before Clementine got back with the water.

'There you go,' said Clementine. 'Mum's making tuna mornay.'

When my phone bounced back to life there were three missed calls from Dad.

'Quick, Clemmy,' I said. 'I need a pic of me in my sling for Bella.'

'I'm not your PA, Alberta!' Clementine protested. 'All you care about is your stupid friends!' She was right, of course, but I still needed to get my news out there and Bella was the perfect person to do it for me. Bella was friends with everyone (including Seth Cromby) and maybe, just maybe, when Sylvie found out about my arm she'd forget about the netball top and about being weird and mean and life could go back to normal.

Clementine attached the picture to Bella's message. 'Okay, so write this: "Hey, Bella... so ended up spending three hours at the hospital thanks to Seth Cromby for breaking my arm"!'

※

Tuna mornay was Mum's go-to comfort food dish and, according to *Tammy Bracken's Guide to Modern Manners*, an ideal fork dish. Eating standing up or with one hand had never been so easy thanks to an ingenious invention known as the Splayd.

As far as I could see Splayds were a weird cross between a fork and a knife and a spoon. I used to love reading the blurb on the box about how some man called William McArthur in Sydney got the idea for Splayds in 1943. He felt sorry for ladies at barbecues who struggled to eat nicely from plates on their laps. Our Splayds were a wedding gift from Granny and Grandad and were usually kept in the sideboard in the good room, neatly filed in a special blue box.

Tammy's Tips

#7 THE SPLAYD

Sometimes referred to as a 'spork', the Splayd is neither a fork nor a spoon. This clever hybrid enables one-handed eating in an elegant and efficient manner. It should not, however, be held like a pencil or used as a shovel.

'Did you take your tablets, Alberta?' Mum asked. 'Has the pain eased off?'

'It's okay,' I said. 'The tablets do seem to work.'

I didn't know what to say to Mum. I knew she was in pain too, but trying her hardest to hide it. I was actually a bit scared of her – the way her eyes were flickering about. She felt like an active volcano. Who knew when she might next erupt? The best thing I could do was try not to annoy her. If only Clementine had come to the same conclusion. But no, she just had to raise the topic of her slumber party. Again! What was she thinking? Her birthday was over a month away. Did she really have to choose that moment?

Fact was, ever since Mum had posted a photo of Clementine's friend Daisy as an example of how *not* to use a knife and fork on *Tammy Bracken's Guide to Modern Manners* Instagram (only to an audience of about five million), Clementine had lost a *lot* of friends. I helped myself to another spoonful of tuna mornay and did my best to change the topic, a handy technique I'd learnt from Dad.

'Mmm, delicious!' I said. 'I just love it when we use Splayds.' Mum was pushing the food around on her plate. Maybe Splayds were just a sad reminder of her and Dad's wedding day? The whole idea of getting married was to be faithful after all, *not* for Dad to be caught having a thing with Ursula Hoffman from Kingfisher Medical Centre. But Clementine just wouldn't let up about the slumber party... or Daisy. I felt Mum's inner volcano rumbling. Why couldn't Clementine feel it too?

'It's just so unfair, Mum!' Clementine whined. 'Just one slumber party!'

'I said "not now"!' Mum snapped.

'Then at least take down the post of Daisy,' Clementine shrieked.

'You're being ridiculous, Clementine!' Mum yelled. 'You can't even see that it's Daisy. It could be any eight-year-old with ghastly table manners.'

Clementine's eyes filled with tears.

'You judge *everyone*! No wonder Aunt Robina didn't want to come for dinner. No one cares about stupid manners! Soon I'll have no friends and all because of you and your boring book!'

Mum slapped her palm against the table as the volcano inside exploded.

'Enough, Clementine!'

There was a moment of absolute silence and stillness like the whole scene had been captured in a photograph. Then Mum picked up her plate, took a deep breath and walked out. Sascha trotted after her but the den door slammed before he made it down the hall.

'Wow, Clementine! You sure know how to pick your moments,' I said.

Clementine's face crumpled. I should have felt sorry for her but it was hard when she behaved like such an idiot. I shovelled in more tuna mornay, free from any of

Mum's scrutiny about manners. It was like the more I ate, the hungrier and hungrier I got.

'I hate her!' Clementine cried. 'If she wasn't so annoying, Dad wouldn't have run away.'

Soon I had finished my plate. 'Come on, Clemmy. Want to sign your name on my cast?'

CHAPTER 7

Finally, there was contact with the outside world. Or with Bella, at least. The news of my accident hadn't seemed to have leaked any further.

Bella Wed 29 December
So sorry about your arm. Six weeks!!! No!!!!!!!!
Does it hurt?
I'm so going to crash Seth's wave tomorrow! 🏄✨
Love u heaps Bertie! 🐞
Are you still coming to the Bowlo for New Year's?
Hope to see you there. Missing our beach dayz! 🐚🐚

There was also a voicemail from Dad. It was nice enough I guess. *How's my darling girl?... that Seth Cromby's going to get a piece of my mind.* Then Dad went all awkward and ummed and ahed a lot. *Look, Birdy... there are things that I don't expect you to understand... I know I've let you all down... it's going to take some time... and about the*

New Year's bash at the Bowls Club... well, it breaks my heart to have to say this, but I think I should give your mum some space right now... I'm sorry, but I'm going to have to sit this New Year's out.

The truth was I hadn't even thought about New Year's Eve. The best part about Dad's message was that he hadn't asked me to call him back. I really didn't want to. What was I meant to say to him anyway – *thanks for dropping a bomb on our family?*

I couldn't help feeling ashamed about Dad and his *thing* with Ursula Hoffman but it was hard not to when according to Georgette at the beach yesterday, the *whole town knows!* How did Dad even meet Ursula Hoffman anyway? Then I remembered one of the days out on the whale boat with Dad and Clementine last winter. We used to go most weekends but Mum stopped coming on account of being too busy writing her book. It was one of those magical sunny winter days when there wasn't a puff of wind, and the ocean was as still as glass.

'I hope we get to see a hunchback,' Clementine had said.

'You mean "humpback"?' I'd teased. And that's when I'd noticed Ursula in the seat across the deck giggling at what Clementine had said. I recognised her straight away from the medical centre. Next thing I know Dad was giggling away too. We saw her another time on the whale boat as well, the day we came across a pod of orcas. I was taking a selfie of Dad and Clementine and me, and Ursula offered to get a snap of all three of us on my phone. Looking back, maybe it was just an excuse to get chummy with Dad. Is that all it takes to start a thing?

There was no point getting out of bed so I just lay there thinking about Sylvie. What if Clementine was right. What if Sylvie was avoiding me too, on account of Mum's book? Clementine said Daisy's Mum was furious about Mum's Instagram post, even though there was nothing to identify Daisy in the photo. It was still Daisy that Mum had used to prove a point – the real point being that Daisy's parents hadn't bothered to teach Daisy proper table manners. That's a sure way to annoy other parents! Maybe Sylvie and Georgette feared being the subject of one of Mum's posts or providing her with inspiration for the sequel to *Tammy Bracken's Guide to Modern Manners*? And you'd hope that if the whole town was talking about your dad having a *thing* with Ursula Hoffman then at least the other parent might not give you any trouble. All I knew was that having problematic parents sure made a broken-armed kid feel super alone.

Outside my window the sky was a silent ocean of blue. Then Clementine clonked past on her stilts and I was reminded that everyone would be down at the beach already, lolling about in the waves, laughing, chatting, eating ice cream and...not missing me at all. I felt my bottom lip quivering of its own accord. There was only one thing that could help.

'Clementine!' I yelled the next time she passed my window. 'Toastie! Pleeeeease...Cheese and tomato?'

'Ugh!' she grunted and clomped off.

'Love you, Clementine!' I yelled after her.

Soon the comforting aroma of burnt butter was wafting down the hall and it wasn't long before Clementine pushed open my door with her foot. She had set up a breakfast tray. She'd even made me a cup of tea. As she put the tray on my desk I noticed her face, lit up with total excitement.

'I've just had the best idea,' she squeaked. I held my breath. Clementine's best ideas were usually only best for her. 'A fish finger hedgehog!' she said.

'A what?'

'For my slumber party. Remember the fish finger hedgehog on YouTube? It's sooooo perfect!'

Oh, I remembered the fish finger hedgehog all right. It was made from two large mounds of mashed potato, one for its body, the other for its head. Fish fingers were poking out of it like spikes. It had green peas for eyes and its nose was a small round of burnt toast. In the video a group of people (the kind of people Mum would call barbarians) were crowded around a table whooping and cheering and singing 'Happy Birthday'. One of them squirted the hedgehog with a squeezy bottle of tomato sauce. Everyone was digging in with their hands and licking their fingers as they used the fish finger spikes as scooping tools to get as much mash and sauce in their mouths as possible. Could Clementine want *anything* more unacceptable to Tammy Bracken, otherwise known as our manners-obsessed mother?

'It'd be perfect, don't you think?' Clementine asked excitedly.

I took a bite of my toastie. The tomato was steaming hot. 'Maybe don't pester Mum about it just yet,' I warned. 'If I were you I'd wait until after her TED Talk. Besides, your birthday isn't for ages.'

'Okay,' Clementine agreed.

I'm not kidding, in less than three minutes Mum and Clementine were having a scrap in the kitchen. You could have heard them arguing from the next street. Mum saying she *refused* to host a party where people were encouraged to eat like ruffians; Clementine accusing Mum of ruining her life. I know Clementine is only eight and has a lot of trouble containing her emotions but seriously, sometimes I wonder how smart she is, like if at *all?* I needed to break the fight up, and let's face it, I didn't have anything better to do.

'Shh! You guys!' I put my plate in the sink. That's when the kitchen landline rang. 'It's probably the neighbours complaining!' I said.

But when I picked up it was Dad and I was trapped talking to him.

'Hey! How's my girl?' he asked. 'How's that arm today?'

'Still broken, Dad,' I said. Mum scurried off to her den, probably so she could pick up the other landline on her desk and listen in.

'I know it is, love,' he said. 'I just wanted to check in, see how you're going.'

'Okaaaaay,' I said. I had never *checked in* with my dad before, especially not over the phone. Was I meant to ask where he was living? Now that he wasn't here for meals, or to drive me around, or help stop Mum raving about manners, I had no idea what to talk about. Besides, I was angry with Dad. What parent turns a simple excursion on a whale boat into a whole-town hoo-ha? An awkward silence descended and it didn't help that Clementine was listening in, hanging off my every word.

'Look, Alberta,' Dad said. 'I'm not proud of what's happened—'

'You mean about what *you* did?' I interrupted.

'Okay...' said Dad. 'I'm not proud of what I did.'

'It wasn't something that just magically "happened", Dad.'

'I agree, Alberta, and I take full responsibility. Still, I was hoping you, me and Clementine could stay connected. It's important... don't you think?'

'I guess,' I said, rolling my eyes at Clementine.

'How about we have an early dinner at Quilty's Diner one night soon? What do you think?'

'Fine' I said, realising that if I agreed to the cringe-worthy future dinner at Quilty's I could at least end the conversation.

'Great,' said Dad. 'Is Clementine around?'

'Here,' I said, passing the handset to Clementine.

Afterwards, I got a message from Mikki Watanabe. Mikki lives in the city but his family have a beach house at the end of our street. When I first saw the message all I could think of was him (and his parents) driving past our place and seeing all of Dad's clothes piled up on our front lawn. I liked Mikki, but it wasn't like we were actual friends. I always thought it was a bit weird they had a beach house in Kingfisher Bay but never went to the beach, not even in a heatwave. Mikki was always off with his video camera someplace, making films. After reading Mikki's message my worst fears were confirmed. He *had* driven past our house (with his parents) and although he didn't mention seeing Dad's clothes piled high on the lawn, as if they could have missed it!

 Hiya, Alberta! We drove past your house yesterday and I couldn't help noticing your arm in a sling. Did you break it? I hope it doesn't hurt too much. I just got back from Japan. Long story, but my grandfather passed away. He was old but he wasn't one bit sick so it was all a big shock and a lot of time spent travelling. If you get too bored at home with your broken arm you could come over to mine if you want to? MW

Suddenly Mikki had a whole lot more appeal. At least he wasn't trying to avoid me! I responded as fast as my one-fingered typing would allow.

Hey, Mikki. I am DESPERATE to get out of the house, so yes, please. I would LOVE to visit! 🙂 I'm free this afternoon? Or tomorrow? I've seriously got zero plans, so any time will be okay. So sorry about your grandfather too. Alberta

CHAPTER 8

That night after dinner Mum wanted to go grocery shopping. She acted all casual about it but we all knew she had taken to night-time shopping so as not to encounter any 'small-town gossipy locals' (Mum's words) during the day. I was surprised she hadn't thought of home delivery, to be honest, but I wasn't going to suggest it because sadly, even a trip to Woolies felt like something to look forward to now.

But grocery shopping ended up being far from exciting. Who would have guessed the first person I'd see would be Seth Cromby! How was I meant to know he had a night job at Woolies stacking shelves? He must have definitely lied about his age. Anyway, there I was with our shopping list, pushing a trolley with Clementine, and there was Seth, squatting in the dairy aisle, unpacking tubs of yoghurt onto the bottom shelf of the fridge display.

Naturally, my first instinct was to run. Well, that was my second instinct really. My first instinct was to throw a carton of oat milk at Seth's ugly face. I did attempt a swift trolley about-turn but it went all wrong. The combination of my one-handed steering (Clementine was zero help) and the trolley's dodgy wheels saw me careening straight across the aisle and into a shelf of feta cheese.

As with most things, Mum's first instinct was very different. Before I could stop her she had bowled straight over to Seth and confronted him. It happened so fast all Clementine and I could do was watch on in horror.

'Seth Cromby,' Mum scolded, 'you are a bully and a coward!'

She pointed back towards me and Clementine, frozen like statues in the cold blue light of the refrigerators.

'What sort of animal... what kind of *barbarian* does a thing like that?'

Clementine grabbed the shopping list and started rolling it into a tight scroll. I just prayed for a sinkhole to appear and swallow me up. But Seth was completely unfazed. He stood up, looked Mum straight in the eyes and said, 'I don't know what you're talking about, lady!'

'*Lady*? Where's your manners, young man? I'm Mrs Bracken to you!' Mum scolded. 'And you're lucky I haven't called the police!'

Seth held his ground. 'Listen, *Mrs Bracken*, I had nothing to do with it. Honest.'

'Honest? Honest! There's not an honest bone in your body!' Mum's voice grew louder. Where was the sinkhole? 'Fancy leaving a young girl injured by the side of the road! You're a disgrace! I shudder to think what sort of man you'll become!'

Seth pushed his half-emptied box along the linoleum with his foot, calm as you like.

'Shudder all you like, Mrs Bracken, but Alberta pranged her bike all by herself.'

'What an absolute load of hogswallop!' Mum looked to me for validation. But I was too busy memorising the ingredient list on a platter pack of tasty cheese and cabanossi bites.

Mum gave up. She knew Seth was never going to apologise or send a card with flowers or do anything that was the slightest bit civilised. Worse than that, he wasn't even admitting he was involved. There were no witnesses so it was his word against mine. Seth could say anything he liked.

Tammy's Tips
#8 MAKING A PROPER APOLOGY

A proper apology has four components. Firstly, acknowledge the behaviour or event that caused the damage. Then, state the reason why your behaviour was wrong – whether it was intentional or otherwise. After that, declare what you will do differently in the future. And finally, use the person's name and solemnly ask for their forgiveness. All this, while offering the person on the receiving end as much time as they need to accept your apology.

'Come along, girls,' Mum said, making sure Seth was still in earshot. 'That Seth Cromby is even more of a coward than I'd thought.'

Mum took hold of the front of the trolley and towed it behind her while I steered with my good hand. Clementine trotted beside her, unravelling the shopping list.

'What about the yoghurt?' she whispered, tugging on Mum's sleeve.

'Clementine, for once in your life just work with me, would you?' Mum snatched the list from Clementine and gave it to me instead.

'Alberta, what's next, please?' she said. That's when I saw some of Clementine's additions... sour worms, Pine Lime Splices, hokey pokey chocolate, party mix.

The whole encounter had put Mum in an even worse mood, if that was humanly possible. But we worked systematically through the list, sending Clementine to pre-check each aisle before we entered to make sure Seth wasn't already there.

'Can we get a burrito kit?' asked Clementine.

'No,' said Mum.

'Ben and Jerry's?' I asked.

'No,' said Mum.

'That's so unfair!' whined Clementine.

'Stop complaining,' said Mum.

But despite Mum rejecting nearly all our requests for sweets and ice cream as we edged our full trolley sideways down the confectionery aisle, different rules seemed to apply to her. 'You get to have your treats,' moaned Clementine as Mum put some Werther's Toffees in the trolley. I gave Mum a silent *she does have a point* face.

'All right,' Mum huffed. 'You two go and get some ice cream. But not that dreadful rocky road!'

Clementine bolted for the freezer section. I followed gingerly behind. The last thing I needed was another collision with Seth Cromby. I poked my head cautiously out the end of the aisle and checked both ways, like I was about to cross a major road. Then I looked back to Mum, standing alone in front the chocolate selection like she was in some kind of dream. She picked up two chunky blocks of Milky Bar Nutty and Crunchy. This was strange in itself because Mum was religious about Fruit & Nut.

But you won't believe what I saw next. I wished my eyes had been playing tricks. I mean... surely Mum knew I was there? But no. If she'd known I was watching she would *not* have done what she did next, and I would *not* have seen what I saw. But she *did* do it and I *did* see it. My mother, Tammy Bracken, world expert on table manners and social etiquette, slipped those two blocks of Milky Bar Nutty and Crunchy straight into her handbag! That's right. She was *stealing* them. Then she just carried on like nothing had happened, whistling to herself as she pushed the trolley towards the checkout. Oh, but there's more. I wasn't the only one who'd seen what Mum did... Seth Cromby saw it too! Or at least I think he did. If he didn't, Woolie's CCTV camera must have captured it, for sure.

My heart pounded as Seth and I eyed each other from opposite ends of the aisle, exchanging a look that could only be interpreted as *I know that you know what I know.* Oh my lord! If my mother got busted for shoplifting it would ruin her entire career. And, considering everything else in her life was a wreck, that would mean ruining her whole life! Mum needed her career more than ever right now. Could Seth be so lousy as to expose her? Well, after Mum's outburst at him in the dairy aisle ... hell yes!

Just then Clementine skipped back with a tub of rocky road ice cream. Rocky road! But weirdly, Mum was suddenly in the best mood ever.

'Oh, there you are, girls!' she said cheerily. 'Let's get going before it melts.'

I still had some hope that Mum putting the chocolate in her bag was just an accident and that soon we'd be paying for them at the checkout with everything else. But that didn't happen. I couldn't help looking over my shoulder. What if Woolies security had seen Mum in the confectionery aisle on CCTV and were waiting to bust her as we left the store? I got an impulse to run and find Seth, try to make a deal with him. Something like, *I won't tell anyone else about you breaking my arm, if you don't tell anyone what you saw.* Beg him, even. But in the end I was too scared. In the end, I just helped Mum with the shopping as best I could with one hand.

Mum was happier on the drive home than she had been in days. But I kept wondering if I should tell her what I'd seen and warn her about Seth.

'You know,' Mum said, 'I've been thinking. Why don't you girls sign up for a school holiday program? How about those drama workshops down at the Rec Centre? That's something you could still do with a broken arm, Alberta.'

'Ew! Drama!' said Clementine. 'As if we don't have enough drama in our lives already!'

Isn't that that truth, I thought.

CHAPTER 9

I woke up the next morning feeling super gloomy. Not just about Mum and the Woolies incident, it was more that I still hadn't heard a peep from Sylvie. I couldn't believe she hadn't shown the slightest bit of concern about my arm. There was no denying it – Sylvie just didn't want to be my friend. Not only that, it felt like she had infected my whole friendship group. I checked my phone for messages. Nothing. I didn't have one friend signature on my plaster, either. Just signatures from Mum and Clementine. Plus one I did myself on behalf of Sascha and another one on behalf of Leroy, the rabbit next door that sometimes comes under our fence. So tragic! At least Mum was still in a good mood at breakfast though, and I did have a plan to visit Mikki Watanabe; two plans actually, if you also count dinner at Quilty's Diner with Clementine and Dad.

'Did I tell you Aunt Robina's going to celebrate New Year's with us at the Bowls Club?' Mum said, as if I would find that exciting. All I could imagine when I thought about the New Year's Eve bash at the bowlo was all my friends having a grand old time without me.

Clementine was leaning into the corner of the bench waiting for her toast to pop up so that she could press it back down again and burn it.

'Oh, Alberta,' Mum said, pouring herself a cup of coffee. 'I almost forgot...I enquired about the school holiday programs too, but the drama group is booked out.'

Clementine and I swapped looks of relief. It was perfect. Not only were we getting out of something we didn't want to do in the first place, but we weren't responsible for spoiling Mum's good mood, either. It was a total win-win. For once I agreed with Clementine. Who needed more drama? It felt like we were living in a soap opera already.

I couldn't help worrying about Seth Cromby and the Woolies incident and what he might do. I mean, he didn't have a problem breaking my arm, so who knew what he might be capable of? Especially after Mum calling him a barbarian.

Mum headed back to the den with her coffee. 'By the way,' she said. 'I'll be practising my TED Talk today, so if you hear me talking to myself, don't go thinking I've lost my marbles!' Mum laughed (she absolutely loved her own jokes) and Sascha joined in too by beating his tail against the lounge room floor.

'Actually, Sascha,' Mum said, 'you can be my audience. Come on!'

Later, when I was ready to leave for Mikki's, I found Mum pacing around the den with her notes and a timer, talking to Sascha who was fast asleep on the floor. I couldn't help noticing the crumpled Milky Bar wrapper on Mum's desk, couldn't take my eyes off of it actually. It took all my strength not to blurt out, *We all know where that came from, don't we?*

'You have a wonderful afternoon, darling,' Mum said. 'And make sure you ask Mikki over here next time. It's polite to return hospitality.'

'Sure, Mum,' I said.

> **Tammy's Tips**
> **#9 RETURNING AN INVITATION**
> *Good manners should always be a two-way street, and all social occasions should have an exchange. Make sure you return the invitation within a reasonable time frame, usually within a few weeks.*

'And make sure you thank his mother when you leave, won't you? Mum continued. 'And use her formal name, unless she tells you it's okay to call her... What's her name again?'

I gave Mum a kiss goodbye. 'Mikki's mum is Junko,' I said.

'Oh dear,' said Mum. 'I should have written a condolence card for you to take over.'

'Mum, you don't even know Mikki's family. That would just be weird!'

CHAPTER 10

Mikki Watanabe's house was one of those low-rooved, brown brick places from the nineteen seventies. His family had bought it from Dad's real estate agency. I remembered the For Sale board out the front and how it described the house as an *Impeccable 1972 time capsule and a retro design lover's dream.*

'Couldn't stand it,' Mum had whispered the day we took a stickybeak at the open for inspection. 'All those low ceilings and wall-to-wall carpet.'

I crunched my way up the gravel path leading to the front door. The air felt cooler in the shade of the huge trees in the front garden. I stepped up to the porch and pressed the bell. Soon Mikki swung open the heavy wooden door.

'Hiya, Alberta. Come in!'

Inside the tiled entrance hall there was a low bench seat along one wall with several pairs of shoes underneath in a neat row. I noticed Mikki was wearing white slippers, kind of like the ones you get in hotels.

'I hope you don't mind?' asked Mikki. 'We take off our shoes inside.'

Mikki reached into some pigeonholes by the door and passed me some slippers. 'Unless you'd rather just wear socks,' he said. 'Sorry, my parents are really pedantic.'

I pushed off my sandals. *Ha*, I thought. If only he knew about Tammy!

'Let me help,' he said, placing my shoes neatly under the bench with all the others. 'It must be hard with just one hand?'

'I'm getting pretty used to it,' I said. I scrunched my feet into the slippers and shuffled behind Mikki. A delicious feeling of accomplishment washed over me. I hadn't considered that there could be manners at other people's houses that Mum had no idea about. In *Tammy Bracken's Guide to Modern Manners* she had not written one thing about shoe etiquette, other than that they shouldn't be allowed on the couch. I wanted to know more about manners at Mikki's. Even if it was just to have one-up on Mum.

'We'd better say hi to my mum,' Mikki said. But the whole idea filled me with dread. I was scared of most parents in general, on account of Mum always shaming me for saying the wrong thing after every parental interaction. I felt like nothing I said to a parent would be right. And I had absolutely no idea what might offend Japanese parents, especially those pedantic about shoes.

I pulled on Mikki's sleeve. 'Wait up...was it your mum's dad or your dad's dad who died?'

'My dad's father,' Mikki said as we shuffled off the tiles in the entry and onto the carpet in the lounge. He pointed to a wooden cabinet near the fireplace. 'You can meet him if you like?' he said.

The cabinet had tiny cupboard doors, which were open and inside there was a candle burning.

'It's a shrine for my grandfather,' said Mikki. 'We still talk to him every day.'

I stopped worrying about meeting Mikki's mum and took a closer look at the shrine. There were three photos in frames. The first one was of a young boy.

'Is this him?' I asked.

'Yep,' said Mikki. 'When he was six.' He picked up one of the frames that held a picture of an old man. 'This one was taken not long before he died.'

My eyes skipped and scanned across all the objects. There was so much to take in. I felt like it might be one of those memory games and any moment Mikki might snap the shrine shut and ask me to repeat everything back. There were two vases with fresh flowers, a stick of incense burning into a brass bowl. A stone tablet with Japanese writing, a Buddha statue, four lychees, a large green apple, some small packets of what looked like biscuits (seriously), an even smaller bowl of rice and a can of Boss coffee.

'We make offerings,' Mikki said. 'To share with Grandfather on his journey to the other world. And to show gratitude to Buddha. Grandfather got a Boss coffee every morning from the vending machine at the station.'

'Oh...'

I was trying to resist saying things like, *Wow or this looks sooo cool*, which didn't feel appropriate when talking about someone's dead relative but was all I could think to say. But was it more appropriate to say nothing at all? For once I was desperate for a manners tip. Inside I screamed, *Mum! What's the right thing to say in a situation like this?*

Mikki's mum was at the kitchen table with a pile of papers that looked like homework.

'Mum, you remember Alberta, don't you?' asked Mikki.

'Yes, of course. Nice to see you again, Alberta,' she said. 'How are you getting on with that arm?'

'Hi, Mrs Watanabe,' I said. 'It's stopped hurting at least. Just have to wait for it to heal.'

'Oh, please, call me Junko. Everyone calls me Junko, even my students.'

I remembered Mikki's parents both worked at one of the universities in the city.

'Okay,' I said. 'Also... my mum sends her condolences.'

'That's nice of her,' Junko said. 'It did come as quite a shock. Just like your arm too, I imagine?'

'Completely,' I said.

'It happened so fast,' Mikki explained. 'One day Grandfather was fine, the next day we heard he had a fall and two days later, by the time we got to Japan... he had passed. I didn't even get to say goodbye.'

'That's so sad,' I said. Mikki was staring out the window in a silent daze. Junko cleared her throat; I think as a way of snapping Mikki out of it.

'Well, Mikki,' she said. 'I'd better get on with marking these exams. How about you show Alberta some of the films you made in Chiba?'

I knew this was our cue to leave.

'Want to?' Mikki asked. 'I'm still editing but I did spend a lot of time filming in one of my grandfather's favourite forests near where he lived.'

'Sure,' I said, following Mikki out of the kitchen.

CHAPTER 11

Mikki had the whole upstairs to himself including a study space along a long wood-panelled wall with a built-in desk. The other walls had green, yellow and orange striped wallpaper. Mikki refreshed his computer screen to reveal a lush green forest.

'It's a cedar forest,' he explained.

'So beautiful,' I said.

I remembered Mikki telling me that he wanted to be a cinematographer one day. He'd even given a talk about it at his school. I'd never met anyone who got so excited about making nature documentaries.

'Do you ever make films about the ocean?' I asked.

'Oh, no,' Mikki said. 'I prefer to make films about trees.'

'Just trees?' I asked.

'Trees and forests,' Mikki said. 'My grandfather taught me so much about trees. He told me the stories from Japanese folklore. Cutting down a tree, especially an old tree, could provoke a curse from the universe.'

'Really?' I asked.

Mikki quickly stopped the video, like he was embarrassed somehow. Did he think it was boring for me?

'I've um...still got a lot of editing to do on that one,' he said.

It wasn't that I didn't like forest videos. I'd just never actually watched one before. I guess trees just hadn't seemed that special since we were surrounded by the Kingfisher National Park. Trees had just always...been there.

There were a bunch of books on Mikki's desk, all stacked neatly in piles. I picked up one with a forest on the front cover. But the title was in Japanese.

'It says, *Shinrin-yoku*,' Mikki explained.

'Shinrin—?' I had already forgotten how to say it.

'My grandfather was a researcher at the UTF,' Mikki said. 'It stands for the University of Tokyo Forests.'

'There's a forest university?' I exclaimed.

'Sure,' said Mikki. 'Japan has more forests than most countries in the world. For my grandfather forests were more important than anything.'

I flicked through the pages of the book.

'It's by one of the professors at the university,' he said. 'My grandfather was one of his researchers.' Mikki pointed to the three characters on the front cover.

'See,' he said. 'This first character is actually depicting a forest. See the three trees?'

森

'Oh yeah,' I said. How cool was it to have letters that were actually pictures of the very thing the letter was describing.

'Then this second one is a wood. See, there are two trees.'

He was right. The character had trees in it, just like the first, but there were two and not three.

'Then this third one means "bathe". See the flowing water on the left and a valley on the right.'

'Cool,' I said.

'So the book title reads, *Forest Bathing*, or ... *Shinrin-yoku*,' Mikki said. 'My grandfather helped prove that being among trees was good for health. Forest bathing is about the practice of walking slowly through the woods, really, really slowly, and bathing in the forest atmosphere.'

I flicked through all the pictures in the book but I couldn't find one of a bathtub anywhere. Mikki must have read my mind.

'It's not about taking an actual bath, Alberta!' he laughed. 'It's like sunbathing. Forest bathing is the same, but instead of soaking up the sun you're soaking up the atmosphere of the forest.'

'So your grandfather invented forest bathing?'

'Not invented. He was one of a team of research scientists. The university did all sorts of studies in the eighties that measured the effects of forests on human health and wellbeing.'

'For real?' I asked, flicking through some of the other books.

'For real,' Mikki said. 'It's why my parents love Kingfisher Bay!'

I had absolutely never considered you could bathe in a forest. Or that a forest could improve your health. To me, the forest was all about providing habitat for wildlife and timber to build things with.

'Does it work in Australia too?' I asked. 'Or...maybe it's just a Japanese forest thing?'

'Alberta, you can forest bathe in the local park if you want to...maybe not as well though.'

Mikki turned back to his computer and scrolled through some of his video files.

'Here, take a look at this one,' he said.

I couldn't believe what I was seeing. It was Kingfisher National Park, *our* national park, the one at the end of our street. But the way Mikki had filmed it...I realised I'd never looked at the forest properly before. I usually just sped through it as fast as I could on my bike. The video was so professional too. Mikki could already be making nature documentaries for real. He'd even made a soundtrack.

'So pro, Mikki!' I said. 'It looks amazing.'

I still had a lot of unanswered questions. The main one being...

'Mikki, do you have to be nude to go forest bathing?'

Mikki laughed. 'No! You can definitely soak up the goodness of a forest through your clothes. Nature has its own electromagnetic frequency. It's just about tuning yourself into it.'

Mmm, I thought. The goodness of a forest. Who knew?

'It all gets a whole lot easier once you realise you can communicate with trees,' Mikki said, and oh so casually too. 'I've been speaking tree for a while now,' he said. 'I learnt it from my grandfather.'

Mikki must have picked up on my confusion. If he knew how to speak to a tree, did that mean he could also read my mind?

'You do understand trees don't use actual words, don't you, Alberta?'

'Sure,' I lied. 'I knew that.'

'Trees communicate more through your own electromagnetic frequency and feelings,' Mikki continued. 'It is possible, if you practise a lot, to *feel* the meanings that are held deep within trees.'

'Mmm,' I said. I was slipping into overwhelm, something I experienced regularly in Maths class.

'But first you have to know how recognise the golden threads and then how to follow them. Only then can you access the feelings of nature. Because did you know, Alberta, that even the earth dreams?'

'Hmm,' I said, thinking... could Mikki be a little bit woo-woo? The dreaming of earth?!

'I can teach you if you like? Just like how my grandfather taught me,' said Mikki. I had a super strong urge to change the subject.

'Are you doing anything for New Year's Eve? There's a bash down at the Bowls Club if you want to come? Families and all.'

'Oh no,' said Mikki. 'My dad's still in Japan tying up my grandfather's affairs and Mum isn't into parties. Thanks all the same though.'

'Fair enough,' I said. Mikki fell quiet, his eyes staring straight past me and out to the sky through the window.

'You okay, Mikki?' I asked.

'I'm okay,' he said. 'Just looking at Grandfather's stuff...' Mikki's eyes filled with tears. 'I don't know... he died peacefully but it just feels so... unfinished... not to have said goodbye.'

'Yeah,' I said. 'That's really tough.'

Mikki wiped his eyes hurriedly. 'Here,' he said taking a small stack of books from the desk. 'These were Grandfather's too. They're the only ones in English. Maybe have a look and we can go up to the forest tomorrow, if you'd like?'

'So like...you're giving me homework?' I laughed. I was trying to lift the mood but Mikki got the embarrassed look again.

'If you don't want to I—'

'Joking, Mikki!' I said. 'These books look *so* special. I promise to take care of them. And I'd love to go to the forest tomorrow!'

CHAPTER 12

When I got home, I went straight to my room with Mikki's books. I felt bad for thinking Mikki was woo-woo, just because I hadn't heard of the things he was talking about. Seriously, after pouring over Mikki's grandfather's books, I couldn't believe how I'd wound up knowing so little about trees. The more I read and the more I googled, the more I discovered just how out of touch I was. I mean, this stuff was actual *science*. When was school thinking of sharing the news? I tried to soak up as much as I could before it was time for dinner with Clementine and Dad. I learnt that trees communicated with one another through huge networks of fungus underground, like a forest version of the internet. I read all about Mikki's grandfather's work and the science behind the interaction of trees and forests and human wellbeing. A forest isn't just a bunch of trees after all. Forests are *global communities of beings!*

Just then Clementine appeared. She was all dressed up like a little girl going to a party, even though it was just dinner with boring old Dad at Quilty's Diner in town. She picked up one of Mikki's books.

'This looks ancient,' she said. 'Want me to make a proper dust cover for it?'

'Maybe,' I said. 'It belonged to Mikki's grandfather, so I'll have to ask Mikki.'

'Is Mikki your new best friend now?' Clementine taunted. She put the book down and opened my cupboard door to check herself out in the mirror.

'You think you're going to win Dad back?' I said. 'With a pretty dress and a ribbon in your hair?'

As soon as I'd said that I wished I hadn't. Clementine didn't answer. She just looked hurt.

'Look, Clementine... the hoo-ha with Mum and Dad. It's got nothing to do with us. We didn't cause it, and we can't do anything to fix it.'

Clementine looked deep into her own eyes reflected in the mirror.

'I *hate* that Ursula Hoffman,' she whispered, loud enough that I could hear.

'Clementine, if you're looking for someone to blame, Dad's your guy!'

'Blah, blah, blah, whatever,' she said. 'Anyway, what are you doing with all these books? It looks like you're studying for a test or something.'

'I'm learning about tree communication and—'

'You're crazy, Alberta! That's the dumbest thing ever!'

I felt myself getting all buzzy and inspired. 'It's not crazy, actually. It's perfect. If I hadn't broken my arm I would never have hung out with Mikki Watanabe today and I never would have learnt about his grandfather or forest bathing either. Don't you see? Breaking my arm seemed like the worst thing in the world, but now I'm suddenly thankful for it.'

'Now you're sounding even more crazy, Alberta.'

'Trees are talking all the time, Clementine, in their own language.'

'Does this mean you're just going to be reading and talking to trees for the rest of the holidays? 'Cause if you are that would be super boring for me.'

'Oh really? Not like your circus training and library book covering? As if that's not boring for me!'

Clementine couldn't argue. She had been down at the library all day. Again. She slammed my cupboard door shut.

'Yeah, well I bet Mikki's toasties aren't gonna be half as good as mine!'

'You're in a super weird mood, Clementine!'

But before we could argue any further Dad's car horn sounded outside.

'Come on, you,' I said.

CHAPTER 13

Mum absolutely never let us to go to Quilty's Diner on account of its classic American cuisine, which *she* says is the worst food in the world. This, of course, meant that for us and pretty much all the kids in town, Quilty's had the best food in the world. We loved the curved booths and the American retro vibe and the way the waitresses put on lame accents as they wrote your order on a pad tucked into their apron. All while chewing noisily on gum, which seemed to be a workplace requirement. I'm pretty sure all their names were fake too. Our waitress was called 'Dolly'. I absolutely couldn't wait to get a job at Quilty's Diner the minute I turned fifteen.

Dolly gave us a large corner booth down the back and we ordered burgers and fries so fast it was like we feared Tammy Bracken might turn up at any moment and force us to switch to ranch salad. But we were safe that night. Mum was at home waiting on an important phone call from England.

'Can I get y'all anything to drink with that?' Dolly asked after taking our food order.

'Blueberry pie milkshake, please,' said Clementine. Dolly scribbled on her pad, then looked up at me.

'How 'bout you, honey?' she asked.

'Make that two, please,' I said.

'What'll it be for you... big boy?' Dolly asked Dad. He blushed.

'A beer, thanks,' he said.

If only Dolly hadn't taken the menus away. At least reading it gave me something to do until the food came. I felt like a bird in a cage in that booth with Dad. At least there was a jukebox near the front door. If things got really desperate I could always go put on some music. I waited for Clementine to start a conversation, because let's face it, she never stops talking. But for the first time in her life Clementine had absolutely zippo to say. The air felt thick with emotions and the aroma of fatty snacks. Then, Clementine started crying. Not exactly the conversation I'd been hoping for, but it sure was better than nothing. Dad shuffled closer to her and put his arm around her.

'Come on now, sweetheart,' he said tenderly. 'What is it?' Was he freaking serious?

'It's nothing,' sniffled Clementine. Was *she* serious?

Dad looked to me like I might have some kind of an explanation.

'Did you know trees can communicate?' I asked. 'Like, actually interact with humans?'

Dad looked annoyed. 'No I didn't know that, Alberta, but thanks. You're a big help.'

'Whatever.' I shrugged. It wasn't me who'd split up the family. It wasn't me the whole town was gossiping about. He hadn't even asked about my arm.

By the time Dolly came back with our order Clementine had perked back up. She blew her nose like a trumpet into her paper napkin. If Mum was here she would have died. Dad's face softened with relief as Dolly appeared.

'Let's see now,' she said, 'We got, ah... three burgers, three fries, two milkshakes and...'

I noticed Dolly making an effort to catch my eye. She gave me a wink, like we were sharing the joke of the century. 'And a nice cold beer for the, ah... *dad of the year*, huh?' That proved it. The whole town *did* know about the hoo-ha.

Dad's cheeks flushed and I gave him a *what were you expecting? It's a small town* look. Thankfully, Dolly's jibe went over Clementine's head. She had already smothered the fries in ketchup and stuffed a bunch into her mouth in an all-out celebration of manners-free dining. For Clementine, this also featured speaking with her mouth full, making sure both her elbows were on the table and that the slurping of her blueberry pie milkshake was the loudest in the land. In between over-sized bites of her cheeseburger she wiped both her greasy hands down the front of her dress.

'Looking forward to the New Year's Eve bash tomorrow?' Dad asked.

'Dad, can I come and live with you?' Clementine pleaded. 'Just till after my birthday?'

This was quite an awkward question given that neither of us knew where Dad was living. If we believed the rumours, he might have shacked up with Ursula Hoffman in her cottage in the middle of the Bunnings car park.

'Gee, well... let me see—'

''Cause there is just no way Mum is going to let me have a hog,' Clementine whined.

'Sorry?' Dad asked.

'Ugh! Don't worry!' Clementine said impatiently, stuffing more fries into her mouth.

'Party food,' I said. 'Fish fingers poking out of gross piles of mash.'

Dad looked bewildered.

'But Mum's just making it all about *her* and that stupid Tammy stupid Bracken.'

'Clementine, Mum and Tammy Bracken are the same person, you know,' I said.

'Shut *up*, Birdy. Daisy might never speak to me again.'

'Daisy?' Dad asked. It occurred to me how much Dad was missing out on by not being home for meals. Would all our catch-ups be just about us filling him in? Would

I really have to live through all of Clementine's dramas twice?

'Mum posted Daisy on Instagram to show the world how *not* to use a knife and fork,' Clementine said.

'Oh dear,' said Dad. 'That was never going to end well.' It was a pity Dad didn't apply that same logic to himself. Did he really believe his thing with Ursula Hoffman would end well?

'Yeah, and now none of my friends will come over, and no one invites me anywhere either.'

'I'm sorry this is happening to you, Clemmy,' Dad said. 'But I'm sure it will settle down. Besides, it's New Year's Eve tomorrow night and I'm sure you and your friends will have a great time, Daisy too.'

The more gripes Clementine shared about Mum, the more relieved Dad looked. I guess it made him feel like he wasn't the only bad guy after all.

'So can I?' asked Clementine. 'Wait, where are you even living?'

'I'm at the Travelodge,' Dad said.

'The one with the pool?' squeaked Clementine. 'And the gazebo? I could have my party there. Oh please, Dad. Please, please, *please*?'

'Well...' floundered Dad. Clementine's eyes swelled with tears. 'Come on, love. I promise I'll help you with your party. We've still got plenty of time.'

'That's if I have any friends left,' Clementine snivelled.

'Clemmy, you wouldn't want to have your party at the Travelodge anyway,' I said. 'Everyone knows it still smells of poo!'

'Alberta, that's a bit unfair, love,' Dad said.

Clementine laughed. 'Ewwww!'

No one dared mention Ursula Hoffman even though both Clementine and I had *big* questions. Would Dad get married to her? Does Ursula Hoffman still have that blind chihuahua, Renaldo, the one that barked its head off when she brought it to the medical centre?

Dad cleared his throat and looked up at the ceiling. His bottom lip started to wobble. 'You know I miss you both terribly, don't you?' It was awkward-as. Especially as so far, I didn't miss Dad one bit. I'd have preferred to be home with my head buried in Mikki's books. I even considered fake-crying, just to get out of the conversation. Thank God Dolly came to clear our plates. She gave me another wink and I felt a tingle of excitement as to what she might say next.

'Can I get you folks some dessert?' she asked. She winked at me again, then looked Dad straight in the eye and said, 'Maybe some hokey pokey, sir?'

Dad's face turned beetroot red. 'Ice cream, of course,' Dolly qualified.

'Yes please!' Clementine squealed. But Dad had already taken his wallet from his jacket pocket and handed Dolly a card.

'Just the bill, thank you,' he said sternly.

'Aw!' Clementine whined. Dolly put Dad's card in her apron pocket and finished stacking our plates onto a tray.

'Why thank you, sir,' she said, smirking. 'Good to see a man who knows his limits.' Dolly turned and went back to the kitchen.

'Mmm,' Dad mumbled. 'Next time I think we'll be going to the Chinese.'

CHAPTER 14

On my way to Mikki's the next morning I could hear the high-pitched screeches of black cockatoos up in the forest. They reminded me of Clementine's arguments with Mum!

I stopped by a she-oak tree, one that I'd passed about a million times. I felt like I had a lot of apologies to make to all the tress in our street that I'd ignored. That day, I saw them with fresh eyes. Apart from getting an A+ for my science report on photosynthesis, I felt like I had taken trees for granted. Now, I saw each tree as an individual being with its very own awareness and unique ability to communicate. I was desperate to learn to speak tree. The sooner Mikki could teach me, the better. Meanwhile, I said goodbye to the she-oak in boring old English, promising to make a page in my journal to not only draw it but write down our future conversations too.

Mikki was in the driveway with the new electric bike he'd got for Christmas. He hadn't used it much yet though on account of his unexpected trip to Japan and

I had completely forgotten him saying he'd dink me up to the forest on it.

'Hey!' Mikki said. 'Look, we're all charged up and ready to go.'

The bike had the cutest passenger seat at the back and a big cargo basket up front, already filled with Mikki's camera equipment.

'Can't wait!' I said. Mikki stowed my bag alongside his camera gear. My heart quickened with excitement. Up until then, bike riding had been ruled out along with absolutely everything else I used to enjoy. And Mikki's electric bike sure was an upgrade too.

'I *love* this thing!' I said.

I saw Mikki's mum inside, walking past one of the large windows. Then, the front door opened and she stepped outside.

'Alberta!' she said. 'I forgot to say the other day... please pass on my congratulations to your mother.'

I must have looked confused.

'For her book,' Junko said. 'Bestseller and all!'

'Oh,' I said. 'Thank you, Junko. I'll tell Mum for sure.'

Junko checked her watch. 'Oh dear!' she said. 'I have to fly! Promise me you'll be careful on that thing, Mikki?' She made a dash for the car. 'And stick to the bike path!'

'We will!' called Mikki. Junko strapped herself into the driver's seat and wound down the window.

'And Happy New Year to you and your family too, Alberta. Have fun tonight!'

'We will!' I called back. Mikki gave me a look, which I could only interpret as *aren't parents annoying*? But at least his mum hadn't launched herself as a world expert on social etiquette while also stealing from Woolies, and at least the whole town wasn't laughing about his father, right in front of his face.

Mikki put the bike on its stand. 'You can hop on!' he said. 'It won't move at all.' I straddled the passenger seat and steadied myself with my good hand. Mikki showed me a bar on the side of my seat where I could hang on. I was relieved because otherwise I'd have to hold on around his waist, which would be awks and also pretty tricky with one arm in a sling. He got himself comfortable on the front seat.

'All set?' Mikki asked, rolling the bike off its stand.

'Good to go,' I said.

When Mikki first started pedalling it felt like a regular bike. But then his legs stopped moving and the bike glided on silently, as if by magic.

'I seriously want one of these!' I shouted. I imagined going to the beach with my boogie board... or making Clementine pay me to take her to school.

We soon reached the playground at the end of our street. It was in front of the entrance to Kingfisher National Park. Clementine and I used to spend whole days there when we were younger and we always had BBQs with the other local families on New Year's Day. Being there made me think about Dad... but not for long. There was a huge stone gateway at the entrance to the national park and a sign saying, *no bikes*. I was expecting Mikki to stop at the bike racks but he just glided on through the gates and into the cool shadows of the trees. A willie wagtail flittered across the gravel walking path as if to welcome us, and spears of sunlight were blinking down from the forest canopy above. Finally, Mikki pulled to a stop.

'Do you mind if I shoot here for a while?' Mikki was already out of his seat and had steadied the bike so that I could step off. 'The track – I love the way it's flickering from dark to light,' he said.

'Sure thing, Mikki,' I said.

'Maybe you could walk ahead a little? It would look so cool in the video.'

I know this sounds tragic, but it was exactly what I'd hoped would happen. When Mikki was packing his camera gear I'd imagined being in one of his nature videos. When Mikki came up with the idea himself, I had to admit, it felt good!

CHAPTER 15

The walking trail led to a creek and we followed its slow downwards arc through the gulley. The air felt swollen with moisture and so much cooler there, among the giant tree ferns. Mikki squatted down with his camera to frame a shot.

'Walk more to the left side of the path,' he said. I could tell he had dropped into movie director mode so I did what I was told and tried my best to forget he was right behind me, watching and filming. 'Walk slower!' he shouted. 'And don't swing that arm so much!'

'Look up every now and again too!' Mikki yelled. It was getting more and more difficult to forget he was there, I can tell you.

I turned my face to the sky—

'Cut!' Mikki shouted.

'Was I that bad?' I laughed.

'Not at all!' Mikki said, tripping on his feet as he lurched towards me. 'I've got an idea! Why don't we make a documentary of our own ... it could be about forest bathing.'

I loved the idea. 'Yes!' I screeched, sounding a little too much like Clementine.

'And you can be the presenter!' Suddenly my love for the idea plummeted.

'No way!' I protested, still Clementine-like. All my previous imaginings about being in one of Mikki's nature videos evaporated. 'You'd be great. Like an eleven-year-old Jane Goodall with her gorillas, but you'd be all about forest bathing instead! It's brilliant... don't you think?'

'Really?' I scoffed. 'A presenter with a broken arm?'

Mikki pointed the camera straight at me.

'Why not? A presenter with a broken arm? I say, yes, Alberta!'

The green light on the camera illuminated.

'Go for it, Alberta!' Mikki said. But I just froze. Whole seconds passed. Mikki gestured with his pointer finger, in a spiralling kind of way, which I could only interpret as, *Come on... hurry up!*

'Mikki, I really don't want to do this!'

But he just kept on filming.

'Just play along!' Mikki said. 'We can edit later. Let's just improvise and see what happens.'

Before I knew it he started firing questions. It sure felt like he'd prepared them earlier too. Maybe Mikki had a secret ambition to be a TV presenter himself?

'So, Alberta, tell me how an eleven-year-old kid in Australia became interested in the Japanese practice of forest bathing?'

'Wait, Mikki!' I said. I couldn't answer Mikki's question, and it had nothing to do with stage fright, either. 'Don't move! There's a—'

'First rule of improvisation, Alberta,' Mikki interrupted. 'Always play along with your partner's offering.'

'I know, Mikki, but there's—'

'It's just fun, Alberta!' Mikki shouted.

It wasn't that I didn't know how to improvise, or play along, or have fun. We did loads of improvisations in Drama and I was always saying 'yes' to people's ideas. It was about the copperhead snake that was rippling across the path between us! Mikki hadn't noticed it because he was only seeing what was in his camera display and he was slowly stepping towards me (and the snake) with his camera. Heading straight for it, in fact!

'Cut!' I yelled. 'Mikki, *listen!*' Mikki peered over the top of his camera.

'Just stop!' I whispered. 'And don't freak out but there's a...snake!' I pointed.

Mikki screamed so loudly that the snake immediately disappeared into the bracken by the edge of the path.

We both stood statue-still. Mikki's eyes were full of terror. Then, when we were sure the snake had gone, we both started laughing our heads off.

'It was more scared than you were!' I said.

'I've never seen a snake before!' Mikki puffed. 'Not in real life.'

After all that the idea of being a presenter in Mikki's documentary felt way less daunting. I mean, I wasn't scared of snakes so why would I be scared of talking in front of a camera? I remembered how Clementine and I used to goof around in the kitchen like we had our own cooking show, and how much I loved being the host in front of our pretend-camera.

Mikki picked up a handful of gravel and threw it to where we had lost sight of the snake.

'Just need to make sure it has really gone,' he said. He tossed another stone in the same direction.

'I think the coast is clear,' I said.

When Mikki was satisfied the snake wasn't going to come back we started where we'd left off, Mikki leading with the same question...

'Alberta, how did an eleven-year-old kid in Australia became interested in the Japanese practice of forest bathing?'

'Well, according to research out of Japan—'

'Go again!' Mikki said. 'Remember to look straight at the camera!'

I took a deep breath and continued. 'According to scientific research the practice of shinrin-yoku, or forest bathing is all about synchronising with the forest environment,' I said.

Mikki lowered the camera.

'Brilliant, Alberta! I knew you could do it!'

I laughed. 'I don't even know what synchronising with the forest environment means!'

'Okay,' said Mikki. 'Follow me and I'll show you.'

Mikki quickened his pace to get ahead then slowed his steps right down, his voice too.

'Firstly, you need to take care of any distractions, like phones. Phones should definitely be turned off.'

'What if you want to take a photo?' I asked. But Mikki didn't answer.

'Next,' he continued, 'you purposefully slow your pace.' I watched Mikki's feet and the deliberate steps he was taking and listened to the crunching sound on the gravel. I tried to do the same with mine.

'Now, once you're free of distractions and you're walking nice and slowly...focus your attention on your breathing.' Mikki took an audible breath in and sighed it out. It was like there was a cool breeze sweeping between Mikki's words. 'Look at all the nature around you, imagine the whole forest breathing with you...with every fresh step you take invite the nature in to calm your mind and body.'

I laughed. 'Except if the nature turns out to be a snake!' Mikki ignored this too. His voice remained calm and centred.

'Notice the many colours in nature, the particular blue of the sky, all the shades of green in the plants and trees,' Mikki said. 'And can you notice, just notice all the different shapes? No need to name or categorise anything...just notice...allow your eyes to drink it all in.'

As I followed Mikki's instructions I felt myself growing more and more relaxed. All the usual forest sounds, the ones I'd barely noticed before, suddenly seemed louder. Colours were more vibrant and illuminated too, and the sunlight flickering between the trees took on a life of its own. I felt time actually slowing down and slipping away, which wasn't so crazy at all, given it was New Year's Eve and time actually was slipping away. Soon the year would be over. My mind couldn't help jumping to the New Year's bash at the Bowls Club that night and how usually Sylvie and I would have made plans to meet up beforehand. But Mikki soon took me back to the forest.

'Really observe all the small details...' he said, '...the leaves, the bark on the trees, the earth under your feet. Notice any movements from the breeze...all the things that usually pass you by.'

Mikki eventually stopped talking and we both ambled along the trail in our own little worlds. Until, Mikki had another idea.

'We could have our own YouTube channel, you know?' he said.

This made me burst out laughing.

'You might laugh, Alberta,' Mikki argued. 'But I subscribe to loads of nature documentary channels on YouTube. People are making really cool videos, even people our age.'

'Really? I thought YouTube was just full of rich kids doing product reviews so they can get free stuff.'

'Well, sure,' Mikki agreed. 'There's plenty of that going on too.'

'Or cooking hacks or slime. Or... boring gaming stuff.'

'Yes, but we could have a really cool channel. I've always wanted to but—'

'You should, Mikki!' I said. 'You totally should.'

'Believe me, I think about it all the time,' Mikki said. 'But I'd be a terrible presenter. Anyway, I just want to shoot film. You could do it though, Alberta. With a bit of practice, you'd be the perfect presenter.'

'I was pretty good with the fake cooking shows my sister and I used to do.' I laughed. 'But gee, Mikki... I don't—'

'Our channel could be amazing... there's nothing on forest bathing and how to communicate with trees!' Mikki's face lit up. 'And my grandfather would be so proud!' he exclaimed.

I think it was that part that got me over the line, the idea of making Mikki's grandfather proud. I wanted that too, I really did. And it wasn't like I didn't have time. What else was I going to do for the rest of the holidays? I decided to go with it, in the full spirit of improvisation – run with my partner's idea.

'Okay, Mikki! Let's do it!'

※

All the usual scenes in the forest had taken on a different, film-worthy light. Mikki and I followed the walking track deeper and deeper into the forest, chatting about how we'd make our first video. Mikki kept stopping to shoot snippets of film. Most of all we needed to agree on a name for our YouTube channel and as we brainstormed, we let ourselves be taken where the forest seemed to want us to go. The ideas were flowing thick and fast, like a game of word ping-pong. But no matter how many names we tried, nothing seemed to stick.

'How 'bout... TreeTV?' Mikki suggested.

'Nah,' we both said in unison.

'Kingfisher Forest Bath?' I suggested.

'Nah,' we both said again.

'All About Trees?' Mikki said.

'Nah,' we said, as one.

'Big World, Little Forest?'

'Nah.'

The brainstorming went on and on. Names like Forest Drama, Studio Eco, Forest Babble, The Tree Tub, Feelin Grovey... but nothing seemed to stick.

'Forest Bath?' Mikki suggested.

'I like Forest Bath but...'

'You know, Alberta,' he said. 'Let's just work on the video today and decide later.'

'Okay,' I said. 'Maybe the perfect name will come to us in a dream? It worked for Albert Einstein. He discovered the theory of relativity after dreaming about cows!'

CHAPTER 16

All that chatting and brainstorming meant Mikki and I soon ran out of conversation. We were walking in silence, Mikki slightly in front, taking steady, measured steps. I became so focussed on Mikki's feet and the soothing, crunchy sound they made that I didn't even notice we'd veered off the main trail and onto a narrow track to the side. Even though this new path had an undeniable 'home to snakes' vibe, we followed it all the same, like the path itself was drawing us in.

Along the way Mikki found all sorts of things to film. A gang of sulphur-crested cockatoos overhead, and every type of tree – stringybarks, peppermint gums, wattles. A lone cloud dabbed against the blue sky, shadows dancing. And he gathered lots of close-ups too; the veins in a fallen leaf, a line of busy ants, a lone feather from a kookaburra's tail, lacy fungus, the most perfect moss-green moss. And one of my all-time favourites... pine needles! The further we followed the path, the more it became scattered with pine needles. Spongy, fragrant, welcoming pine needles.

Soon, the native forest gave way to a mysterious grove of towering pines – all standing in neat lines. It was a whole other forest, hidden within the forest. Mikki squatted with his camera, panning across the rows of grey gnarly trunks, then up to the sky. I weaved in and out of the trees. Deep pillows of pine needles were mounded around the base of each trunk. It felt like the perfect place to sit down, and all the while it seemed like the pine trees were observing Mikki and me ... with great interest.

'Mikki! Did you know this was here?'

'Not at all!' Mikki said. 'The strange thing is being here feels just like visiting the conifer forest in Japan, near my grandfather's home in Chiba. I'm getting shivers!'

'Me too,' I whispered. 'It's so so quiet.'

Around the perimeter of the trees there were some rotted-out wooden posts, maybe once belonging to a fence. We found a rusted-out gate leaning against one of the bigger trees and some crumbled bricks on the ground next to sheets of rusty tin, like from a roof. Mikki turned a blackened half-brick over with his shoe.

'Looks like there used to be a house here,' he said. 'This would have come from a fireplace.' He pointed to a piece of rusty metal on the ground. 'An old oven door, see?' I don't know how he knew it was an oven door, but I took his word for it.

'Whoa!' I said. 'So someone actually lived here?'

'Sure looks that way. The same someone who planted this pine grove, probably,' Mikki said.

'Must have been so long ago. These trees must be one hundred years old!'

'Maybe even older,' Mikki said.

I stood on the old brick fire place and cast my eyes across the pine grove. The trees were mostly all the same size but there was one that was clearly bigger and taller than the others, the tree with the rusty old gate leaning against it. Mikki took the gate and moved it over by the old brick chimney. Then he went back to the tree and circled around it, running his hand across its dark lumpy bark.

'It's weird,' he said. 'This reminds me so much of my grandfather. I feel like he's right here.'

CHAPTER 17

When I got back from the forest I could hear Mum and Aunt Robina laughing their heads off from the back deck. They sounded like a couple of galahs.

'Here she is!' Mum said excitedly as I stepped outside. They were all dressed up for the New Year's party at the bowlo, sipping champagne and eating disgusting oysters.

'How did your film project with Mikki go?' Mum asked.

'It was fun,' I said. 'We actually found a little pine forest inside the forest.'

'How intriguing!' Aunt Robina said. 'How's that poor arm of yours?'

'It's okay,' I said. 'Just have to wait it out, I guess.'

'Speaking of waiting,' Mum said. 'Your sister's been dying for you to get home. She's been on that pogo stick for hours!'

I was secretly hoping Clementine might have heard something from Sylvie or one of my other friends. I knew it was a long shot but maybe she'd seen one of them at the library and had news of some kind of a pre-party plan. Last New Year's Eve a bunch of us from school met at the front beach before going to the Bowls Club. But I knew that was just wishful thinking. Truth was, there probably was a plan. I just wasn't included.

'Be a love would you, Bertie?' Mum said. 'Help your sister get ready. We'll need to get going soon.'

When we finally arrived at the Bowls Club the party was in full swing. Even from the car park you could see people crowded all over the balcony.

'Do you think Ursula Hoffman might be here?' Clementine whispered as we got out of the car. 'Or her chihuahua, Renaldo?'

'Shh!' I giggled, shepherding Clementine inside.

The club house had been decorated with coloured balloons in the shape of letters, spelling *Happy New Year* and there was a mirrored disco ball spinning above the dimly lit dance floor in front of the stage. Clementine and I scanned the room for people we knew. It seemed most of the adults were outside on the balcony, while the kids were clustered inside. The Mayor of Kingfisher Bay, Mr Pizzey, was weaving in and out of the crowd selling raffle tickets. Clementine rushed towards him, pulling me along with her by my sling.

'Hello, Mr Mayor!' Clementine said. 'Is Harriet here?' Harriet was Clementine's friend from school and Mayor Pizzey's daughter.

'Well hello, girls!' Mayor Pizzey said. 'And don't you look pretty in that dress, Clementine!' Vomit! Mayor Pizzey was seriously so out of touch he still thought the only thing girls wanted to hear was how pretty they looked. Still, Clementine lapped it up, especially as Dad hadn't mentioned a thing about her special dress the night before, even when she'd wiped her burger-and-fries-stained hands all over it.

'Let me see,' Mayor Pizzey said, scouring the room. 'I think I saw Harriet at the bar. The staff have made some fabulous mocktails for you kids.' Clementine made a beeline for the bar, leaving me stranded with Mayor Pizzey.

'And how's that arm of yours, Alberta?'

'Still broken,' I said. Awkward silence.

'I could do with some help selling raffle tickets,' Mayor Pizzey said. 'What, with such dwindling tourist numbers this year, the Kingfisher Bay business community sure needs a bit of extra support.'

'I could definitely get my mum and Aunt Robina to buy a couple,' I said, seeing it as a perfect opportunity to escape. 'I'll go ask them now.'

Mum was outside on the balcony with Aunt Robina. I don't know why they wanted to come to the party actually; they weren't even talking to anyone else, I guess because of the small-town gossip Mum was always complaining about. I was halfway through telling them about the raffle tickets when I saw Bella arriving with Sylvie,

Georgette, Pip and Harrison. It was so obvious they had all met up before coming. I felt my eyes pool with tears. I still couldn't believe Sylvie had turned everyone against me over a stupid netball top.

'Just going to the loo,' I said, escaping Mum and Aunt Robina before they noticed I was upset.

In the bathroom, I turned on the tap and washed my face with cold water. I really didn't want to go back out to the party. Would Sylvie even respond if I said hi? Or would I spend the rest of New Year's Eve selling raffle tickets for Mayor Pizzey? Just then, Bella burst through the door.

'Oh my God, Birdy!' she said, 'We've been looking for you everywhere!' Bella gave me a big hug. She didn't seem to notice I was upset.

'Well, you didn't look very hard,' I said. 'You could have messaged me!'

'I feel awful!' Bella said. 'There was nothing organised, not properly. Harrison messaged me about a last minute meet-up at the beach. But he said he'd invited Seth Cromby. Of course we wanted you to come … we just didn't think you'd want to bump into Seth!'

Bella gave me another big hug and I patted her on the back with my good hand. She was right. I totally wouldn't have wanted to see Seth, but I still wished they'd invited me.

> ### Tammy's Tips
> #### #10 INVITING PEOPLE WHO YOU KNOW CAN'T COME
> *Receiving an invitation lets a person know they are loved and wanted. Getting invited makes them feel they are valued in your life. Even if you know your friend or relative won't be able to attend your occasion, invite them anyway. It's a kind gesture and an expression of friendship.*

'Wait! Seth's not here, is he?' I asked.

'No way!' Bella said. 'He didn't turn up to the beach and when Harrison messaged him, Seth said he'd been grounded! Apparently, your dad called his dad and told him what Seth had done to your arm and Seth's parents went nuts!'

'No way!' I suddenly felt a little guilty for being such a grinch with Dad. 'He never said a thing!'

'Anyway,' Bella said. 'We're all dying to sign your plaster. Look! I've even gotta Sharpie!' Bella reached into her shorts pocket and found the pen. I breathed out a huge sigh of relief, even though I still felt like something wasn't quite adding up. None of what Bella had told me explained why Sylvie hadn't messaged or called when I broke my arm. But I soon put my anguish aside. I was just happy all my friends were there. It would have been a pretty sad New Year's Eve glomming onto Clementine's friends.

Sylvie and the others were on the dance floor. Not dancing, just huddled together sipping mocktails. Each one was in a proper cocktail glass with a pineapple swizzle stick and one of those little paper umbrellas. Sylvie gave me a hug. Then all the others did too. They were all super excited about my immobilised arm, like having a cast and a sling was the coolest thing ever. Bella gave Sylvie the Sharpie pen.

'Oh my gosh!' Sylvie laughed. 'Under the spotlight! I don't know what to write!'

'Just sign your name!' Bella shouted over the music.

I wriggled my arm out of the sling to make it easier, even though revealing I had signed my own cast as a dog and a rabbit was dead tragic.

'Ha ha... It was Clementine's dumb idea!' I lied.

It was such a relief to be having a laugh with my friends again, until Mum came to say hello, which seemed to make Sylvie act all weird again. She was polite enough at first, like anyone behaves when talking to a parent, especially if that parent also happens to be a world expert on table manners and social etiquette. And it's not like Sylvie's shy or anything. She's known my mum since we started kinder. But for some reason Sylvie couldn't even look at Mum. It was like Sylvie had stopped acting weird with me but had now taken up acting weird with my mum instead. It's not as if Mum hadn't returned the netball top.

'Just going to get another mocktail,' Sylvie said, even though hers was still half-full. Then she scurried off. I looked to Bella for some kind of explanation, but she avoided my gaze. Sylvie didn't get another drink. Instead she just did a lap of the room, watching and waiting until Mum had left. Then she joined us again, chatting and laughing like her usual old self.

Close to midnight Mayor Pizzey stepped onto the stage to make some announcements, mostly about how the people of Kingfisher Bay needed to pull together and support one another even more in the new year ahead, on account of the unfortunate poo incident and how it had driven the summer tourist dollars away. Then he gave himself a big plug as Mayor of Kingfisher Bay and listed all the improvements he had made and how excited he was about the future of the town so long as he was voted in again as Mayor at next year's council elections. Was he kidding? Everyone knew the poo incident was Mayor Pizzey's fault. Hands down, he had caused the livelihoods of hundreds of families to be literally flushed down the drain that summer. It was a relief when he stopped self-promoting in time to draw the raffle.

'Now!' he announced. 'Do I have any volunteers to pick the winning tickets?'

There was high-pitched screeching from the audience. 'Me! Me!' It was Clementine and Harriet.

'Come on up!' Mayor Pizzey said.

Clementine and Harriet ran up on stage and giggled their way through drawing the winning tickets from a cardboard box. There were three prizes in all. Mr Lawson from the hardware store won first prize – dinner at the Italian restaurant in town. Second prize was a garden voucher from Kingfisher Nursery that went to Mrs Licciardi from Banksia Crescent, and third prize, a meat tray from Kingfisher Organic Meats, went to Oliver Holten from Clementine's class at school. Clementine and Harriet couldn't stop laughing on account of Olli being vegetarian.

'What's Olli meant to do with a whole bunch of sausages?' Clementine giggled.

'Lame prizes!' Harriet said. 'I was totally expecting first prize to be a car!'

Mayor Pizzey ushered Clementine and Harriett off stage. It was almost the new year.

'Now...let's all charge your glasses,' Mayor Pizzey announced. 'It's time for the countdown...ten, nine...' Everyone joined in, shouting the numbers at the tops of their voices. '...three...two...one...Happy New Year!'

The DJ played the Mariah Carey version of 'Auld Lang Syne', and everyone in the clubhouse hugged and kissed and wished one other 'Happy New Year'. Then Sylvie hugged me and I couldn't help apologising (again) about her netball top. I just wanted to make sure we didn't carry any bad feelings into a squeaky-clean new year.

'Birdy, don't be silly,' Sylvie yelled over the music. 'I'm the one who should be sorry... I've been a crap friend!'

'Happy New Year!' Bella interrupted. 'Love you guys soooo much!'

'Group hug!' Sylvie shouted, pulling Georgette in too. Georgette grabbed Pip by her shirt and before we knew it Harrison had bombed our hug as well. 'Happy New Year!' we all shouted. For some reason, in that moment I wondered what Mikki was up to and felt a bit sad that he wasn't celebrating New Year's. But I realised he'd probably be happily sleeping and who knows – maybe he'd come up with a name for our YouTube channel? Mikki didn't seem to care for parties much anyway. He probably thought it was just as much fun to be shooting videos in the forest. Come to think of it... so did I!

CHAPTER 18

After the party Mum and Aunt Robina stayed up laughing their heads off in the kitchen until the birds were up. And you might have thought Mum would sleep away the morning but no... there she was, looking all fresh and knocking on my bedroom door by seven. This is what I blame for my terrible night's sleep and for why a name for our YouTube channel hadn't come to me in a dream like I had hoped.

'I just need to ask you and Clementine one small favour,' she said. 'Oh, and Happy New Year again, darling.'

Soon Clementine and I were sitting on the good couch in the front room, rubbing our tired eyes. It seemed like only yesterday we had been there while Mum dished up the bad news about Dad. But it wasn't long before we learnt there was more bad news to come. Mum wanted me and Clementine to be her live audience so she could practice her TED Talk! Don't ask me why it was so urgent. It was the weekend after all and I'd planned to spend the day with Mikki in the forest. This felt like a new kind of torture.

'Oh, Mum!' Clementine protested.

'Just once. I promise,' Mum said, handing Clementine the timer. 'You know TED Talks have a strict eighteen-minute maximum.'

'Eighteen whole minutes!' cried Clementine.

'Come on, girls. It's the last favour I'll ever ask of you,' said Mum. 'I promise.'

Clementine and I both rolled our eyes. I can't tell you how many times Mum had promised us that the current favour she was asking was the *last* favour she'd ever ask. We both knew there'd be another one, most likely tomorrow. Fortunately, I am highly skilled at zoning out – an attribute that gets me into a lot of strife at school but for moments like these it's a total gift!

> *Tammy's Tips*
> #11 MAKING PROMISES
> *Every fulfilled promise builds respect and integrity and shows you are a trustworthy, honourable person. Never make a promise you can't keep.*

Clementine switched on the timer and Mum began. That's when I zoned straight back to thinking up YouTube names again and about all the things Mikki had told me about his grandfather and how sad it was that

Mikki didn't get a chance to say goodbye to him before he died and how cool it was to have made a new friend, even though once the holidays were over Mikki would be going back to the city. I thought about all the new things I'd learnt about trees, even if I didn't understand what Mikki was talking about when he mentioned golden threads and the dreaming of earth. It was then I remembered the journal Uncle Gus had given me for Christmas. I wanted to get started on a tree journal straight away, a place to gather all my learning in one place to make up for all the science that had been left out at school. I was pretty sure it was still in Mum's car, right where I'd left it after Christmas. Finally, Mum finished her talk.

As Mum rummaged through her bag for the keys I couldn't help thinking about that second Milky Bar she had stolen. Was it still there, or had she conveniently eaten the evidence?

'Check the boot,' Mum said. 'I think I saw it the other day.'

But all I found in the boot were some of Clementine's stinky old runners. Next I checked the back seat – no luck there either, although I could imagine Clementine kicking it under the front seat, especially if she was cross for having to sit in the back. I padded under the passenger seat with my good hand. 'Aha!' I said out loud. I felt the hard cover of the journal straight away and pulled it out. But there were other things under the seat too. It felt like clothing. I reached in as deep as I could, extracted it all and piled it all up on the back seat. The weird part was that all the clothing was brand new – three pairs of exercise leggings, four lycra training tops and two T-shirts, all with swing tags intact. And that's when I got shivers. The swing tags were from Kingfisher Sports. That was Sylvie's family's store. Then it got worse – the gear didn't just have Kingfisher Sport's swing tags but also those plastic store security tags, the type that usually get taken off when you pay. I gasped out loud. Mum hadn't paid! She must have just shoved the gear into her bag, just like the Milky Bar incident at Woolies.

I searched frantically under the other seat, hoping to find something to erase the picture that had just painted itself vividly in my mind. Maybe I'd find a Kingfisher Sports bag, a receipt even, you know – the kinds of things that could prove Mum actually bought all that gear. But there was nothing. There was no denying it. My mother, Tammy Bracken, world expert on table manners and social etiquette, was a verified shoplifter. Not only that, she had stolen from our friends, and not just a couple of chocolate bars either. This was an actual haul. I flashed back to the night before at the bowlo. Finally it made sense why Sylvie had been acting so weird. And come to think of it, Sylvie's parents had kept their distance from Mum the whole night too. It was all so obvious now. Mum must have been seen! Sylvie probably knew and wasn't allowed to say anything. Did this mean Sylvie's family had told the police instead? Were they about to do a raid any moment?

Just then, I heard Mum open the back door. Had she suddenly remembered what she'd stashed in the car?

'Did you find the journal, Alberta?' she called. I quickly stuffed the clothes back where I'd found them, grabbed the journal and closed the car door. My heart was pounding, like I was the one who'd done the wrong thing. Mum was waiting by the back door.

'Thanks, Mum,' I said, giving her back the keys. 'It was in the boot, just like you said!'

I paced around my room in circles. My brain felt like it was going to explode. Every little part of me wanted to take Mum on. Talk about double standards! How could Mum have made such a fuss about poor Daisy's improper use of a knife and fork, not to mention badgering me and Clementine on a permanent basis about every little thing... and the *whole time* she's out stealing things from stores? And not just any store, our friends' store! None of it made any sense. It wasn't as if Mum couldn't afford exercise gear or chocolate. Her book has sold squillions and Mum hates exercise anyway!

Soon I had a pressure headache. Where was Dad? Did he know about any of this? Was I meant to report my own mother to the police? I'd seen on a movie once that if you knew someone was committing a crime but you didn't report them, then that made you part of the crime too. An accessory.

I remembered Miss Hicks in Year Four teaching us about mindfulness in the school gym when everyone in the town was worried about the bushfires. She said that human minds were just like monkeys and it was natural for the mind to jump around and chase thoughts, just like monkeys chase bananas. That's exactly what my mind was doing. It had been completely taken over with banana thoughts – like Mum in jail, her career in tatters, and our family needing to leave town. I was so stressed that I actually started to clean up my room. Voluntarily! In the end I decided not to say anything about the clothes. At least not for a day or two.

Mum came into my room when I was getting dressed for Mikki's and I told her about my idea for a tree journal.

'You've always loved science,' Mum said. 'I'll never forget that exploding volcano you made out of baking powder and vinegar!'

'Muuuuuuum!' Clementine yelled from the kitchen.

'Speaking of volcanoes,' Mum said. I saw her whole body stiffen. 'Would you excuse me, Birdy?'

Moments later I heard the familiar rumble of Mum and Clementine's argument, not that I could hear everything they were saying. Just the odd phrase like 'crass fish fingers' from Mum and 'ruining my life' from Clementine. Seriously, when was Clementine going to give up about her party?

CHAPTER 19

All the way to the forest Mikki and I brainstormed more YouTube names. It was the perfect thing to keep my banana thoughts under control. We rehashed some of the ones we had rejected from last time and did our best to come up with some new ones. When we got to the pine forest Mikki headed straight back over to his favourite tree, the one that reminded him so much of his grandfather. He gave it a long hug, which I found a bit embarrassing, and I didn't know where to look so I explored some more over by the broken-down house. I turned over a brick with my shoe, and watched the dark-dwelling insects burrow frantically into the pale pine needle litter underneath. I noticed Mikki wiping his eyes as he was taking things out of his pack.

'You okay there, Mikki?' I asked.

'I'm okay,' Mikki said. 'Just having a conversation with my grandfather and this tree.' Mikki leaned a photo frame of his grandfather against the trunk of the tree. I wasn't sure whether he planned to leave it there and if he did I was already worried about what might happen to the photo if it rained.

'I'm making a small shrine here,' Mikki said. 'A bit like the one we have at home. I can't stop hearing Grandfather's voice in my head.'

'Aw! I'm sure he's missing you too, Mikki,' I said.

But I also felt like the less I said the better. I didn't want to intrude on Mikki's conversation with his grandfather. Even though I was dying to know what the tree had actually said. Mikki carefully placed two red apples next to the photo. Given that Mikki had never seen a real snake before I hoped he wouldn't get upset when those apples became a meal to real possums. But I didn't say anything. Realists can be such downers.

'The tree said it would help me with the memory of my grandfather, and also to say a proper goodbye,' Mikki said.

That's when I got chills. It was the idea of a tree helping with memories. 'Oh my gosh, Mikki! *The Memory Tree!* Wouldn't that make the perfect name for our YouTube channel?'

Mikki's face lit up. 'Mikki and Me and the Memory Tree. I love it!'

⚘

We got straight into rehearsing our first intro, in front of the Memory Tree – me playing the clunky presenter, Mikki filming and directing like a pro. Every time I mucked up, he just kept on rolling.

'Try again!' he said. 'You'll get it this time, Alberta!'

'Sorry! Here goes...' (Throat clearing noise.) '...Hey, there! Thanks for watching. I'm Alberta Bracken, and behind the camera is my good friend, Mikki Watanabe.'

I patted the trunk of the Memory Tree.

'And here we are, in Kingfisher Bay, Australia. Mikki and I discovered this little pine forest right in the middle of the national park and it's become one of our favourite places. And *this* big guy... we've named the Memory Tree. It's the inspiration behind our new channel, *Mikki and Me and the Memory Tree.*'

'Cut,' snapped Mikki, and I thought I'd done something wrong for sure.

'What?'

'No, you're doing great,' he said. 'I just want to shoot the next bit with you walking towards the camera.'

I was glad for the chance to rehearse my next piece in my head, as I made my way to the track.

'There is good!' Mikki hollered. 'Now, turn back, talk straight to the camera and walk... but not too fast!'

'Got it!' I shouted back.

'Eyes straight to the camera!' Mikki yelled.

'Okie dokes!'

Mikki started counting me in. 'Three, two, one... and... action!'

I didn't have time to be nervous. I had to be *on*.

'*The Memory Tree* is all about forests and the cool new science on tree communication.' Without taking my eyes from the camera I could sense I had already made it halfway back to Mikki.

I slowed down the tiniest bit. 'We've got loads of great videos coming up, so subscribe to our channel and look out for something new.'

Mikki signalled *cut*. 'Okay, cool! We'll pick it up again on the main trail.'

Mikki was filming everything out of order but he said it didn't matter. 'It will all make sense in the end. It's all in the editing, Alberta.' And I believed him too. We picked up our pace, headed back to the main forest trail then down the gully to the creek.

'Well, here we are, deep in Kingfisher National Park in Australia. And lucky for us, this gem is just a bike ride away. It's here we'll be exploring the ancient Japanese art of shinrin-yoku, or forest bathing – all thanks to Mikki's grandfather—'

I gestured a frantic *cut* signal to Mikki. But he kept on filming. Why did I have to go and mention Mikki's grandfather? And all the stuff about Japan. It seemed like Mikki should be the one talking about it.

'Mikki, you should be the presenter for this part, not me.'

Mikki's eyes filled with tears – proof that I had upset him. He turned off his camera.

'No, it's nothing you said, Alberta.'

Everything felt so heavy all of a sudden and I definitely felt like we should take a break, stop for the day even.

'I feel kind of happy and sad at the same time,' Mikki explained. 'Anyway, I'd be the worst person in front of the camera. Believe me. I'm far more valuable behind the scenes. And forest bathing isn't just a Japanese thing. That's the whole point. The science is here for the whole world to share.'

The forest fell into shade. If I was at the beach, the sun would be melting over the horizon, soon to disappear.

'It feels like time to get home,' I said.

Mikki was deep in thought. He sighed. 'You know, my grandfather did love pines.'

'So do I, Mikki. So do I.'

'Let's just get one last chunk!' Mikki said. He got his camera into position and before I could argue he was counting me in.

'Well... I'm sure you already know that being in nature makes you feel good, but thanks to scientific research we now have actual proof that forests have a bunch of positive effects on humans. So... make sure you tune in to our next video on shinrin-yoku. Yep, that's forest bathing. Just like a relaxing hot tub, bathing in a forest calms the mind and soothes the nerves. All without getting wet!'

Afterwards, I hung at Mikki's while he did some editing. I was starving, and if I didn't have Tammy Bracken for a mother I would have just come out and asked Mikki if he had any snacks. Fortunately, I was distracted by watching Mikki work. I couldn't believe how all the snippets he'd gathered that day turned out making so much sense – the passing clouds, water swooshing down rocks, a sunburnt pine cone. Mikki connected it all into a story. I was seeing the forest through Mikki's eyes and it was absolutely magical.

Mikki's hands danced effortlessly across the keyboard. It was like watching a concert pianist. His fingers floated between keyboard and trackpad, flicking scenes from the forest on and off the screen. The whole experience would have been perfect if I didn't have to watch myself on video too. Terrifying! At times I had to cover my eyes.

'Don't worry,' said Mikki. 'Once I've finished you'll like it, I promise.'

'Seriously, Mikki, how did you learn how to do all this?' My tummy started growling.

'It's like anything,' he said. 'I've learnt loads online... and practice too, of course. We do have one obstacle though, Alberta. And I'm hoping you can help.'

'Sure,' I said. 'If I can.'

'We're under thirteen, right?' said Mikki. 'So we're going to have to get a parent to open our YouTube account. I can't ask *my* parents because Dad's still in Japan and Mum already thinks I spend too much time online. I know exactly how it would go. They'd talk about it for about ten hours on the phone and then say no anyway.'

'That's the obstacle?' I asked.

'So,' Mikki continued, 'I thought you could ask one of you parents. They seem... nice?'

If Tammy Bracken was to describe my reaction she would definitely use the word 'unsightly' and the word 'snort' combined with the words 'unfortunate laugh'. But really... Mikki didn't know a thing about my parents. There was no way I could ask Mum! Not without copping a lecture on cyber safety and internet predators. As if that hasn't been drummed into us enough at school. And Dad? Well... as you know, it's complicated.

'They're really our only hope,' Mikki said.

'Okay, I'll ask my dad,' I said, even though the idea of Dad blabbing about it all to Ursula Hoffman was a total cringe.

By then I was just dying to get home to eat something. As I was walking back I thought about the segment we'd filmed earlier, me talking to a bunch of make-believe subscribers. Would we even get any subscribers? Mikki had showed me lots of young filmmaker channels on YouTube, and loads of nature documentary channels too. I didn't know half of that stuff existed but who was I to judge? I mean, if someone had told me millions of people were going to go nuts about manners I wouldn't have believed that either!

But I did know I felt excited to get home and message Bella about our channel. Excited made it feel easier to ask for Dad's help too. Most of all... I was excited like crazy to get back to the forest, to do it all again.

CHAPTER 20

Dad picked me up early Monday morning. I hadn't spoken to him about calling Seth Cromby's parents and I was super grateful that it amounted to Seth getting grounded, but I still couldn't find the words to thank Dad. I felt all mixed up with feeling angry with him at the same time. Then there was the stuff about Mum. I really did want to talk to him about that too. But more than anything I wanted Dad's help with our YouTube channel so even while it was the perfect opportunity for a one-on-one with Dad I didn't say anything that morning on the way to his office.

'So what are you going to do on the YouTube?' Dad asked.

'Dad, do you even know what YouTube is?' I was dealing with a guy who let his messages from Ursula Hoffman come up on the family iPad, remember?

'Aw, that's a bit much, Alberta! You were crazy about my eggs Florentine!'

'You got that on YouTube?'

'Not only that,' Dad said, 'I think you'd agree my scrambled eggs are the creamiest in the land, not to mention I do the sweetest mac 'n' cheese, the fluffiest rice, the—'

'Okay, okay, I take it back!' I laughed.

Kingfisher Bay Real Estate was in the middle of the main street, sandwiched between Ocean Shores Coin Laundry and Shelley's Street Style Fashion Boutique. Across the road was Kingfisher Sports, from which my mother likes to steal exercise gear to shove under the seat of her car. As my eyes swept past Woolies and all the other stores I couldn't help imagining Mum shoplifting from every one of them. I was so relieved when Dad turned into the car park where all the shops were out of view.

It was still only 8:15 a.m. so Dad and I would be the only ones at his work for at least another half hour.

'Absolutely desperate for a coffee,' he said, getting out of the car. 'How 'bout I open up and you kickstart my computer?'

Dad jiggled his keys in the back door lock, and pushed open the door to the agency. Then he punched in the code to turn off the alarm.

'You remember where all the lights are, don't you, Birdy?'

'Sure, Dad,' I said.

The lights flickered on in Dad's office. The first thing I saw were all the family photos in frames on Dad's desk.

Our family. The photos seemed so out of place now. I felt my throat tighten at one of Mum and Dad's wedding day. Why hadn't he put that one away? Mum looked so happy in her shiny bride's dress, and there was Dad in his navy-blue suit with a flower in the lapel. My instinct was to lay the photo facedown. Seeing it there just made me cross.

That's when Dad came back with his coffee and I blurted out. 'Maybe you should put this one in your drawer?' I said. 'I mean, what would Ursula think?'

Dad's eyes flashed with what looked like rage, but he took a deep breath and acted calm as anything. He took the photo and carefully placed it back upright on his desk. 'Should we get this thing done, Alberta?' he asked. 'I've got a lot of appointments this morning.'

'Okay, Dad,' I said, wishing I'd never mentioned the photo or Ursula Hoffman.

He switched on his computer, and we both waited in silence while it came to life.

I opened YouTube, clicked 'Create New Channel', then typed in *Mikki and Me and the Memory Tree* in the space where it asked for a name. Dad filled out all the account stuff but not without asking a million questions, because parents just love to do that when they know they've got you captive.

'Alberta, I have to ask you – ' Dad's tone was way serious ' – could you be pursuing fame?'

'Of course not!' I said. 'We're making nature documentaries, Dad!'

'Well, I did a bit of research about all this and I need to make sure you understand about privacy, not just your own but the privacy of others too,' Dad said.

'Dad!' I argued. 'It's just for fun over the holidays.'

'And how are you going to protect against trolls? Perhaps we should think about disabling comments?' By then, the only comments I wanted to disable were Dad's. That one and the next hundred Dad comments that followed. It was actual torture just to keep myself nice but there was no way out of it. I knew I'd be parent-free soon, over at Mikki's sharing the good news that our channel was real.

※

'Do Mikki's parents know about all of this?' Dad asked as we pulled up outside Mikki's. Dad had only ever met Mikki's folks a couple of times, back when they'd bought their house. 'Maybe I should have a word?'

That was a scene I wanted to dodge, for sure. Dad didn't really mean it anyway. He was running late for his meeting.

'It's cool, Dad.' I said, getting out of the car as quickly as possible. 'Thanks for all your help!'

'And don't slam the door!' Dad shouted...just as I slammed the door.

'Sorry!'

But it turned out I wasn't free of parents after all. After Mikki answered the door, he told me that he and his mum were in the middle of a FaceTime chat with Mikki's dad in Japan.

'Come and say hi, if you like?' Mikki said. 'We won't be long!' I felt all the excitement for our YouTube channel turn into pressure and awkwardness as I followed Mikki into the kitchen. I did manage to tell him I'd removed the obstacle though.

'Great news!' Mikki whispered as Junko patted the chair next to hers and invited me to sit down. Mikki took a seat next to her on the other side. Mikki's dad's face was on full-screen view on Junko's laptop.

'You remember Alberta, don't you?' Junko said.

'Yes, of course,' Mikki's dad replied. 'How are you, Alberta? Mikki's been telling us about your project. Sounds very interesting.'

'Hi, Mr Watanabe,' I said nervously, not knowing what on earth to say next. Judging by the silence, neither did either one of Mikki's parents. It was a total relief when they all started speaking in Japanese, while I just sat there like a lump. I couldn't help thinking about Mum again and wished that I had said something to Dad after all. I really needed to share the burden. Not even Google had any advice for kids with parents who steal.

Finally, Mikki started speaking in English again. 'Got to go, Dad,' he said.

'Okay, Mikki, speak soon. Nice to see you, Alberta. Look after that arm!'

Afterwards, Mikki and I set about adding a description about our YouTube channel.

Mikki and Me and the Memory Tree features videos by young nature documentary filmmaker Mikki Watanabe and presenter Alberta Bracken. Together we make videos about trees and forests and how humans can learn the language of trees.

Mikki showed me his edited version of our first video. I couldn't believe how polished it looked. Even watching myself talking was half bearable. 'Ready to publish?' Mikki asked and before I could even squeak he'd pressed the 'Publish' tab.

'There,' he said. 'It's done!'

I got chills all over. To think our little video had been launched to the world. It was such a strange feeling, like when Clementine and I had entered a competition to come up with a new flavour of crisps. All that brainstorming and excitement, then just silence and waiting.

CHAPTER 21

Next morning, I woke up thinking about Mikki and the Memory Tree. I'd never had a grandparent pass away so I had absolutely no idea what it might be like to say goodbye, or, in Mikki's case, to not say goodbye. Mikki's Memory Tree was in a completely different country from the trees in the forest where his grandfather lived. But Mikki said the distance between two trees is irrelevant as the hearts of all trees are the same. That's when I logged into YouTube. I couldn't believe it. There were already two subscribers to our channel! And one of them was from Italy! They had both left comments on our first video too. In total we had twenty-one views and likes.

Polly Outdoors 1 day ago
Love this! Can't wait for more on forest bathing.

Massimo Paolini 1 day ago
You are fortunate to have such beautiful forest near to you home.

Reading the comments gave me tingles. I actually didn't expect anyone to even look at our video, at least not so soon. But seeing those comments – it sure felt good to be appreciated, even if it did make me feel self-conscious. I called Bella straight away, hoping to chat before she went to the beach. We stayed on the phone while she watched the video.

'So cool!' she said. 'Can't believe you pulled this together practically overnight!'

'Ha ha! Thanks, Bells. Gotta give Mikki most of the credit though,' I said. 'I really didn't think anyone, would watch it. I need to pay far more attention to wardrobe.'

Bella laughed. 'What about that polka dot dress?' she said. 'I used to love that one ... anyway, Berts, I have to fly. Harrison's mum is giving us a lift to the surf trials.'

After the call I searched everywhere for the dress but couldn't find it anywhere. This could only mean *one* thing! I stomped down to Clementine's room and barged in.

'Did you take my spotty dress?' I asked.

'Why? Are you dressing up for Mikki?' Clementine taunted. 'I thought you weren't into looking pretty for boys!'

'Don't be an idiot, Clementine. I just need a change of outfit. We're making another video today.'

'Again? This is starting to get boring, Alberta,' Clementine whined.

'Not like your dead-end circus training. That's not boring one bit!'

'Alberta, everyone knows the circus will be back next year. They only cancelled the shows at Kingfisher Bay because of the poo incident!'

'Are you sure you haven't seen that dress?'

'Did you look in your messy drawers?' Clementine asked.

Clementine followed me back to my room. I soon found the dress crumpled up with my T-shirts. 'Ah ha!' I said, pulling the dress out of my bottom drawer.

'It's all crinkly,' Clementine said. 'I wouldn't believe anything from someone in a dress like that.'

'Shut *up*, Clementine!' I snapped.

'I could iron it for you...' she offered. 'I could help up in the forest too.'

But as temping as it was to have Clementine iron my dress, (God knows how I was going to manage it with one hand myself), we both knew where it would lead... to the three of us on Mikki's electric bike and that was a definite no, even if I felt a bit mean excluding her. I didn't want to be responsible for Clementine, I didn't want to listen to her complaining and I didn't want to feel even more self-conscious when I did my presenter act with her watching. Besides, Mikki and I had a huge day planned. I just couldn't deal with Clementine too.

'Maybe next time,' I lied. 'But could you iron my dress anyway?'

Clementine's face crumpled. Then she ran to her room crying and slammed the door. Next thing I know I'm getting a lecture from Mum.

'Oh, Alberta, can't you just show a little kindness towards your sister?'

Oh. My. God. Was she serious? Was it 'kind' for Mum to steal from Sylvie's family and to almost ruin our friendship? Not to mention her being unavailable as a parent for the entire school holidays. Why was it up to me to entertain Clementine? Under the circumstances, Mum's 'kindness' rant just made me cross.

'Um...I'm not her mother. You are, Mum. Remember?'

Mum pulled her brow into deep furrows. Her eyes flared with anger.

'Alberta Bracken! How *dare* you?' she scolded.

But she must have known I had a point, because before I could even make a fake apology she had marched off to Clementine's room.

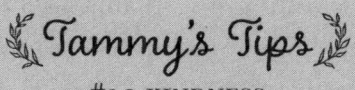

#12 KINDNESS

Kindness is at the heart of good manners. As the author Henry James once said, 'Three things in human life are important: The first is to be kind. The second is to be kind. And the third is to be kind.'

Mikki and I were getting all our gear together and packing it into Mikki's bike. Like me, Mikki was feeling super encouraged by our YouTube responses.

'We've got an audience now,' Mikki said. 'They'll be waiting for our next upload.'

It did feel a bit like having homework, or like having a pet that needed feeding and looking after. Our YouTube channel was definitely something I wanted to nurture, but it also felt like a lot of responsibility. Was this how it felt to be a parent? I felt relieved to not have Clementine tagging along.

'It really will be quite a lot of work,' I said, 'to keep posting new videos all the time.'

'Yes, but you know what they say... if you love your work it doesn't feel like work,' Mikki said.

The morning sun streamed through the trees, casting flickering light across the path as we glided along the main forest trail. Mikki pulled the bike to a stop and took out his camera, setting off a gang of kookaburras into cackles from the high branches of a banksia tree.

'There's a word for this in Japan,' he said as he stopped filming.

'For what?' I asked, thinking he might be talking about the kookaburras.

'This light – the way the sunlight is filtering through the leaves and the trees. It's called komorebi,' Mikki said.

'That's so cool,' I said. 'Here we just call it "glare".'

A pair of rosellas whizzed low across the path and Mikki squatted to capture them on film. Afterwards, we parked Mikki's bike by the side of trail and headed straight for the smaller path to the pines. The further we walked, the less we spoke. Soon, we were in complete silence and I wondered whether Mikki was planning another conversation with the Memory Tree, and if he was, whether he'd prefer to be alone. I wish I knew the right thing to do when it came to conversations with trees. For all the manners Mum had drummed into me I had no idea about forest etiquette.

I slowed my pace and allowed a gap to open up between us, hoping to give Mikki some time alone with the Memory Tree. From a distance, I could see the apples he'd left last time had gone. But the photo frame was still there, leaning against the trunk. I watched him take a hoodie and one of his grandfather's books out of his pack. He sat down next to the offerings and folded the hoodie into a cushion and wedged it between his back and the tree's gnarly trunk. Then he closed his eyes.

I made my way quietly over to the old fireplace and paced around the fallen-down house. I couldn't help thinking of who used to live there. Kids like us maybe, living out whole lives among the pines? Or could it have been a hideout for someone dodgy? And all the black bricks in the fireplace – what kind of meals had been cooked there? My thoughts were disrupted by the most gentle whisper of breeze, which had the effect of reminding me of lines I needed to rehearse for our next video... *the key to entering into the forest bathing experience is to first walk mindfully in the forest, then open your senses to absorbing its goodness...*

'The Memory Tree agrees!' Mikki shouted.

'Agrees to what?' I shouted back.

'About the name for our channel.'

'Oh... that's great,' I said, making my way over to the Memory Tree. I was feeling a bit left behind. I also wanted to speak to a tree.

'Hey, Mikki,' I said. 'Do you think I'm ready to learn to speak tree?'

Mikki's eyes took to the sky. He seemed concerned. 'First,' he said, 'you have to create the right conditions... in yourself.'

Mikki invited me to take his place sitting at the base of the Memory Tree. Then he started circling slowly around it.

'Just take some time to settle,' he said. 'And when you're ready... close your eyes.' As soon as I did Mikki's footsteps sounded louder. He took a long, even breath in, which made me want to do the exact same thing. I filled my lungs with air, and I felt the edges of myself fading into the forest. I remembered from my reading how trees act like the lungs of the earth, and I was comforted to imagine all the pines breathing too, and wondered what it was like for them to have Mikki and me visit again, and for all of us to be breathing together. Then I thought about how weird it all was, to be in this forest... breathing with Mikki Watanabe and a bunch of trees, instead of boogie boarding out in the surf with my friends.

Mikki must have sensed all my thinking.

'See your thoughts coming and going,' he said. 'Like passing clouds.'

Problem was, my thoughts weren't passing like clouds. They were more like multiplying rabbits. Thoughts everywhere. Then, all the rabbit thoughts started hopping around. I even thought about what Clementine might be up to. That's how crazy my thoughts were! And Seth Cromby... I wondered how long he'd been grounded for, and gosh... what if he did report Mum about the Milky Bar incident at Woolies?

'Now,' said Mikki, 'as your breath settles, open your eyes and just let them be soft and to wander.'

The sound of Mikki's voice interrupting my thoughts made me feel like I was in school, vagued out in Maths with Mr Schmidt telling me off for staring out the window. I did my best to focus and follow Mikki's instructions exactly. After all, I was desperate to learn to speak tree. I allowed my eyes to meander the depth of the forest, from the vastness of the sky to one solitary pine needle. An ant, travelling solo, made its way across my shoe.

'Just keep breathing slowly and deeply,' Mikki continued. 'Nothing at all to do... just you in this forest with these old pine trees...and as you notice your eyes wander you'll soon see something in particular has drawn your attention towards it.'

Mikki was right. As my eyes cast a gentle net across the forest, soaking up the glowing orb of sun behind trees, the fallen-down house and the rusted-up fence, the gate off its hinges, the pillowy pine needle floor...and then my eyes settled on a single pine cone; it somehow stood apart from all the others. It had long ago burst open, seeds released. It looked as old as the pine forest itself. Mikki kept talking, like he knew exactly where my mind was at.

'Observe it in as much detail as possible,' he said.

Who *was* this Mikki Watanabe, some kind of wizard? the rabbit thoughts asked.

'Notice every little part of it...and when you are completely immersed in seeing it, *really* seeing it and nothing more...then you just have to ask yourself one question. How does it feel?'

I was still studying the pine cone when I couldn't help thinking, (which I knew I wasn't meant to be doing), about how I didn't really know Mikki Watanabe or his family. Could they be part of a cult? No. Back to the pine cone.

'And I don't mean how does it feel with your hands,' Mikki continued. 'It's about reaching out with your senses, and asking how does it feel with your heart?'

'Okay,' I said, and this time I harnessed all my attention and focussed on nothing else but that pine cone. To do this I imagined any rabbit thoughts transforming into clouds...and passing. Once they were gone I asked myself, *How does it feel?*

'Now, you just wait for a response,' Mikki said. 'You'll feel it.'

I waited. But nothing happened and I didn't feel anything at all, which super bothered me because I was usually a quick learner. Except for in Maths. Definitely slow there. And now...this business too, it seemed.

'The pine cone had nothing to say to me, Mikki,' I whined. 'I did absolutely everything you said.'

I could tell Mikki was disappointed, like me not being able to speak tree had made him just that one bit more alone in the world. But he did his best to reassure me all the same.

'It's okay, Alberta,' he said. 'Most people live their whole lives without fully understanding their senses.'

'It was the rabbits, Mikki!' I giggled.

'You just need to practise. I promise you, soon you'll get a feeling sense of an object's aliveness. That's when you know you've made a connection with its wildness. Keep going, Alberta.'

But I was less enthused. And clearly not a natural either. The language of trees? Learning Japanese felt like it might be easier.

※

Mikki and I prepared for our next video in front of the Memory Tree. Mikki took two new apples from his pack and placed them carefully next to the photo of his grandfather and the books. He also set down a small bowl and squirted some water into it from his drink bottle.

'More offerings for Grandfather,' he explained, 'to help guide him onto the next life.'

'How will you know when it's time to say goodbye, Mikki?' I asked.

Mikki looked a little sad. 'I guess I'll just know,' he said. 'Hey, I've been thinking. We had planned to do our next video on forest bathing, but we probably should talk about hub trees first?'

I had already read plenty about hub trees, the biggest and oldest tree in a forest, and how they help others in the tree community by sending sugars and nutrients through the forest's underground network of fungus. Hub trees can even detect stress signals if other trees are under attack, like by leaf-eating caterpillars. That's when a hub tree releases chemicals that attract caterpillar-eating wasps.

I agreed. 'It makes sense, I guess. The Memory Tree is definitely the hub tree in this little forest.'

Mikki laughed. 'That's what the Memory Tree said too!'

I gave up on any ideas of talking to the Memory Tree that day, given that I'd failed at communicating with a pine cone. Instead, we immersed ourselves in our filming, even though I still had creases in my spotty dress.

'Hi, everyone, Alberta here and thanks for tuning into our channel, *Mikki and Me and the Memory Tree*. Well, here we are again in Kingfisher National Park, where we're just mad about forests and trees, so make sure you look out for more of our videos. I know we promised a video on the Japanese art of shinrin-yoku, or forest bathing, and this is still coming, we promise you that. But today is going to be all about what scientists are now calling "hub trees". Hub trees are also known as "mother trees". If you want to know more, check out the work of Suzanne Simard.'

Mikki cut.

'A bit too much of a rant?' I asked.

'All good,' Mikki said. 'Just that the light is really amazing at the moment.'

Mikki was right. All the pine trees were illuminated in the most beautiful golden light. He set about filming from a few different angles.

'Pity we don't have a test on this stuff at school!' I called out after him. 'I've never memorised so much information!'

'Great!' yelled Mikki. 'Keep rehearsing for the next bit!'

Mikki lay on his back at the base of the Memory Tree. He pointed his camera up the trunk so he could film the length of it, all the way to its crown. When he was done I took up where I'd left off with presenting.

'Throughout human history,' I continued, 'in the mythology of almost every culture in the world, trees have played a sacred role. Humans have always had deep relationships with trees, for births, weddings, funerals, burials and worship. Or, to help us say goodbye to our ancestors …'

Mikki promised to send the video before he uploaded it onto YouTube that night, just to make sure I was happy with it. I knew I would be. When it came to anything to do with filming I trusted Mikki's judgement completely. I had only just finished dinner when I found the hub tree video was in my inbox. It was amazing. Everything I'd feared were too long and ranty had been pieced apart until there was hardly any of me and my crinkly dress at all. Rather, Mikki had used my voice for narration over the top of his beautiful cinematography. I gave him the go-ahead to upload it and logged onto YouTube myself. I was surprised to see even more new subscribers and comments from yesterday's intro video.

Sy Mason 5 hours ago
Alberta and Mikki … keep producing great vids … and maybe we might see you on TV one day! 🎥 🎬 🌲 📺

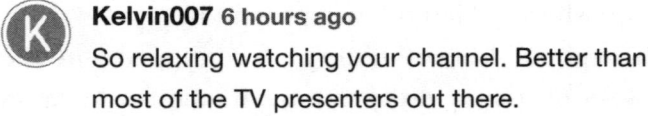

Kelvin007 6 hours ago
So relaxing watching your channel. Better than most of the TV presenters out there.

ProjektQ 6 hours ago
👏 Like it!

But then... There was this one...

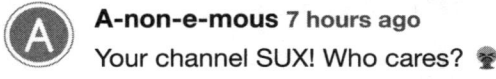
A-non-e-mous 7 hours ago
Your channel SUX! Who cares? 💀

Ouch!

CHAPTER 22

Parents like Mikki's who worry about him spending too much time online are right. I was already hooked, especially after getting all those comments. I logged onto YouTube the moment I woke up. That's when Mikki messaged me too.

Alberta, have you seen the comments under the hub tree video? Call me!

I scanned through the messages.

Polly Outdoors 4 hours ago
Another cracking video. Keep it up guys!

NatureBoy 5 hours ago
I have to say that these aren't just videos, they are pieces of art. I hope you guys never stop. Love and Respect. ♥ 🔺

TheodoreGoldFilms 5 hours ago
Inspiring, inTree-ging and awesome work guys.

A-non-e-mous 7 hours ago
Can you guys seriously get any dumber? See those white stakes in the ground? Means those pines have been listed for removal. That whole pine forest is getting cut down you dweebs!
Next time you visit your big old hub tree... think CHAINSAWS!!! Sayonara Memory Tree!! ☠ ☠
See Ya, Wouldn't Wanna Be Ya!!! Ha ha ha...!!!!

My heart started pounding and I felt cold all over. I called Mikki straight away.

'Who *is* this A-non-e-mous creep?' I clicked on the name.

'I already checked,' said Mikki. 'He's no one. Nothing. Just some empty profile with a bunch of deleted videos.'

I clicked on the hub tree video and played it with the sound off.

'There *are* white stakes in the ground!' I cried.

There they were, clear as the morning – squat wooden stakes, some only just visible above the pine needle floor. My stomach sank. 'How could we have missed them?' I whispered.

'I did notice them actually,' said Mikki. 'But I didn't know what they meant.'

'Could it be true? Or might this A-non-e-mous just be some sad troll with nothing better to do?'

'I did some research,' said Mikki. 'The wooden stakes are called survey markers and yes, they could mean that some kind of agenda is in place.'

None of it made any sense. Why would anyone want to chop down a forest of perfectly healthy trees?

I imagined the Memory Tree towering over the pine forest, so grand and majestic, deeply rooted into the earth. And Mikki's shrine with its offerings and the spirit of his grandfather. Mikki had told me pine trees were special to his grandfather because they were unchanging, evergreen. They were also seen as symbols of resilience and longevity and could ward off bad luck and evil spirits. But it sure felt like the pine's luck had run out that day. For all a tree's cleverness in defending itself from insect invasions or adapting to times of fire or drought, it had absolutely no defence against some cold-hearted redneck with a chainsaw slicing its life away, easy as butter. I could hear Mikki tapping away on his keyboard on the other end of the phone. I felt physically sick as I stared blankly at my screen. And then a new comment appeared.

AbiFilms just now
Hey guys. You should definitely check with your local council. If any trees are coming down in a national park, they're the ones who'd know. Good luck! Such a beautiful pine grove and the Memory Tree has such a presence.

'Mikki, can you reply?' I asked. 'Takes me ages to type with one hand.'

Mikki and Me and the Memory Tree just now
AbiFilms thanks so much! We will definitely get to the bottom of it. There is just NO WAY we're going to let anything happen to those trees. We will save the Memory Tree no matter what!

A-non-e-mous just now
Ha Ha! Can't wait to watch you try! Capital L for LOSERS!

'Mikki? Are you still there?'

'Yes... sorry. I'm looking at the Kingfisher Shire Council website. There's a field where you can put through an enquiry to the Natural Resources Officer.'

'Are you going to?' I asked.

'I did,' Mikki said. 'I guess we just wait for him to reply.'

'Mikki, I do know Mayor Pizzey.'

'Even better!' exclaimed Mikki. 'Let's give him a call!'

'Maybe I can get my dad to talk to him?' I suggested. This whole thing felt kind of... parental.

'It's just a phone call, Alberta,' he said. 'Anyway, you should come over... I'm dying to go check on the pines.'

CHAPTER 23

Mikki and I left the bike on the main trail and ran as fast as we could to the pine grove. Mikki went straight to the Memory Tree and wrapped both his arms around its knobbled trunk, just like you see kids hugging some animal character at Disneyland. My hug was more of a one-armed affair obviously, just a gentle lean in. Once again Mikki's apple offerings had been taken by the creatures of the night, but the other objects were still there, just where Mikki had left them. Mikki took two cans of Boss coffee from his pack and added them to the shrine.

'No more apples?' I asked.

'Thought I'd mix it up a bit,' Mikki said. That's when I noticed the white survey markers, right around the perimeter of the pine forest. I couldn't believe I hadn't seen them before.

I wondered who had hammered them in. In my imagination I saw brutish men with mallets, their thick hairy legs in boots stomping across the pine needles. The air was clouded with dust. The forest was no longer our secret. Now it had a creepy vibe, and I felt like people could be watching us. I looked up to the treetops gently scraping the sky, and I could have sworn each tree was leaning in and hoping we could help. Was it the trees that had lured Mikki and I up here in the first place? What must it be like to be so wise and alive yet plugged so deeply into the earth that you can't run? If the pines really thought we could help... how?

After Mikki had finished with the Memory Tree we were ready to make our next video. 'Can we shoot it back at the creek, though?' Mikki asked. 'It feels a bit sad here today.' It was like Mikki couldn't get out of the pine forest fast enough. I practically had to trot to keep up with him. He was in a sombre mood all right, we both were. We hardly spoke the whole way back to the eucalyptus gully. I guess we both felt defeated in our own way.

Mikki got his gear ready to film.

'You good to go, Alberta?' Mikki asked. I gave him a thumbs up even though I wasn't feeling good to go at all. I was just going to have to fake it.

'Hiya, it's me again, Alberta, and my good friend Mikki is behind the camera. Thanks for tuning in and hi to all the new subscribers to our channel. We're so excited to bring you this video about shinrin-yoku, or the Japanese art of forest bathing, from the shade of this beautiful eucalyptus gully.'

Mikki stopped me to direct some non-speaking scenes – stuff like me stepping across stones in the creek, walking across a fallen log. Then he asked me to look around the forest slowly in all directions while he followed my gaze, as if my eyes were the camera.

'You might have seen our earlier video about how trees can communicate with one another, but have you ever thought about how trees and humans might interact too? In fact, Mikki's been speaking tree for years, haven't you, Mikki? It's all about understanding the language of nature. It's not about words. We're talking about a language of vibrations.'

'Cut!' said Mikki.

'Gee, Mikki,' I said. 'You sure it's not sounding too... out there?'

But Mikki ignored me. He was on a roll. He directed me over to a gully gum. 'How 'bout standing here for the next bit?' he said, checking his watch. I got into position.

'When you're ready, Alberta,' he said.

'The first thing you need to do, if you're wanting to get on the same wavelength as trees is... to switch off your phone, of course!' I took my phone out from its hiding place in my sling and pressed the 'off' button. 'Now... let's take a wander!'

As I got walking I noticed Mikki was filming my feet and each one of my slow and considered footsteps, like every last step had a beginning, a middle and an end.

I was relieved to know that for this segment, it was mostly my feet that were the star of the show.

'Feel each muscle in your feet pressing against the earth,' I continued. 'Check in with your thoughts. Is your mind busy and distracted or do you feel it slowing down with each footstep? Listen to the noise your feet are making. Are you here, right now, or is your mind someplace else? Shift your thinking back to your feet and what's happening right now.'

For the next location Mikki got me to sit cross-legged on a huge granite boulder surrounded by southern blue gums.

'And...action,' he said.

I pulled a long breath in. 'Hopefully, by now, you're leaving the outside world behind. Look around. Look deeply at all that there is – just these trees in this moment.' I softened my gaze, and kind of let my eyes go a little blurry and out of focus, like Mikki had taught me.

'And now can you deepen your observation? Really notice the colours... have you ever noticed just how many shades of green there are? And the shapes... any movements in the trees? Any wildlife? Observe everything in detail... the bark on the tree trunks, all the different layers of the forest... and can you also observe any changes in your body? Maybe your breathing feels slower, maybe there's a feeling of relaxation, of peace? This is how it feels when you've connected deeply with a forest. The wellness you feel... that's the feeling of the forest feeling seen, and the forest seeing you back. Any peace you feel is the forest actually responding.'

'Okay, cut,' said Mikki.

'Oh, Mikki, was that just the most woo-woo rant ever?'

'Not at all!'

''Cause it sure sounded like crystal healing to me!' I laughed.

Mikki laughed too. 'Don't worry, Alberta,' he said. 'The magic happens in the edit, remember?'

And I knew Mikki was right. By the time I got to see the video, all the tiny macro scenes Mikki had filmed – seed pods, fern fronds, footprints, moss... a loveliness of ladybugs – would all be peppered with my words. I could already see how good he'd make it look.

When we had finished filming I lay down on the granite boulder, my back soaking up its warmth. My eyes were drawn far into the distance to a patch of sky, perfectly framed by trees. A solitary cloud drifted into sight, then wisped itself away again, off into an endless indigo sky.

CHAPTER 24

The Kingfisher Shire Council was a squat brown-brick building at the back of the Recreation Centre. Mikki and I were fifteen minutes early for our meeting with Mayor Pizzey. The meeting that I still didn't even want to go to. Mikki couldn't get over how Mayor Pizzey had agreed to meet with us, even though I'd told him ten times that Mayor Pizzey knew our family because Clementine was friends with Harriet at school.

Mikki was fussing with his bike lock at the racks outside on the footpath. That's when I noticed some posters on the electricity poles and wandered over for a closer look. They were all about reminding people to shop local and support the businesses that were missing out on tourists because of the... poo incident. Suddenly, I heard someone calling my name and looked about to find where it was coming from. It was Bella! She was at the bus stop over the road, with her surfboard.

'Hey!' I yelled back. 'Why aren't you at the beach?'

'I'm trying!' Bella yelled back. 'Had some stuff to do this morning, then missed the bus!'

Bella waited for a gap in the passing cars then made a dash across the road, leaving her things at the bus shelter. She had a colourful new rash vest on, with surf company branding all over it.

'Gonna be another half hour,' she said, a bit hoarse from all the yelling. It felt so great to see her. Even though she'd been following *Mikki and Me* online, it wasn't the same as actually hanging out.

'Cool rashie!' I said.

'Thanks! Did I tell you I'm getting sponsored now?' she asked. 'So much free stuff!'

Bella took a swig of water from her similarly branded drink bottle. 'And I made the girls under twelve division... at the Junior State Surf Title trials. Let's hope I make it through to the finals!'

'No way!' I squealed. I gave Bella a huge hug. 'I knew you would, though. When are the finals? I'm definitely coming!'

'Love you to come, Birdy!' Bella said. 'But it's a three-day event this year. Miles away too, up at Ocean Tides 'cause of the poo incident.'

Mmm, I thought, no surf competition at Kingfisher Bay this year. Another thing ol' Mayor Pizzey had goofed up. How was I going to keep a straight face in our meeting? Mikki finished locking his bike and came over to where I was chatting to Bella and said hi.

'Oh! And guess what?' Bella said excitedly. 'You'll love this, Birdy, Seth would have definitely made the cut for the boys division but couldn't come to the trials and won't be in the finals 'cause he's still grounded!'

Bella was right. I did love it. The news made me feel positively gleeful.

'So, what are you two doing anyway?' Bella asked.

I noticed Mikki checking his watch. 'Got an appointment with Mayor Pizzey,' I said.

'I think we should film it too,' Mikki said. 'For our channel.'

'Love your films, Mikki!' Bella said. 'I had no idea that old pine grove even existed.'

It suddenly occurred to me that Mikki had planned to make a video of our meeting with Mayor Pizzey all along. Why else would he have brought his camera gear? I felt uneasy. If Mikki was going to be behind the camera, then that meant I was going to have to do all the talking. I felt like a chess piece, forced into position in Mikki's game.

Mikki and I said goodbye to Bella and made our way inside. Whenever I protested about Mikki's plan, he cut me off.

'You do want to save the pine grove, don't you?' he asked impatiently.

As the automatic glass doors slid open we were greeted by a cold blast from the airconditioner. The foyer inside was library-level silent, while the voices of doubt in my head grew louder and louder. What was I even doing here? Who were we to think we could change anything?

Mayor Pizzey had three photo frames on his desk, just like Dad. I immediately recognised Clementine's friend Harriet in a family photo taken down at the beach. Talking about Harriet felt like a natural conversation starter but Mayor Pizzey ruined it by asking me how things were going at home, his head cocked to one side in a fake-caring kind of way. I was tempted to tell him about the horrific situation with Dad being allergic to Ursula Hoffman's blind chihuahua, Renaldo, but instead I thought I'd throw him off track completely, which really did seem to work.

'You mean with Clementine? We're waiting on test results. But there's still hope. So nice of you to ask, Mayor Pizzey.' Mikki gave me a look.

'Well, sure…okay. You want to tell me more about this little project of yours?' said Mayor Pizzey, looking at his watch.

'We're interested in the small grove of elder pines in the middle of the national park,' Mikki said.

'And it looks like there was once a house there too,' I added.

'That would be old Fullerton's hut,' said Mayor Pizzey. 'He was one of the first gold prospectors in the valley. Lived up in that forest for years.'

'Was he the one who planted all the pine trees?' Mikki asked.

'Yes, but don't ask me why!' Mayor Pizzey scoffed. 'Stumbled across a natural clearing in the forest and he went and put in a bunch of pines. Still, I guess that's what most settlers did back then, right after building a house.' Mayor Pizzey checked his phone. We needed to get straight to the point.

'Mayor Pizzey,' I said, 'we're here because we heard that all the trees in that pine grove are going to be cut down.'

The look on Mayor Pizzey's face could only be interpreted as *and what would be the problem with that?*

'Shouldn't be there in the first place,' Mayor Pizzey scolded. 'Pines are classified as invasive weeds nowadays.'

'Weeds?' Mikki exclaimed. 'They're magnificent, wise, robust, healthy trees.'

'They're intruders, Mikki! Pine trees don't belong here and it's council's responsibility to restore crown land to its pre-colonial condition.'

My heart sank. The way Mayor Pizzey was talking, it sounded like a done deal. But he still hadn't given us a solid answer.

'So it's true then?' I asked. 'Kingfisher Shire is going to destroy those trees?'

'Once they're removed—'

'You're talking about an actual massacre,' Mikki whispered.

'Look...in a few years the area will be revegetated with more appropriate native tree species.' Mayor Pizzey checked his watch again, then took a deep breath. 'Council has already approved an action to remove those trees.'

'*Remove*,' Mikki whispered.

Mayor Pizzey shuffled through some papers on his desk. He opened a manila folder, flicked through some documents and quickly snapped it closed again, perhaps because Mikki was taking too much of an interest with his camera.

'Alberta,' Mayor Pizzey said in a scary-calm tone, 'I want you to understand that restoring this section of the forest... removing non-native vegetation, replanting... it all creates jobs, and that's what Kingfisher Bay needs right now, with everything that's gone on this summer.'

I really wanted to bring up the poo incident and how it was all his fault but I managed to resist.

'In fact,' Mayor Pizzey continued. 'We've already engaged a local arborist.'

I could feel every pine tree in the forest, silently screaming. There we were, all listening to the same horrible story. I could hardly breathe. It was like the forest had already been lost. And it was devastating.

'When will it happen?' I asked quietly.

'Three weeks from now,' Mayor Pizzey said abruptly. He pushed back his chair, stood up from behind his desk and extended his hand. It all played out in slow motion. Was he kidding? There was no way I was going to shake that man's hand. I didn't care if it was bad manners. Mikki and I stood up and walked out.

CHAPTER 25

You're not going to believe what Mikki told me on the phone later that night. He'd been sorting through what he filmed at Mayor Pizzey's office. In particular, the sneaky film he'd captured when Mayor Pizzey was looking in that manila folder on his desk. Mikki told me he'd zoomed in on one of the documents. There was a logo that he recognised, a tree logo. The writing underneath said, *Paul Cromby – Arborist.* Paul Cromby – that was Seth Cromby's dad!

'Remember Mayor Pizzey said Kingfisher Council had already hired a local arborist to cut down the forest?'

'Seth's dad!' I shrieked.

'Exactly!' Mikki said. 'And you don't need to be Einstein to work the next bit out too!' I was definitely having a non-Einstein moment because I had no idea what Mikki was talking about. I was just reeling from how much destruction the Crombys had brought to my life.

'A-non-e-mous!' Mikki exclaimed. 'Don't you get it? A-non-e-mous is Seth! He'd know all about the forest because of his dad!'

'*Oh. My. Gosh!*' I said. 'But wait ... that doesn't explain how Seth knew about our channel from practically day one.'

Mikki blushed. 'Um, that part was possibly because of me.'

'Possibly?' I asked.

'Well, it was my mum, actually,' he said.

'Mikki, you need to tell me what's going on!' I demanded.

'Seth's dad came to our house,' Mikki said. 'Mum's been worried about that huge tree in the front getting tangled in the power line. I heard my mum telling him about my films and our channel. He must have gone and told Seth.'

'Parents are such blabbermouths!' I said. 'Oh ... I didn't mean your mum, Mikki, I—'

'Alberta, all I know is that if it wasn't for Seth Cromby trolling our channel then we still wouldn't know about the council's plan. At least now we can do something about it.'

After Mikki showed me how he'd edited the video (us making total nuisances of ourselves at the council), I felt like we'd suddenly changed from being a couple of nerdy nature enthusiasts to strident young eco-activists fighting for the rights of trees. He wanted to publish it right away. That's when I noticed we'd got a whole lot more subscribers, including Sylvie, Georgette, Pip and Harrison too.

GeorgieGirl 1 hour ago
So this is what you've been up to?? Go Berts!!!
🍃 ❤️ 🌲 🍂

Abe C 2 hours ago
Guys, you should so fight this. When are people gonna understand trees have rights too?

GreenGal 8 hours ago
When I was eight, my family sold our house and bought a cheaper one. At first the house seemed way too small but it had a huge garden almost ten times the size of the house. Big green gardens and large trees have such a way of transforming one's mind. All of us spent a large portion of our day outside relaxing, playing, eating, gardening. The garden kept everyone away from the TV and phones and computers. I'm in my twenties now but these were the best years of my life.

A-non-e-mous 10 hours ago
All I've got to say is... You better Hurry Up losers (sound of chainsaws) Mwa ha ha!!! ☠️ 👏

Massimo Paolini 10 hours ago
I love that you are fighting this fight. Why your mayor think trees don't belong in your country? How can anyone live with themselves who cut down these beautiful trees?

'Exactly!' said Mikki. 'That's what we'll say to Seth's dad.'

'Mikki, as if we're gonna be *talking* to Seth's dad!' I had a sinking feeling that Mikki was going to embroil me in another one of his plans.

'Sure we will,' Mikki said. 'Let's get up early tomorrow and catch him for an interview before he leaves for work.'

'No way, Mikki,' I protested. What about when Seth found out? I sure wasn't about to tell Mikki about the Milky Bar incident, but with Seth already grounded he could spill at any time. Mikki had *no* idea! 'I'd rather skip talking to any of the Crombys if that's okay?'

'Come on, Alberta!' Mikki pleaded. 'I'll be filming the whole thing. Seth's dad will be on his best behaviour. Believe me.'

But the only thing I believed right then was just how far Mikki was willing to go to create a good story for our channel. What next? Would Mikki suggest I chain myself to the Memory Tree while Paul Cromby's gang of tree-choppers fired up their chainsaws? All while Mikki captured it on film?

'Seriously, Alberta,' Mikki said. 'It will just be a conversation. You have nothing to fear. I promise.'

☙

I had barely woken from a menacing dream in which Seth Cromby was stalking me, when I was out the front of our house to meet Mikki. No time for breakfast. By sunrise I was gliding down Seth Cromby's street, in the dawny silence, on the back of Mikki's bike. Seth's dad's ute was parked outside their house, directly below the illuminated street lamp.

'Perfect lighting!' Mikki said, as we hid the bike behind some shrubs next door. There was a solitary light shining from inside the Cromby's house. My tummy was growling like there were actual bears inside. Even Mikki could hear it.

'We'll be home again in no time,' Mikki assured me. 'He's not going to want to talk for long.'

I was hoping like crazy that Seth wouldn't be up. His dad used to give him a lift in the mornings – to the oval for footy training or to the rock climbing centre or the gym. But that was all before he was grounded. Then suddenly, the front door opened and Seth's dad had quietly let himself out. He was walking down the driveway towards us when Mikki gave me an encouraging prod (shove) in the back.

'Rolling,' he whispered, pointing the camera at Paul Cromby's car. 'Three, two, one, and...action!'

Seth's dad was already by the driver's side door of his car. Any moment, he'd be driving away. 'Here goes!' I whispered, stepping out of the shadows.

'Mr Cromby...excuse me? Mr Cromby!'

'Who's there?' Seth's dad sounded genuinely startled.

'Mr Cromby, hello...it's me, Alberta Bracken,' I said. By this time I was fully visible in the light of the street lamp. A bunch of magpies started chortling from the heights of next door's trees.

'Mr Cromby, if you don't mind—'

'Look, love, if this is about your arm, like I already said to your dad, Seth's been grounded for as long as it takes for him to apologise,' he explained.

'No,' I said. 'It's not about that – ' (although I did like the idea of Seth apologising) ' – we'd like to ask you a few questions about the old pine grove up in the national park,' I explained.

That's when Seth's dad saw Mikki. 'Hey! Get that camera out of my face! This is private property!'

'Actually, Mr Cromby – ' Mikki said, from his vantage point behind me ' – the street is technically the public domain.'

'I know you,' Paul Cromby said, 'the kid from Waratah Street? Your mum told me about the videos. She didn't mention this though, sneaking up on a bloke on his way to work.'

I had to talk fast. Any moment now Seth's dad would be driving away.

'Is it true, Mr Cromby,' I asked, 'that you plan to cut down a whole grove of perfectly healthy pine trees?'

'Listen, sweetheart, I'm just doing my job. I'm not the one making the decisions, okay?' Seth's dad got into his car and started up the engine. I tapped on the driver's window. As he opened the window halfway, Mikki positioned himself behind me, hoping to get a good angle.

'But you're still enabling it, Mr Cromby,' I said. 'By accepting the job you'd—'

'Look, if I didn't do the job the council would find ten other blokes who'd jump at the chance,' he said, closing the window again. 'I don't have time for this...' His voice faded as he put the car into gear, ready to drive off. I knocked on the window again.

'But, Mr Cromby—' I pleaded.

'Out of my way, love!' Seth's dad yelled through the glass. 'Those trees are coming down and there's nothing you can do about it!'

CHAPTER 26

Riding back to my place I was relieved that the encounter with Paul Cromby was over, but felt a familiar anguish about Mikki meeting Mum. She'd always find something picky to say about my friend's manners and give me a lecture after they'd left, like them licking their fingers was my fault. But by the time we'd arrived and Mikki had taken off his shoes and filed them neatly by the front door, I knew Mum wouldn't find much to complain about. Besides, she was probably already busy practising her TED Talk and snacking on stolen chocolates to notice much about anyone else. I took my shoes off too, not just because Mikki did, but to make sure we didn't wake Clementine with our footsteps. Let's face it, Clementine made a better impression when she was asleep.

I was wrong about Mum snacking on stolen chocolates. She was in the den, wearing some of the stolen workout gear instead, from the stash I had found in her car. She had fresh new trainers too. Her hair was pulled into a neat ponytail. She sure looked like the mothers she usually criticised for gossiping at Pilates. She must have read the quizzical look on my face.

'Alberta, everyone knows a good workday wellness routine is the cornerstone of success,' she said playfully. She was clutching a bunch of notes, probably trying to learn her talk off-by-heart. She soon noticed Mikki standing closely behind me.

'Mum, this is Mikki.' I turned to Mikki. 'Mikki... my mum.'

I knew I'd done the introductions all wrong, or a shortened version of something nearly right, but before Mum could give me one of her looks, Mikki had already reached out to shake her hand.

> ### Tammy's Tips
> **#13 INTRODUCING A FRIEND TO AN ELDER**
> *When introducing a friend to an elder, always address the older person first. The person being introduced should come second. For instance, 'Mum, this is my friend Sarah... Sarah, this is my mother, Mrs Tammy Bracken.' You might also add a snippet of information that could spark an easy conversation such as, 'Mum, you might have seen Sarah at netball?'*

'Pleased to meet you, Mrs Bracken, and congratulations on the worldwide success of your book.'

Mum loved what Mikki said so much she actually blushed. 'Oh, thank you, Mikki. That's very kind but...'

'Mum, we're staaaaaaaarving!' I said, pulling Mikki by his sleeve towards the kitchen.

'Mikki, come have some brekkie?'

I knew Mum would soon be following right behind, with a million questions about what on earth we'd been filming that morning in the dark. I hadn't even poured Mikki a juice when she started. Mikki was quick to answer. It was weird, like he actually *enjoyed* talking to parents.

'We had to conduct an interview, Mrs Bracken, for our—'

'Oh, Mikki, please, you can call me Tammy,' Mum interrupted.

Mikki perched on a stool at the kitchen bench. 'Oh, thank you, Tammy,' he said. 'It was for our YouTube channel,' he continued.

'Oh yes,' said Mum. 'Clementine did mention some kind of... what was it called again?'

'YouTube,' I said. 'It's—'.

'Alberta, I know what YouTube is!' Mum snapped.

Mikki looked a little embarrassed. I bet Junko wouldn't snap at him in front of a friend. 'We started our own nature channel,' he said. 'It's all about trees.'

'Oh yes, the thing Clementine was crying about,' Mum said. She was trying to load on the guilt but it didn't work one bit.

'Anyway, we heard that Seth Cromby's dad was going to be cutting down our special forest and we needed to find out if it was true,' I said.

'Alberta! I thought we'd agreed you'd stay well away from that horrible bully!'

'Yes, but Mrs Bracken... Tammy... we just needed one quick interview for our next video and it was perfectly safe because Seth was still asleep,' Mikki said enthusiastically. Meanwhile I was fighting off an unwelcome vision that had appeared in my head – Seth asleep and dribbling into his pillow. Ew!

'Alberta,' Mum scolded. 'I don't want you going near that Cromby house again! Especially not turning up there unannounced in the dark, like some... criminal!'

Mikki looked away. He probably wasn't used to people bickering like they do in our family. Or having a mother accuse you of being a criminal. Given Mum's little *shopping* secret, it sure felt like a cheap shot!

Clementine appeared in the doorway wiping her eyes, her hair in a complete tantrum. If Mikki wasn't there she would have most definitely caused an argument with Mum.

'Oh, hi, Mikki,' she said. 'I really like your tree videos.' See, Mikki was already a calming influence.

'It's a team effort really... Alberta does all the talking.'

'Yeah, she's good at that,' Clementine mumbled cheekily.

After breakfast Mikki and I were keen to get started editing our video and Mum suggested we set up on the dining room table in the front room. If only Mikki knew what a big deal it was for Mum to offer that. Maybe she was worried it would never get used again, like for Christmas or family gatherings?

Mikki had caught some really cool footage of me appearing from the darkness outside Seth Cromby's house, but I can't tell you how cringeworthy it was to see myself acting all *A Current Affair* interviewing Seth's dad. I couldn't bear it if Clementine saw. If only the front room had an actual door.

'Aaagh! Make it stop, Mikki!' I said. But he just ignored me and put his headphones on instead, immersed in a world of his own. I logged onto YouTube on my laptop. It was so exciting to see what might have hatched overnight.

'Seriously?' I shrieked, tugging on Mikki's sleeve. He took off his headphones and paused his screen. 'Mikki, you're not going to believe this!' I swivelled my laptop around so that Mikki could see.

'We've got two thousand and three subscribers!'

'Whoa!' Mikki said.

I scrolled down to the comments section.

'I might read them later, Alberta,' Mikki said. 'Just dealing with a small technical hitch.'

Lisse Boinn 5 hours ago
Alberta has a great career ahead as an inspirational speaker.

Yasaar El Abed 5 hours ago
Many thanks for this wonderful video, wish for you all the best.

Eric Normson 4 hours ago
Hi guys, I watch all your vids and love them because they are always so uplifting. I can't wait till you show us how to talk with trees!

Big Drop Outdoors 4 hours ago
Wow! Thanks, guys, for taking us along on this journey. You absolutely have to save the Memory Tree and all the other pines. Go for it guys. Fight the good fight.

GeorgieGirl 5 hours ago
Rocking it Birdy! Can't wait for more. ♥ 🍃 🏆 🌲

Sylvie500 5 hours ago
Missing you at the beach but saving a forest is so cool Berts! Go for it!! 🐞 ♥

There were loads more comments too, but Mikki interrupted my reading them. He'd had another one of his bright ideas – one that put me totally into the spotlight. Again!

'Really happy with how this video is shaping up, Alberta,' he said. 'We'll just need to add a few pieces of voiceover.' I still wasn't ready to look at it, preferring to wait for Mikki's final edited version.

'Okay, cool,' I said, skim-reading what seemed like hundreds of comments.

'And then we need to totally expose A-non-e-mous,' he said. 'Show our two thousand and three subscribers who he really is.'

The back of my neck prickled at the thought of it.

'Aw, Mikki, I don't think that's a good idea,' I said. 'Can't we just ignore A-non-e-mous? He'll get bored soon and find something else to do.'

'I'd like to believe that, Alberta,' Mikki said. 'But it seems unlikely.'

I watched Mum walking down the hall in her stolen leisure wear. Everything started to feel hopeless. I really didn't want to bring more destruction into my life by antagonising Seth Cromby. It was hard enough dealing with the imminent destruction of the pine forest. In my mind's eye I saw the Memory Tree and the shrine Mikki had made for his grandfather. I just couldn't see how exposing Seth Cromby was going to help. The truth was, in three short weeks, those men would be coming for our little forest. And as much as I was pumped about our channel having so many subscribers, I couldn't see how a bunch of supportive comments was going to help. It was just us.

How were a couple of eleven-year-olds *ever* going to save a forest?

CHAPTER 27

When Mikki left Mum took Sascha for a dawdle around the block. It was the perfect opportunity to take a snoop through her wardrobe. Boy, did I strike gold! Mum had a total haul, all stuffed into her top drawer. Three pairs of jeans, all brand new, all presumably stolen. There were *four* silk shirts, a striped jumper, two belts, three pairs of the same earrings. It was all from Penelope's by the Sea – a fashion boutique in town. I was so immersed in my chilling discovery that I didn't notice Mum had come home.

'Excuse me!' Mum said, clearly annoyed. 'I don't go rummaging through *your* things, Alberta!' She pulled me away from the wardrobe, pushed the drawer closed and slid the mirrored doors shut. But I just couldn't pretend any longer.

'Mum, *what* are you doing?' I exclaimed.

'No, Alberta, the question should be what are *you* doing? I have a right to privacy. My things are—'

'*Your* things? Are you sure about that, Mum? How long has this been going on?'

'How long has *what* been going on? I don't need to justify myself to my own daughter. Now, if you don't mind, Alberta, I'd like you to stay out of my room!' Mum ushered me to the door but I resisted.

'Mum, the make-up at the back of the bathroom cabinet, the gym gear stashed in the car – there's still security tags on half these things! Are you really going to deny it?'

Mum's cheeks reddened. 'Alberta, what on earth are you talking about?'

'I'm talking about shoplifting, Mum! You know, stealing? And from Kingfisher Sports too. No wonder Sylvie hasn't been talking to me and why do you think her parents totally ghosted you on New Year's Eve? I saw you stealing at Woolies too. Hardly good manners, Mum. Someone could report you to the police at any moment!'

'How ridiculous!' Mum scolded, brushing the creases out of the quilt cover on her bed. Then she rearranged all the cushions into two neat rows.

'Alberta, I simply don't have time for this. I'm under a lot of pressure with this TED Talk, my American publishers are being *very* difficult about my next book and in case you haven't noticed – ' (volume increase) ' – I'm also trying to deal with your father bringing *total* disgrace to this family with that Ursula Hoffman!'

'Believe me, Mum, your American publishers will be a lot more difficult when you tell them you're writing your next book from jail!'

'Enough, Alberta!' yelled Mum. She used exactly the same tone she'd use on Clementine. Then she disappeared into the bathroom and slammed the door, also a lot like Clementine.

I went straight to my bedroom to call Dad. I needed to handball the whole thing. It was hard enough trying to work out how to save the forest. It shouldn't be up to me to save a parent as well.

'Mmm,' Dad sighed when I explained the situation, and that Mum was denying it. 'I was hoping it had stopped.'

'What? You mean this is a thing? Like, Mum's got—'

Dad cut me off. 'Look, there are things you don't understand, and why should you, you're eleven. But let's just say it hasn't been easy...your mother's overnight success—'

'How can that be a bad thing, Dad? Isn't it everyone's dream?'

'I haven't helped either,' Dad said. 'There's been a lot of strain on our marriage.'

'Too much information, Dad! Like you said, I'm eleven. I just need you to deal with this!'

I could hear Dad pacing. I didn't know what else to say.

'Leave it with me, Alberta. I promise to keep an eye on it.'

And that was that. Dad just hung up.

CHAPTER 28

Mikki and I headed back to the forest. I wanted to learn to talk tree more than ever and was desperate for Mikki to give me another lesson. We spoke about it all the way down the trail. How could I talk about tree communication on our channel if I hadn't even mastered it myself? That day it felt like the pines were calling us more than ever, even louder than the birds.

'Communicating with a tree is no different to using any of your other senses,' said Mikki. 'When you touch, you feel through your fingers, don't you?'

'Sure,' I said.

'And you can taste, smell, see and hear?'

'Like... obviously, Mikki!'

'So why believe it stops there, with just five senses? Because that's what they tell us in school, right?'

'Yep,' I said, hoping Mikki would stop asking me questions and just get on with it.

'Your five senses are just the most basic ones. But

humans actually have more than twenty different senses, did you know that?'

'No way!'

'Tree communication requires us to use our basic senses but we also need to develop other senses too. It takes some training, Alberta. Many of our senses have been forgotten, but they're ready to be remembered at any time.'

Our footsteps synched into the same rhythm. I thought about what Mikki had said. How hard could it be? I'd only been alive eleven years. My forgotten senses couldn't be that far away! And I liked the idea of training. Even if just to compete with Clementine.

'Can I start training today then, Mikki?' I could already see the pines in the distance and there was a light scattering of pine needles across the path.

'You can warm up at any time by yourself,' Mikki explained. 'Start by trying to get a sense of one of the trees calling to you. You'll feel drawn to it. When you do, go to it and start tuning into its vibrational frequency. Remember how you prepared the other day, with the pine cone? You can even give it a hug!'

Gosh, I thought. If Sylvie and Georgette only knew just how far I had ventured away from boogie boarding!

When we got to the pines Mikki and I peeled off in opposite directions. We didn't even have to talk about it; we both knew Mikki needed time with his grandfather at the Memory Tree. I wandered over to the old fireplace, brushed the pine needles off the bricks and sat down. I took a long breath. Tiny particles of dust were suspended in the air, spiralling down in spears of light. In the distance, a bunch of crows cawed.

I was keen to immerse myself in Mikki's warm-up exercise, desperate to remind my forgotten senses that they did, in fact, remember how to feel a tree. For the next few breaths I closed my eyes. Then I opened them and let them gently meander the scene in front of me. I gave my eyes permission to go wherever eyes might want to go. Eventually they settled on a single tree. It wasn't any different to the other pines around it, apart from a neat mound of pine needles that had gathered around its trunk in a slightly different shape to the others. It looked like a pillowy question mark. It felt like an invitation. Soon, I was sitting down under the tree, with my back against its knobbly trunk. 'Hey, tree,' I whispered.

I breathed out any thoughts that weren't about right here and right now and this tree. Thoughts about the forest getting cut down and my shoplifting mother and the conversation I'd had with Dad and the way he'd so casually said, 'I was hoping it had stopped'. I tried to comfort myself with the other comment Dad had made, the 'I promise I'll keep an eye on it' one, but... to be honest, the whole hoo-ha with my parents... I felt like I couldn't rely on either of them anymore. Then I thought about how Mikki would be finished at the Memory Tree soon and how I did have to get on with trying to remember how to sense that tree even if the sensing a pine cone failure still hung heavily in my mind.

I was as ready as I was going to be. I tipped my head back against the trunk of the tree and my eyes followed it all the way to the sky, where its crown was swaying ever so slightly in the breeze. Then I asked myself... how does it feel?

I knew what was *meant* to happen, I knew I was *meant* to experience a burst of feeling. One of Mikki's books explained that once you could sense a tree's aliveness then the tree could sense your aliveness too, and together we'd be connected to the dreaming of earth. But all I could think about while trying to feel the tree's aliveness was just how short-lived that aliveness might be. If Mayor Pizzey got his way there'd soon be no aliveness left in that tree at all, or any of the trees in the pine grove. Knowing this, and sitting with that tree... it felt like I was keeping a dirty secret. To be honest, I couldn't feel the tree's aliveness one bit. All I could feel was guilt.

Fortunately, Mikki had felt a whole lot more. He said all the pines were aware of the impending danger. I knew this meant the larger trees would have already offloaded nutrients out of their trunks and leaves and into the soil to support the next generation of saplings, no matter what species they might be. Mikki had tears in his eyes. He said the Memory Tree had already sent chemical messages through the enormous fungal network underground. It had already accepted its demise.

'It's unbearable,' I said. 'Did any of the trees say what they want us to do?'

'Exactly what we are doing,' Mikki said. 'Follow the golden threads of our intuition.'

'I still don't get what you mean by that,' I said.

'It's about when something captures your attention and maybe you don't even know why, when you get that kind of impulse, trust it and follow it home. For it came from deep inside the world.'

'I just—'

'Golden threads touch all of us every day,' Mikki interrupted. 'But it's usually only the artists and children who take the time to follow them.'

I still wasn't sure about all the golden thread stuff. And I had zero idea how to follow one either.

'Don't worry, Alberta,' Mikki said. 'I know we're on the right track. The golden threads of my intuition says our next video should be about the vibrational frequency of nature. We need to act fast.'

Mikki wanted to shoot the video down by the creek again and far away from the Memory Tree. As we hurried along we chatted about what information we (I) should include. I was relieved to have read a little about vibrations, even if I wasn't sure if any of it was science. I thought of that quote from Einstein, the one that's all over the internet – 'Everything in life is vibration.'

I couldn't help thinking that even if it wasn't Einstein who'd said it, even if it was somebody else... it still felt true. Soon Mikki had found a good location where the light was just right. By the time he had set up his gear, I felt like I was ready to go.

'You'll need to project your voice over the sound of the water,' Mikki said, shuffling me under one a giant fern frond. 'It makes the perfect umbrella!'

Mikki looked at his camera screen. 'Amazing!' he said. 'Ready?'

※

'Hi, guys, it's *Mikki and Me*, up here in our local forest and today we're going to be talking about vibrations. You may have heard that everything in the universe is made up of invisible energy vibrating at different speeds or frequencies. But what does this actually mean?

'Well, physics nerds like Einstein knew that everything in nature, the whole world actually, is vibrating, all at different speeds, even the cells in your body! The vibrating is a way to store energy and everything is vibrating at its own rate. This is what Einstein called frequency. This tree fern, the water in the creek, objects like your bike, even our thoughts and feelings are vibrating at their own frequencies.'

Mikki stopped filming.

'Cool, Alberta. You actually sound like you know what you're talking about,' he said. Somehow this didn't feel like a compliment. 'Let's change it up though.' Mikki directed me back up the main trail. 'I want you to wander down to the water... like you're the only one here!' Mikki sounded excited, like he was already seeing the finished video in his head. I did what he had directed. 'Yes, there. Perfect!' he shouted. Then he counted down from three and we were rolling.

'Like I mentioned earlier, every one of us is vibrating at our own frequency,' I said. 'Everything in the universe... it's all just energy vibrating... but at different speeds. That's how we can feel separate from what's around us, like from other people, trees, animals and objects. The fascinating thing is, science is now suggesting we are more connected than we know... like we're all swimming around in the same ocean of energy. Physicists call this the "unified field". Isn't it amazing to think we're all silently quivering in one big sea of vibrating energy?

'Interestingly, animals, particularly birds, can tune into and read the vibrational frequency of potential predators and other dangers. It's with their powers of perception that animals sense the world around them. They rely on this far more than their sense of sight or sound. Humans can do this too. We're all born with our powers of perception wide open. But sadly, we slowly forget how to use them. And did you know humans actually have access to not just five senses, but more than twenty? I'd better point out that I've forgotten how to tune into most of my senses too. But with training and practice, I'm hoping that can change, and eventually I'm hoping to speak tree. Mikki already can of course... isn't that right, Mikki?... Mikki's been talking tree for years!'

After what felt like a long rant I was thinking we'd be finished for the day, but Mikki had another idea.

'This is all excellent content for our channel, but I was thinking that if we're going to save the pine forest we need to appeal to actual decision makers. And all those people are on Twitter.' Now it was Mikki's turn to rant. 'I saw a piece about that woman who campaigned to save all those beautiful old mountain ash in the Toolangi State Forest. She spoke to the local council, sure... but also to the Minister for the Environment.'

'Oh yeah,' I said. 'She had lots of good tips for staging an effective eco-campaign.'

'So let's go back to the Memory Tree and record a quick tweet,' Mikki said.

Eco-activists. I couldn't help feeling like an impostor. I mean, wasn't it pretty much yesterday we were just... having fun? And when we started our YouTube channel it was never meant to be an eco-campaign.

And if I had felt awkward about our meeting with Mayor Pizzey at the council, I felt positively terrified at the idea of a video speech to the Minister for the

Environment. It's scary enough talking to parents! But none of my fears or excuses outweighed the importance of saving the forest. If I did nothing and the pines were destroyed... I knew I would never forgive myself. As the pine grove came into sight I knew I had no choice other than to fight for it. For all trees. I guess that made me an eco-activist after all.

Mikki ran his fingers down the trunk of the Memory Tree. 'No matter how it turns out,' he said, 'at least Grandfather will know that I tried.'

'Yep,' I said. I was all fired up. 'Let's do it.'

※

'Hey, there, people. It's Alberta and Mikki here again, up in the Kingfisher National Park. Firstly, a huge shout-out for all the help and support we've been getting from our subscribers from all over the world. We really couldn't do this without you. So... thank you!

'For those who might not know, Mikki and I are trying to save this beautiful little grove of pine trees. We've only just discovered that in a matter of weeks this community of magnificent, wise and healthy trees will be "removed".

'Mayor Pizzey from Kingfisher Shire Council, we have this to say to you. How can you and your council be serious about climate change when you are "removing" over one hundred perfectly healthy trees that have been proven to reduce carbon in the atmosphere?

'You justify this act of violence against nature by saying these pine trees are invasive weeds. Really? Isn't a weed just a word white men use for things they haven't found a use for? If you want to understand invasive species, Mayor Pizzey, just take a good look at our colonial past. These trees weren't the ones who invaded this country. Look at them! Each one is a living, breathing, contributing being. Should it really matter that they are not an Australian species? When it comes to life on this planet, is one species really more valuable than another?

'And Eleanor Doyle, how can you call yourself Minister for the Environment but be letting this and any act of vandalism towards trees occur? Isn't it your job to understand the value of trees, forests and wild places in our care... and to protect them?

'Mayor Pizzey, Minister Doyle, and anyone else who might be watching, we *urge* you to stop the senseless destruction of these healthy, resilient trees. These trees are loved. These trees are valuable, and most of all, these trees have a *right* to exist. Thank you.'

Mikki switched off his camera 'Whoa!' he said. 'You should seriously get into politics, Alberta!'

'Are you kidding?' I scoffed. 'Then I'd have to hang around with people like Mayor Pizzey and Eleanor Doyle!'

Mikki and I laughed but I knew that soon Mikki would

be uploading that video for all the world to see. My heart started pounding just at the thought of it.

'It's okay for you, Mikki,' I said. 'You get to hide behind your camera!'

CHAPTER 29

Afterwards, up in Mikki's study, we still had to record some narration before Mikki could weave his technical magic and pull it all together. It took a lot longer than we thought.

'Would you like to stay for dinner?' Junko asked. 'I've made Mikki's favourite fish pie.' But I had promised Mum I'd be home by six, and with all my heightened emotions I didn't have the appetite for fish pie.

'Thanks, Junko,' I said, 'but I have to get home.'

Junko looked over Mikki's shoulder at the pine forest scenes on his screen. 'Your grandfather would have loved to see this, Mikki,' she said. 'And I was going to tell you this at dinner, but your dad called while you were out. He'll be home the day after tomorrow.'

'Cool,' said Mikki, his slender fingers dancing across the keyboard. 'Maybe he can help with our campaign.'

When I got home the house was in complete darkness. As I switched on the light in the hall, Sascha trotted down to greet me. He sat up obediently at my feet, pleading with hungry eyes.

'Aw, Sascha,' I said, patting his head. 'You need some yum-yums! Where *is* everyone?'

Then I heard whimpering coming from Clementine's room.

There she was. Lying on her bed clutching L'éléphant – a large, very ugly velveteen elephant she'd had since she was two. Clementine had arranged L'éléphant's trunk so that it wrapped around her neck like it was giving her a hug. Sascha followed me to Clementine's room, stepping up and down on the spot as if to say, *Look, I've been dealing with this for hours so can someone just feed me now, please?*

I perched on the edge of Clementine's bed and swept L'éléphant's trunk from her teary face. 'Hey, what's going on, Clemmy... Where's Mum?'

Clementine pushed me away. 'She went to dumb old Officeworks,' she snivelled. Was Clementine crazy? Mum splurged big time at Officeworks. She'd buy you anything if you told her it was educational. But I couldn't help imagining another scenario too, one where Mum's bag was full of stolen fluoro markers and lunch-room chocolates.

I brushed Clementine's sticky hair back from her face. 'You didn't want to go?' I asked. I still had no idea what was wrong.

'Dad wants to go to the Chinese tomorrow night,' Clementine said.

'Oh, come on, Clemmy, the Wing Ho won't be that bad. You love lemon chicken.'

Clementine sat up. 'God, Alberta! It's not about the food!' she screeched.

'No! I just meant—'

'Shut up, Alberta! You don't even care one bit that Dad's living at the tragic Travelodge, you don't care about his ... *thing* with that Ursula Hoffman, or that his own dog, Sascha, is practically dying of old age while he's hanging out with a blind chihuahua called Renaldo. Don't you get it? Dad's not coming back! And you, Alberta Selfish-Bracken, *you* don't even care!'

It was a total relief to hear Mum coming in the back door.

'Girls!' she called. 'I've bought home a treat for dinner!'

Clementine's eyes lit up. She frantically mopped her face with L'éléphant's trunk (what that poor stuffed animal has been through!). That's when I caught the undeniable aroma of fish 'n' chips wafting down the hall.

'Come on,' I said. 'We can talk about it with Dad tomorrow. Try not to get so upset.'

I couldn't wait to get online and see if Mikki had posted our video. But Mum had some 'absolutely marvellous' news and wanted to celebrate, which meant dinner was going to take ages. Mum had set three champagne glasses on the table, two of them already filled with orange juice.

As Clementine and I took our places Mum popped the champagne cork and filled a glass for herself.

'Well, it's official,' she said, raising her glass. 'I found out today that *Tammy Bracken's Guide to Modern Manners* is going to be made into a Netflix series! Can you believe it?' I actually *couldn't* believe it to tell you the truth.

'Oh my God, Mum!' Clementine shrieked. 'Do we get to go to America?'

Mum laughed. 'I don't know about that, Clementine!'

'That's incredible, Mum!' I said, clinking her glass with mine. Really incredible, I thought.

'It's amazing, Mum!' Clementine said.

But inside the whole thing felt fraught. Not just the bit about a TV series on manners (seriously, who would watch it?), but given Mum's *problem*... let's just say I was glad we were having dinner with Dad the next night. He needed to think of something fast!

※

As my laptop sprang to life I saw Mikki had already posted the video on YouTube. Now everyone in Kingfisher Bay and across the world would know about our campaign to save the pines. The idea of it made my heart quicken... again. I scrolled down to the comments and notifications. People thought I was brave! They used words like 'gutsy', 'awesome', 'unstoppable'. Someone even called me a 'force'! Me! I had never thought of myself that way. I had never really fought for anything before.

And now I could feel the strength and support from all those comments coursing through me. I felt fierce, wise, strong... like a tree.

But still, I couldn't sleep that night. Clementine's words about Dad kept repeating themselves in my head and maybe I was being selfish but I hadn't been that worried about Dad or his thing with Ursula Hoffman. I couldn't tell Clementine that I was more worried about our mother being a professional shoplifter. And there was absolutely no need for it, either. Mum could easily pay for the things she had stolen. So... why? I might have been feeling wise and strong like a tree but I needed some answers! At four in the morning there was only one thing for it... Google!

It was almost light by the time I'd finished my research. The answer was clear: Mum needed therapy!

CHAPTER 30

By the time Dad picked us up for dinner I had a whole speech prepared, one that could be delivered in the time it would take for Clementine to go the bathroom at the Chinese restaurant. Fortunately, the toilets at the Wing Ho were way out the back. I'd have loads of time.

'How's your tree project going, Alberta?' Dad asked in the car.

'It's not a project, Dad. It's a campaign.'

'Haven't you heard? Alberta's an eco-activist now,' Clementine said smugly. 'She even tweets.'

'Well someone has to do something,' I said, 'when none of the adults seem to care.'

'Oh, don't be like that, love.'

'They're going to cut down Mikki's Memory Tree,' Clementine said. 'And the rest of the pine forest too.'

'Clementine, can you stop!' I said. 'I'm perfectly capable of speaking for myself.'

'They're making a TV series out of Mum's book,' Clementine said.

'Clementine!' I scolded. 'Mum asked us not to tell anyone!'

'She did not!' Clementine yelled. 'And Dad's not just anyone!'

'Clementine,' Dad said, 'how 'bout you tell me what you've been up to?'

I couldn't help jumping in. 'No, let me tell you... mmm, let's see... this week Clementine covered a hundred library books and spent a grand total of three million hours on her pogo stick. Oh, I forgot to mention the stilts. Add another two mill—'

'Shut up, Alberta! It's better than trying to talk to a tree!'

'Is it though?' I asked. 'Is it really?'

Dad pulled up out the front of the Wing Ho. Usually at this time of year you couldn't get in. But now it was almost empty. Just the red glow of ceiling lanterns above rows and rows of vacant tables.

'Now, girls,' Dad said. 'I hope you're not going to keep this bickering up once we're inside?'

The waiter offered us a window table but Dad said he'd prefer the one down the back, in the corner, near the fish tank, I guess to hide from any gossipy locals. It suited me fine, though, I wasn't in the mood for bumping into anyone either. Not to mention the spectacle of Clementine using chopsticks, no matter how many times she's been told they weren't designed as a stabbing implement.

We hadn't even sat down yet when Clementine wanted to order. Dad made a *just slow it down a little* gesture with both hands, like he was pushing down a helium balloon. 'Let's just all take it easy, huh?'

'*Fine!*' said Clementine. She started spinning the lazy Susan around, to see how fast it could go before the bottle of Kikkoman soy sauce flew off.

'How old are you, three?' I mocked. 'Can you *stop?* The waiter's coming.'

After we'd ordered, Dad said he had something important to say. The first thing I imagined was that he and Ursula Hoffman were getting married, or worse – having a baby. Can you imagine? Dad cleared his throat.

'What I want to say to you both...' he began. 'I want you know that what's happened between your mother and I... none of it is your fault.'

'Dad!' I scoffed.

'Yeah, Dad,' said Clementine. 'Mum already told us that every little bit of what's happened is all your fault.'

Dad looked shocked. 'Your mother said that? Oh, okay then... I'd just read that sometimes children can feel responsible for—'

I couldn't help laughing. 'Dad, *you're* the one who ran off—'

'Please, Alberta! I hardly ran off—'

'Mum threw him out remember?' Clementine shrieked.

'Shh!' Dad urged, looking over his shoulder. Then Clementine leaned in close.

'Remember the clothes all over the lawn, Bertie?' she whispered.

I could see the waiter approaching with our food.

'Shut up now, Clementine!' I whispered back.

'You two, please!' Dad said. 'Look, maybe we'll talk after our meal?'

'Here we are,' the waiter said. He put two plates onto the lazy Susan. 'Lemon chicken and special fried rice for you. I'll be straight back with your Mongolian beef.'

Clementine spun the lazy Susan so that the lemon chicken was directly in front of her. Then she started spooning food into her bowl like she hadn't eaten in ten years. Dad gave her stern eyes.

'We're *sharing*, Clementine,' he said. 'Understand?'

Clementine filled her bowl then went quiet. It wasn't because Dad had told her off. She was just hoping Dad and I would busy ourselves talking so that she could shovel extra spoonfuls into her bowl without us noticing. Share plates with Clementine around was never a good idea. When the waiter returned with our Mongolian beef I asked for a fork. I was definitely at a competitive disadvantage with chopsticks.

> **Tammy's Tips**
> **#14 PROPER USE OF A LAZY SUSAN**
> *When eating at a table with a lazy Susan, always check if anyone is taking food from a dish before you spin it around to yourself. When it's your turn, always spin it clockwise, and try to keep the serving dish on the lazy Susan when serving food into your own bowl, even if that means moving your bowl closer.*

Dad was staring into his bowl with watery eyes. Was this how it would be from now on, meeting up in restaurants to argue? Was Dad about to cry? Everyone knows kids can't handle it if their parent cries.

'Dad? Are you okay?' I asked.

Dad cleared his throat. 'Look,' he sniffed. 'You're not the only one fighting for something here, Alberta. If you know what I mean?'

The problem was I didn't know what Dad meant. Not one bit. I gave him a confused look. Clementine spun the lazy Susan again, piling Mongolian beef on top of her lemon chicken.

'What I mean is...' Dad said. 'You're trying to save your... what's it called...?'

'Memory Tree!' Clementine said with her mouth stuffed full.

'And I've seen the videos you and ... who is it ... Mikey?'

'Mikki!' Clementine shrieked.

'I can see you're really fighting to save something,' he said. 'And don't get me wrong, I think it's great.'

'It won't work,' said Clementine. 'As if anyone's going to listen to Alberta!' It took all the restraint I could muster not to punch her in the arm.

'Would you just let Dad finish, Clementine?'

'What I'm saying,' Dad continued, 'is that I'm fighting for something too, okay?'

'Okay...' I said, still a little confused.

'I made a mistake. With Ursula. I don't know how it happened. Your mother's been so absorbed with her book this past year ... it hasn't been easy.'

'Tell me about it!' said Clementine, wiping her face with her napkin.

'But I'm hoping she'll give me a second chance. I just want you two to know that.'

Clementine laughed. 'As if Mum's going to give you a second chance while the whole town's talking about you and that Ursula Hoffman!' With that I did actually punch Clementine in the arm.

'Ouch!' she complained.

'Nothing is more important to me than you three,' Dad continued.

'What about Sascha?' Clementine argued. 'Or is Renaldo your new best friend too now?'

'Of course not, Clementine!' Dad said.

'How could you trade Sascha for a blind chihuahua, Dad!' Clementine taunted.

'Wait,' I said. 'I don't get it. Does this mean you're coming back, Dad?'

Clementine's eyes lit up. 'Are you, Dad? Are you?'

'Look, I'm not perfect,' Dad continued. 'Parents aren't perfect. I know you kids think they are but—'

Clementine started laughing uncontrollably.

'Do you want another punch, Clementine?' I taunted.

'Parents are just people,' Dad said. 'People who make mistakes, people who lose their way. Your mum has every right to be angry. She should have been able to enjoy her success without... I'm just hoping that one day she can find it in her heart to forgive me.'

Finally, Clementine went to the bathroom and I could talk to Dad alone, even if he was almost crying.

'Dad,' I said. 'I did some reading and what Mum's been doing... it's called "nonsensical shoplifting", and it's an actual *thing*. She needs to get help, Dad. I read that some people shoplift as a way of dealing with stress and loss. I'm worried sick about it, Dad. People know, and if they went to the police—'

'Alberta! She's not going—'

'I can't tell you how many lipstick testers I found stashed in the back of the bathroom cabinet, Dad. Like... ew! Testers!'

I felt tears welling up in my eyes too. 'Oh, great,' I said, looking over my shoulder. 'Here comes Clementine.'

Dad squeezed my leg under the table. 'Try not to worry, love,' he said reassuringly. 'But I agree, your mum needs help. As soon as she starts taking my calls... I'll talk to her, I promise.'

Clementine sat back down at the table, wiping her wet hands on the legs of her jeans. She scanned the lazy Susan for anything still worth eating.

'Can we get fried ice cream?' she asked.

CHAPTER 31

Talking to Dad definitely helped, even if it was quite a rushed conversation. I did feel less worried about Mum. Now I could focus all my energy on saving the pine forest and the Memory Tree. And the idea that Dad might come home? Well... I sure wasn't going to be saying anything to Mum. Let's be real, I could count on Clementine to do that!

I lay in bed thinking about our video and about how everything in the universe is vibrating with the same life energy, but just at different speeds or frequencies. Even my thoughts had their own vibrational frequency. Apparently, feelings like anger and fear vibrated at lower frequencies than say feelings of courage, acceptance and peace. I had also read that nature has a very high vibration, which if you can tune into it, is why forest bathing can make people feel so much better.

What I realised was that ever since breaking my and Dad leaving and Sylvie acting weird and discov Mum's shoplifting habit, I'd been experiencing a low-frequency emotions. No wonder I couldn't communicate with trees. My vibrational frequency had been way lower than nature's. When I realised this I got a buzz of inspiration. Maybe it was a golden thread? I was determined to follow it.

I crept down the hall so as not to wake anyone, especially anyone nosey and noisy like Clementine. Mum's bedroom door was still closed. I took a peek into Clementine's room – risky, I know, but I needed proof that she was fast asleep. Sascha was snoring on his bed in the lounge.

Outside, at the bottom of the garden, was an old Moreton Bay fig tree. There it was, as wide and full and magnificent as ever. The whole tree was twittering with parrots flitting about its branches. The ground was damp under my feet. I took a cushion from one of the garden chairs.

'Good morning, Fig,' I whispered. I ran my hand down its smooth (also lumpy), grey trunk, then nestled the cushion into a rounded hollow where it met the earth, sat down and crossed my legs. Had the tree sensed me? What might it be like for a tree to receive an early morning human visitor?

I could hear Mikki's voice in my head, that first day he'd taught me how to synchronise with the forest, to breathe and take in all there was to observe around me: the figs shiny leaves above my head, the yellow ones on the ground. When I closed my eyes, my mind flooded with thoughts and memories – how Mikki's dad would be arriving later that day and how excited Mikki was to see him. Then I focussed all my attention on sound: the chattering early morning birds, a car door closing in the far distance, a creak from the bough of the tree. And when my ears were fully satisfied with noticing every sound I shifted my focus to the spaces between the sounds, the vastness of the silence. A dog barked. My breathing in waves like the ocean. I felt my back, warm against the tree trunk, a tingling sensation rising up my spine.

More thoughts appeared. I hadn't even checked YouTube that morning. There were sure to be comments and messages overnight. But I did my best to ignore it, or anything else that wasn't happening right now. Back to the coolness of the air, my back against the tree, breath coming in, pausing, breath going out, the rumble of a distant truck on the highway, breath coming in, tummy gurgles, breath going out. Soon, an illuminated purple orb appeared inside my eyelids and I watched it expand. As I did, my physical body felt like it was disappearing, like I was actually merging into the tree. That's when I asked myself... *How does this tree feel?* And waited.

What I felt was so subtle I could have easily missed it. It's hard to explain but I knew I was feeling the language of that tree. It was a completely new feeling. It was the deep, wild hum of nature. And it had been there in that tree all along, waiting.

When I got back inside there were eight messages from Mikki! They were all about one of our subscribers on YouTube, a guy from Italy called Massimo Paolini, and his video called *The Music of Plants*. Massimo had visited a place called Damanhur. Mikki said it was in northern Italy, up near the Alps. At Damanhur, researchers had developed technology that captured the vibrational frequency of plants and turned it into sound. I called Mikki as soon as I'd watched Massimo's video. 'I couldn't believe what I was seeing!' I said. Massimo was at an outdoor concert where the music was being played by... plants! It wasn't music as we know it though. The plants weren't playing an actual tune. It was more like a bunch of sounds and tones.

'Me either,' said Mikki. 'So clever that the vibrational frequency of a plant can be turned into sound. I think they used a synthesiser.'

'This is insane!' I said. 'It means the plant actually has a voice. Can you imagine if—'

'I know!' said Mikki. 'Did you watch any of his other videos? There's one where Massimo's fruit salad plant is playing its own music, just sitting there on his desk.'

'Would it work with trees?' I asked. I couldn't help wondering what sounds the fig tree might have made. Or... Mikki and I both fell into silence. The back of my neck prickled and my whole body shivered.

'Are you thinking what I'm thinking, Alberta Bracken?' Mikki asked excitedly.

'Hell, yes!' I squealed. 'Let's have a concert in the pine forest and invite the whole town! This is how we save the trees, Mikki!'

CHAPTER 32

When Mikki opened the door I saw a suitcase in the entry space. His dad was home. I suddenly felt like I shouldn't have been there. God knows how awkward it would be if Mikki was at our place and my dad walked back in the door. At least the Watanabe's didn't have a version of Clementine!

'Dad's just freshening up before breakfast,' Mikki said. 'And you're invited too.' I loved that idea. With the excitement of communicating with our fig tree for the very first time, then Massimo's video and the whole forest concert idea, I had completely forgotten about eating.

Up in Mikki's study he told me he had messaged Massimo and arranged a video chat so we could ask a few questions about his plant-music device, and whether it could be used with big forest trees too.

'He's soooo much older than us,' I said. 'Like twenty-something, for sure.'

'That's okay, Alberta. Let's make a list of questions so we're prepared,' Mikki suggested.

Then Junko called us down for breakfast.

'I hope you don't mind,' said Mikki. 'Mum's prepared a Japanese breakfast. It's kind of a special occasion.'

To be honest, the breakfast looked a lot like dinner to me. The kitchen table was neatly set for four, and in each place there was a bowl of steaming rice, a second bowl of soup, a smallish plate of fish and another with what looked like a rolled-up omelette. Then there were tiny dishes with a bunch of things I didn't recognise. Mikki must have read my mind (again) because as soon as we sat down, he pointed to each of the dishes and whispered, 'seaweed, pickled vegetables, fermented soybeans.' There was also a tiny cup of green tea. Mikki's dad was smiling at me from across the other side of the table. I guess he wanted to see my reaction.

'Don't worry, Alberta,' said Mikki's dad. 'Most days we have toast and cereal.'

I laughed. 'Or burnt toast if you're at our place!' I said. 'This looks far more delicious,' I said, completely lying about the concept of eating fermented soybeans for breakfast.

'How much longer for that arm of yours?' he asked. It was the question all adults seemed desperate to ask.

'Still a few weeks, Mr Watanabe,' I said. I took a sip of tea, which tasted slightly of grass. And I wasn't sure whether there was a right or a wrong way to approach eating a Japanese breakfast, so I just did whatever Mikki did and hoped for the best.

'I've been following your channel,' Mikki's dad continued. 'And all your good work to save those beautiful trees.'

'If only the council thought pine trees were beautiful,' I added.

'We're planning a protest,' Mikki said. He cut a chunk of salmon with his chopsticks and added it to his bowl of rice. I mimicked him exactly. 'In the form of a forest concert. If we can make it work.'

'Oh, I just love the idea of a musical protest,' Junko said. 'And I guess you'd know some local musicians, Alberta?'

Mikki and I exchanged looks. We both knew it wasn't quite time to explain to Mikki's parents that the local *musician* we had in mind was an actual tree.

'Kind of,' I said, struggling to know what to say next.

Luckily, Mikki jumped in, and we got off the topic of the forest concert entirely. I enjoyed every part of the breakfast too. Even the fermented soybeans! I did wonder what Mikki's parents might have heard about my parents, though. But I was soon cured by the sour, zingy burst of pickled cucumber. It was a completely new taste for me...at breakfast. It reminded me of all the new things I'd learnt about vibrations too. And now that I'd handballed all my Mum worries over to Dad, it was easy to recall the feelings of calm I'd discovered earlier that morning...when I'd tuned into our fig tree.

Mikki checked his watch.

'We have to go,' he said. 'We've got an important meeting to get to.'

※

Mikki was right, Massimo Paolini did have a lot of experience with plants and music but he had never used his plant-music device on a tree, especially not a huge old tree with pine needles instead of actual leaves.

'It should work,' Massimo said. 'As long as you can make a successful connection. The device comes with two electrodes, one is a metal spike that gets pushed into the earth at the base of the tree, then there's a clasp that goes onto the leaves. That's how the device can read what's happening inside the tree, and tap into its unique intelligence.'

Mikki and Massimo talked tech for what felt like a very long time – all about probes and electrodes and types of cables and MIDI output and SD cards. They talked about what we'd need to connect the device up to external speakers and the software required if we used a PC. Then they talked about sound parameters and pre-sets and filters and electromagnetic interference and base frequencies and musical scales. They finally spoke about things I could understand. And I could tell Mikki was convinced that a plant-music device like Massimo's would work for our forest concert. We had already talked about doing a crowdfunding campaign to cover costs.

'So...' said Mikki. 'Where do we buy one of these plant-music devices and... are they expensive?'

'I want to tell you something,' said Massimo. 'I am so in love with the Memory Tree and all the beautiful pines in your forest. It would make me so happy if I gave you my plant-music device... really, it would.'

'Oh no,' said Mikki. 'I mean, thank you, Massimo, but we couldn't accept.'

'But why?' Massimo said. 'Your forest concert will be the most wonderful event and not only for the people in your town. It is such a beautiful, peaceful protest. You should livestream it on YouTube for all the world to enjoy. Please let me help you. I am so happy for it.'

I nudged Mikki under the table. It all felt so right. I hoped like anything Mikki wasn't going to get all proud about it and say no. I had to interject.

'We would love this, Massimo. Thank you! But it would just be a loan. We could send the plant-music device straight back to you afterwards?'

'This is fine with me,' he said. 'If you have your own speakers the device itself is not very big. I can ship it straight away by express.'

CHAPTER 33

I was soooo excited about the the forest concert! I could already see it so clearly in my mind. Especially the look on Mayor Pizzey's face when he heard the voice of the Memory Tree. Surely the Kingfisher Council wouldn't let Seth's dad chop the pines down then. Would they? Mikki and I were almost done designing a forest concert poster at my place. I thought I'd almost gotten away with having a friend come to visit without Clementine and Mum having one of their arguments too. Sadly, no. We could hear them arguing in the kitchen and soon Mum was storming down the hall, yelling at the top of her voice, 'Oh, Clementine, will you just give it a rest. Please!' I was so embarrassed. Compared to the peaceful breakfast we'd had with Mikki's family that morning he must have thought our place was an actual zoo. Mum slammed the door to her den, and I noticed Mikki's brow crinkle with the shock of it.

'I'm sorry, Mikki,' I said. 'I think there is something actually wrong with my sister. Honestly.'

'You want to know what I think?' Mikki asked. I wasn't sure that I did. He probably thought Clementine needed to be tranquillised. I know I did.

'Don't worry, Mikki,' I said. 'Clementine will get her stilts out soon. With any luck she'll fall off and knock herself out!' Mikki didn't see the joke.

'Your sister needs a job. She's a very bored girl. Why don't we get her to help with the forest concert? We've got such a lot to do,' Mikki suggested.

Of course, Mikki was right. Not just that Clementine was bored but we did need some help. We had so many ideas for the forest concert but every single one of them added about ten more jobs to our list. Marketing the event was the most important thing to start with but we couldn't start advertising the event without a poster and then we'd need to put them up all over town and who had time for that? We also had to make a new video that day in the forest. Organising a forest concert using a device we didn't even have yet, then convincing the whole town to come along and the whole world to tune in on YouTube was definitely ambitious, and the biggest thing either of us had ever done. And there was a horrible feeling of time running out.

'We could use some help putting the posters up, for sure,' Mikki said. 'Maybe Clementine could take care of local marketing?'

'I guess if she had something to do she might not cause so many arguments with Mum,' I said.

Clementine was beside herself with excitement when I offered her the role of Forest Concert Local Marketing Coordinator. She couldn't wait to put up posters in town and called Dad straight away to ask him to help with printing.

'He said he could do it today at the office,' she said. 'In colour!'

'Nice work!' I said, and I meant it too.

Dad picked Clementine up on his lunch break. I could hear the muffled tones of he and Mum having a conversation on the porch, and Clementine stomping about after being sent away. The fact that Mum and Dad were actually talking felt like a good sign, so long as they didn't explode. I didn't want another zoo scene in front of Mikki.

'After we've printed the posters,' Clementine said excitedly, 'Dad said he'd help put them up, you know, like on poles and in shop windows!'

'Thanks a bunch, Clementine,' I said. 'There's heaps of sticky tape in the craft box.'

'Yes, thank you, Clementine,' Mikki added. 'You're already a most impressive Forest Concert Local Marketing Coordinator.'

Clementine's whole face lit up as Mikki gave her a USB. 'Here's the file for the poster,' he said.

'Can you check out the op shops too?' I asked. 'We need to get lots of picnic rugs.'

'I will!' Clementine said, racing out the door. 'Bye!'

'Everyone needs to feel useful,' Mikki said. 'And we'd better go too, Alberta. We need to check in with the Memory Tree. I mean, it's going to be the star of the show and we haven't even asked for its permission. Let's get up to the forest before we lose too much light.'

CHAPTER 34

By the time Mikki and I got to the pines the sun was dropping behind the trees, which cast long, long shadows across the forest floor.

'We need to start filming straight away,' Mikki said. He set to work gathering quick snippets around the Memory Tree. Then he checked his light meter.

'The light's a bit muted,' he said. 'But actually, I think it's perfect. It suits the solemn nature of what you'll be talking about.' Mikki directed me to my position in front of the Memory Tree and before I knew it, the recording light was illuminated. No time for rehearsal. I'd just have to wing it.

'Hey there, tree loving people, Alberta here again and I'm with Mikki up in our favourite little forest inside the forest here at Kingfisher Bay. As you can see, it's late in the day, but this video is really important so we wanted to get it out there as soon as we could.

'Firstly, if you're new to our channel, welcome, and we hope you'll check out our previous videos, beautifully filmed and edited by Mikki Watanabe.

'Behind me here is the Memory Tree and some of you may already have learnt that this tree, and all these magnificent pines, are currently under threat. That's right, the Kingfisher Shire Council plans to cut down each and every one of them!

'Mikki and I want to thank all our subscribers for the support you've given us so far in fighting against this injustice. Your encouragement has been completely overwhelming and has really given us strength to fight for these trees.

'Today we want to send special thanks to Massimo. If you haven't checked out his channel you really should. Mikki and I are so inspired by Massimo's video about plant music. That's right! Plants and trees can make sound...with a little help from technology, of course. And that's when Mikki and I had a vision...as part of our campaign to save these trees we'll be hosting a peaceful protest and inviting the whole of Kingfisher Bay to a forest concert, right here among these pines. And our star performer will be none other than this one – the tallest and wisest and oldest tree in the pine grove – our very own Memory Tree.

'We'd like to send a huge thank you to Massimo for not only sparking the inspiration for a forest concert, but for being our technical support and also sending us his plant-music device, all the way from Italy. Thank you, Massimo. We absolutely couldn't do this without you and we can't wait for the parcel to arrive.

'So... please join us here at Kingfisher Bay on January twenty-six for our livestreamed forest concert hosted by Mikki and me and our beloved Memory Tree. We'll let you know more as we get closer to the date but for now we're asking all our supporters to send tweets and messages to the people who can stop the mindless killing of these beautiful beings. We've provided all the links below. Every voice helps. On behalf of all trees in this forest, please let your voice be heard.

'To the state Minister for the Environment, Senator Eleanor Doyle, Mayor Pizzey from Kingfisher Shire Council, and especially to Paul Cromby, the arborist who has agreed to cut down these trees... if you're watching... we have reserved the front row at the forest concert especially for you. Until next time, thanks again for the support and it's goodnight from Mikki and me.'

That night Clementine was buzzing with excitement. Mikki was so right. She just needed gainful employment. At dinner there was absolutely no mention of her slumber party and she hadn't bounced on her pogo stick all day. She was too busy putting up fifty forest concert posters all over town.

'I saw Bella and Sylvie,' Clementine said. 'They were super impressed with the posters!'

'Can't believe my little sister sees more of my friends than I do!' I laughed. 'I'll call Bella later. She'll get all the grommets to come.'

'Serious?' asked Clementine. 'Won't that mean Seth Cromby will come too?'

To tell you the truth, I hadn't even thought of that. 'Hopefully he'll still be grounded,' I said. 'Did you remember to check out the op shop?'

'Of course!' Clementine said. 'There were loads of cheap picnic blankets and cushions. Dad said he'd help me get them next time. At least people won't get pine needles in their bums.' She laughed.

'Nice one!' I said. Clementine was shaping up to be more helpful than I'd thought.

'Yeah, and then when Dad dropped me home Mum spoke to him for like ... three whole minutes!'

'Did she let him inside?' I asked.

'No, it was through the car window.'

'Was the car window open?' I asked.

Clementine laughed. 'Bertie!'

'Well, was it?' I asked again.

'No,' Clementine finally admitted. 'But it's still better than her not talking to him at all!'

It felt like it had been such a huge day but there was still so much to get done. I lay on my bed and imagined myself on the night of the forest concert, addressing a crowd of actual people. This felt far scarier than just chatting away to Mikki's camera in the forest. And we still didn't know for certain the date the council planned to cut the forest down. How could I find out? That's when I put through a call to Bella. She had total cred with Seth Cromby and could surely extract some information.

'Hey!' I said. 'Clemmy said she saw you today?'

'She's so funny,' said Bella. 'She was arguing like crazy with Audrey Nancarrow at the bookshop about putting a poster in the front window!'

'Clementine? Arguing?' I joked. 'Are you sure you got the right person?'

'Ha ha!' said Bella. 'Clementine won in the end!'

'Hey, do you know if Seth Cromby's still grounded?' I asked.

'Nup. He must have done some serious grovelling because his parents ended up letting him come to the State Surf Titles next week. Just to watch though, 'cause he missed the trials. I'm actually getting a ride with Seth's parents. I hope you don't mind, Bertie? You know I'd love you to be there.'

'That's okay, Bella,' I said. 'I'm really sorry to miss it but... you know...'

'I get it,' said Bella. 'Awkward!'

'I do have a huge favour to ask though...' I said.

I stayed up way too late reading about vibrations. I felt like I really needed to cram before the next video and there was so much information to sort through.

Some of it was proven science, like Einstein and the laws of physics, but there was also lots of stuff about energy and vibrational frequency that hadn't been proven. And sometimes science just didn't have the tools to test if something was true or not. So, just because something wasn't proven by science didn't always mean it wasn't true. I kept this in mind as I read that when your vibrational frequency is high, it actually let more light into your being. That meant – whatever you can imagine you can also attract into your life, that there's a like-attracts-like thing going on.

If I believed this (and I think I did), it meant that whatever I imagined about saving the Memory Tree and the forest I could ultimately make it happen. Up against the cold reality of the trees being cut down, I felt relieved that my beliefs and imaginings could help. It was the only thing that offered hope. It was time to imagine in as much detail as possible how we would save the Memory Tree and the forest. I had to actually believe that miracles could happen.

CHAPTER 35

Massimo emailed some information about how the plant-music device worked. This was a relief because if I was going to be hosting the forest concert I needed to have the facts really clear in my mind. I watched a video about the sacred woods at the Damanhur community in Italy, the place where Massimo had first seen the music of plant device in action. In the video live musicians were playing instruments while the plants chimed along in the background. Our concert was going to be different though, of course. Ours would have only one musician – the Memory Tree.

From what I could understand, the Memory Tree, once hooked up to the plant-music device, would send a signal, like a pulse in the form of its vibrational energy. The device feeds the pulsating energy into a synthesiser, which transforms the tree's energy into sound. Our forest concert would be the first time anyone in the audience would have heard a tree have its voice in a way that humans could understand, through sound. Maybe then, people would see all the pines as more than just invasive weeds, or some problem that needed 'removing'. With a voice, for the very first time, the Memory Tree could express itself not as an object, but as a light-giving, sensitive being, vibrating with aliveness.

This was the scenario I came back to whenever fears crept into my mind, like being heckled by someone in the audience. I couldn't flounder. I had to have all my knowledge right there at the forefront of my mind. Mikki's grandfather's research had already proven that nature vibrates at a high frequency and that humans could tap into this too. This is why forests are so powerful; trees can help raise the speed of energy vibrating inside us... I mean, isn't that amazing? All humans need to do to commune with trees is set up the conditions to be open to nature's vibrations.

Mikki called to say the courier service had told him a parcel was on its way.

'I can't believe it!' I said.

'Can you be ready in five?' Mikki asked. 'My mum said there's literally hundreds of posters up around town. She even saw someone taking some down! I thought we'd agreed on fifty with Clementine?'

'Mmm,' I said. 'Not at all like Clementine to go overboard.'

'I think we better go check it out,' he said.

Junko was right. As we rode into town on Mikki's bike we saw forest concert posters on every electricity pole.

Mikki laughed. 'Clementine's a hard worker,' Mikki said. 'And we do need to promote the concert but—'

'There is actually no hope for that girl!' I said. As we got closer to the town centre there were posters stuck to every possible surface. Clementine had even poster-bombed the Give Way sign near the library.

'How did she even achieve this?' I said. 'I can't imagine Dad was involved.'

Mikki pulled up outside the library. I counted ten forest concert posters on the public noticeboard near the front door.

'Clementine's actually gone insane!' I said.

That's when Mikki and I bumped into Dad, who said he had just bumped into Mrs McGlashan from the council, who had just spoken to Mayor Pizzey, who said the posters had to stop. Not only that, Mrs McGlashan said that Mayor Pizzey had insisted any public event held on land in Kingfisher Shire required written permission from the council and a permit!

'It's just a bit of red tape,' Dad said. 'Nothing that can't be sorted out, with time.'

My heart sank low, dragging my vibrations down with it.

'Time!' I exclaimed. 'The very thing we don't have. If we don't get a permit for the forest concert, we won't save the trees! Why is Mayor Pizzey being so mean?'

When Mikki and I got back to our place Clementine was in the kitchen burning toast.

'Clementine... the posters. There's about a million all over town. What the hell?'

'God, Bertie, you're the one who put me in charge of marketing!' Clementine squeaked.

'Now we have to get a dumb permit and we might not be able to have the forest concert at all!'

'There's just no pleasing you is there, Alberta?' she screamed.

Mikki looked a little embarrassed.

'You did do a very thorough job, Clementine,' Mikki said.

'Thank you, Mikki,' Clementine said. She opened the fridge and practically stuck her whole head inside looking for the butter. Then she slammed it shut. I could hear Mum coming down the hall. Next thing I knew Clementine would start another argument.

'Come on, Mikki,' I said, shuffling him into the lounge. 'We need to find out about this permit business.'

'Can I help?' Clementine asked.

'Not your department!' I scolded.

The Kingfisher Shire Council Special Event Permit Application had a squillion questions, including ones on things we had absolutely no idea about, like insurance and whether the police, road authorities, fire department and ambulance needed to be advised. And you couldn't just make stuff up, either. You had to attach actual proof. If that wasn't hopeless enough, the guidelines said we'd have to wait four weeks for a permit *if* our application was even successful.

'I hate the council!' I cursed. 'Why do they ruin everything?'

Somehow Mikki was able to stay calm, even though Clementine made a point of walking past the lounge room window on her circus stilts about ten times.

'See? This is what I have to deal with!' I said, pointing at my impossible sister.

'Let's just stay focussed and submit the online form,' Mikki said. 'For most of the questions we can tick "not applicable". Then ... maybe we can find someone to—'

'Need any help?' Mum asked.

Mikki and I explained the situation to Mum, who did her best to reassure us. She knew everyone down at the council.

'You'd be surprised at what you can achieve when you employ good manners,' she said. 'Let me see what I can do.'

'That would be amazing, Mrs Bracken,' Mikki said. 'Thank you!'

Mikki's eyes were full of hope but he was probably the only person in town who didn't know about Mum's nonsensical shoplifting problem. As far as Mikki was concerned, my mother was simply Tammy Bracken, world expert on table manners and social etiquette. If only my mother was *just* that!

> ### 🌿 Tammy's Tips 🌿
> #### #15 INFLUENCING OTHERS
> *People are more likely to support your cause if you listen carefully, show respect and demonstrate good manners. This is why good manners are your secret weapon to influencing others.*

After submitting the permit application Mikki and I studied the instructions for the plant-music device.

'When it arrives,' Mikki said, 'we need to be ready to go.'

We familiarised ourselves with all the components – a black metal box with a bunch of dials, two reels of electrical cable – one with the metal spike at the end, and one connected to a metal clamp.

'Just like Massimo explained,' Mikki said, 'the device measures the electromagnetic vibration of a plant in two places – through the roots by pushing the probe into the soil and also through the plant foliage or leaves.'

My heart sank low.

'Wait!' I said. 'How are we meant to get to the Memory Tree's foliage? Its closest pine needle clusters are up about ten metres high!'

'Uh-oh,' said Mikki. All the hope drained from his face.

'It's not like I can climb a ladder with this arm!' I said. Clementine clonked past the window again on her stilts, doing her best to be seen. 'If only those stilts were a bit higher!' I said.

'Don't look at me,' Mikki said. 'I'm absolutely terrified of heights.'

'Perfect!' I huffed, sarcastically, and slumped my head down on the table.

Then I remembered how powerful thoughts can be, and how slumped-out, head-on-a-table kind of feelings were definitely of low vibration and not at all the kind of feelings that would help. I had to perform a brain intervention, fast. I picked my head off the table and closed my eyes, imagined myself as an antennae, reaching out to the universal field of all potential.

'What are you doing?' Mikki asked.

'Imagining the Memory Tree making music,' I said. 'You should too, Mikki.' For the next few minutes, Mikki and I sat with our eyes closed, deep in our imaginations. I was sure I felt my heart expanding with higher vibrations. In my mind Mikki and I had already saved the forest. Yes, we had!

CHAPTER 36

Mikki was desperate to put a video on YouTube in case anyone had any clever tree-climbing ideas that didn't involve one of us actually climbing a tree.

'We don't need to go all the way to the forest,' he said. 'How 'bout I come over to your place? We could shoot it in front of your fig tree?' But I felt unsure. What if Clementine bombed our video on her stilts?

'Come on, Alberta,' Mikki said. 'We could introduce Clementine on the video too.'

'Okay,' I said. 'We'll see you soon.'

While Mikki was making his way over, I needed to explain a few things to Clementine about the video-making process. This was harder than it sounded. Clementine refused to stop jumping on her pogo stick for the whole conversation. Talking to her seriously gave me a sore neck.

'Firstly, promise to only step into frame when I'm ready to introduce you.'

'I promise,' said Clementine.

'You need to watch Mikki. He'll give you a hand signal when the time is right, okay?'

'Got it.'

'Then when he says "cut", you stop talking, okay?'

'Der!' said Clementine. 'As if I don't know that!'

'And for the rest of the time you have to promise to be quiet... no pogo-sticking, no stilts, no walking on hands, no—'

'You're not the boss of me, Alberta!' Clementine shouted.

'See, that's where you're wrong, Clementine. This time, I actually am your boss!'

'Muuuuuuuum!' Clementine screamed, jumping with even more conviction.

'Shh! Mikki will be here soon and you're sure looking crazy!'

Just then Mikki appeared with his camera gear. Clementine stopped jumping straight away.

'Who's looking crazy?' Mikki asked.

'Not me!' said Clementine. But Mikki wasn't really listening, he was already squatting in front of the fig tree to line up the best angle for our video.

⟵

'Hey, guys, Alberta here and today I'm at home with another tree that's really special to me, this Moreton Bay fig. Mikki and I are just about to head back up to Kingfisher National Park where we're getting ready for our forest concert event, which we're hosting to save the Memory Tree and all the other pines in our favourite little forest inside the forest. We want to say thanks again for all your support and encouragement for the forest concert. Can you believe we already have over sixty people attending and two hundred and twenty registrations for the live stream? This is awesome!

'Today you're going to meet the newest member of our team who also happens to be my sister, Clementine. Come and say hi, Clementine!'

'Hey!' Clementine said, smiling and waving at the camera.

'Clementine's been helping out with marketing here in Kingfisher Bay and on the night of the concert she'll be taking care of the livestream. Mikki will be capturing the whole thing on film. I can't tell you how excited we are. It's going to be such a special night so please tell your friends and ask them to tune in too. And don't worry if you miss it. You'll be able to watch it anytime here at *Mikki and Me and the Memory Tree.* But for now, if anyone out there can help us... we need to find a way to hook up a wire to the Memory Tree's foliage. It's way too high for a ladder to work so if you have *any* ideas, no matter how far-fetched... please leave a comment after this video.'

We couldn't believe how quickly the responses started flooding in.

AbiFilms just now
Hey! I know a guy who climbs trees and he uses a crossbow and a fishing reel to get the ropes up there. 📓 I hope you can work it out.

Bananaboy12 just now
If I lived in Australia instead of Norway I would for sure come and help. Good luck. Can't wait for the concert. 🎼 🌲

Massimo Paolini just now
Did you receive my parcel yet? Perhaps try the fire department? LOL

Quantum108 just now
Maybe the Memory Tree could help come up with an idea?

TomLovesTrees just now
I am SO THERE for this concert... Be tuning in from Albany WA. You guys are awesome!

AriellaWaterSprite just now
Can't wait to see how you solve this one but I know you will. Loved meeting Clementine too. My little sister is soooo jealous!! ♥ 🌲 🌲

A-non-e-mous just now
I've got an idea or two up my sleeve... stay tuned!

Sylvie500 just now
Guys, the forest concert sounds so awesome! Love *all* the posters!!! I really want to help too. Berts, I'll call you later to find out how!! 🌲 👋 ♥

It was so nice to get a regular message from Sylvie again, even if it was just on YouTube with all the others. It felt like old times. I remembered that day on the beach when Sylvie's weirdness had started, the day I'd broken my arm. Bobbing out in the ocean on my boogie board her weirdness had felt like being swept up by a wave. I remembered feeling I just had to accept it and ride it out. Somehow I knew that Sylvie and I would never talk about the reasons she'd been acting so weird. We didn't need to. I knew she felt sorry for ghosting me when I broke my arm and that it was all because of Mum's little (well, big, actually) shoplifting spree at Kingfisher Sports. At least her parents hadn't gone to the police, just blabbed about it to everyone in town instead, including to Sylvie. None of it was ever about her and me or the silly netball top. From that moment I realised my friendship with Sylvie was back on track and that was all that mattered. The comment from A-non-e-mous was less comforting though. I shuddered to think what that creep had up his sleeve!

We were almost ready to go to the forest when Bella called. She was full of encouragement about our video and she also had some exciting news of her own. Bella had won the girls under twelve division at the Junior State Surf Titles at Ocean Tides.

'Though you know they're calling us "Poo Point" in Kingfisher Bay now?'

'Bells, I knew you'd win. So happy for you. You're better than anyone else by far!'

'Aw, thanks! How's it going with the forest concert? Can't believe how many posters I've seen around town!'

'Typical Clementine!' I said. 'But I have to admit she has been a big help.'

'Speaking of help,' Bella said. 'Sure looks like Clementine had some too.'

I wasn't sure what Bella meant by that but I suddenly remembered she'd got a ride with Seth Cromby's parents to the surf comp.

'Hey, did Seth's dad mention anything about the forest?' I asked, hopefully.

'Nah, sorry, Berts…' she said. 'I really want to help out with the event though. Sylvie and Georgette do too.'

'Ha ha. The Three Foresteers!'

Bella laughed. 'We can keep an eye on Clementine too!' she said.

CHAPTER 37

Mikki and Clementine and I looked high into the branches of the Memory Tree, trying to find the best bunch of pine needles to wire up the plant-music device. It felt like a daunting mission.

'That's sooo high!' Clementine said. 'Higher than the Seven for sure.'

Clementine was referring to the seven-metre diving platform at the baths. There were three platforms – the Five, the Seven and the terrifying Ten. Clementine was right, those pine fascicles were as high as the seven-metre platform ... only without a ladder or a pool to jump (fall) into below. How were we meant to get the wires up there without eventually asking a parent for help? If Mum or Dad knew what was involved they'd shut the forest concert down for sure. Parents just love that kind of thing. I turned my back on Mikki and Clementine and the Memory Tree and wandered over to the old fireplace. There were still broken bricks on the ground and I busied myself picking them up, one by one, and adding them on to the stack I'd made that very first day we'd discovered the pine grove. I guess I got completely immersed in the task. So immersed that I hadn't noticed what Mikki or Clementine were doing or that an unwelcome guest had arrived. Can you imagine my horror when I discovered Mikki and Clementine over by the Memory Tree, chatting away casually to... wait for it... Seth Cromby!

I knew straight away that Seth's appearance in the forest had something to do with Clementine. It was so obvious. I know every shifty look on that face!

'Just listen, Birdy!' she begged. 'Please! Seth wants to help. He's got important information and—'

'It's true!' Seth interrupted. 'It's about the forest concert. I found out Dad's got his team lined up and ready to cut down the trees that very same day. By the time of the forest concert... well, the trees will be gone!'

My mind was racing. Surely this was some kind of a trap? What else would you expect from a guy that broke your arm and then trolled you online? It didn't make any sense that Seth would help now. And why would he dob in his own dad?

'Just thought you guys should know,' he said solemnly.

I noticed Mikki was avoiding my gaze. 'Were you in on this too, Mikki?' I asked.

But Mikki remained silent. He just kept staring up the trunk of the Memory Tree, which confirmed my worst suspicions.

'Oh my God!' I yelled.

'Don't be angry, Alberta!' Clementine said. 'I know Seth hurt your arm but since then he's been so helpful with the—' Clementine tried to swallow her words.

'With the what?' I demanded.

She looked away. 'With the ... posters,' she whispered.

'What's wrong with you people?' I yelled. So it was Seth who'd helped Clementine put up the posters all over town? I felt like I was stuck in a washing machine with Seth Cromby. I couldn't get away from him. It was just Seth Cromby and me, spinning round and around.

'It was my way of saying I'm sorry for hurting your arm, Alberta,' Seth said.

'Hurting it!' I yelled. 'You broke it, Seth Cromby! You broke my arm.'

'I know I did,' he said. 'And I want to make it up to you. I want to help save your trees.'

'Oh yeah!' I argued. 'How's *that* going to go down with your dad?'

'I don't care!' he said. 'I know I was a dick trolling your YouTube channel, but—'

'You're such a faker, Seth Cromby. Why don't you just come clean about what you really want?' I was sure he was going to hold something over me about Mum and the Woolies incident.

'Shut up!' screamed Clementine. 'Don't you see? Seth Cromby is the only person in Kingfisher Bay who can climb the Memory Tree!'

Seth nodded in agreement. Mikki too.

'She's right,' said Mikki. 'Seth's rock-climbing skills are exactly what we need. And it will make a great video too.'

Seth nodded again.

'Climbing that big boy would be a total breeze,' Seth said, 'and, sure, my dad will be mad as hell, but seriously, I really want to help save the forest.'

CHAPTER 38

When Clementine and I got back home Dad's car was parked in the drive. Inside, he and Mum were in the kitchen having a cup of tea. Their conversation fell into silence as soon as they saw us. They both just sat there looking weird.

'I've got some good news for you!' Mum said. 'I called Mayor Pizzey and while he is concerned at the sheer number of posters that have been put up around town, he's granted you a permit for the concert! Isn't that wonderful?'

'That's so rubbish!' Clementine shrieked. 'What's the point of a permit when the trees will already be cut down before anyone even turns up!'

'What do you mean?' asked Dad.

'What we mean,' I said, 'is that while he's granted a permit for a twilight forest concert, he's also approved the trees being cut down that very same day!'

'Yeah, so what's the point?' Clementine cried. 'Mayor Pizzey just told you what you wanted to hear, Mum. And you fell for it.'

Mum clunked her teacup onto its saucer, stood up and stormed out of the kitchen.

'Well,' she said, 'we'll soon see about that!' Dad was left sitting there looking helpless.

'I, ah...I suppose I should get going,' he said. He stood and put on his jacket. 'Bye, girls,' he added, giving me a kiss. I wondered what he'd said to Mum. Had he done what he'd said when he promised he'd take care of Mum's little (big) problem?

I dashed outside to catch Dad before he drove off. I was desperate to find out what was happening with Mum. On the way I overheard Mum talking sternly on the phone in her den. Dad was just starting to reverse out of the drive as I knocked on the car window. 'What is it, love?' he asked. He seemed impatient.

'Did you speak to Mum?'

'Alberta, I said I'd take care of this. Haven't you got enough to think about with the forest concert?'

'Dad!' I whined.

'Look, it's going to take some more talking but we've agreed on a plan.' he said.

'Is she going to see someone...like a shrink?' I asked.

Dad took a deep breath. 'Your mother and I had a good talk and, in the end...well...we're both going to see someone actually. Together. A relationship counsellor.'

'But what about that Ursula Hoffman?' I asked. Dad looked like a blend of embarrassed and fed up. At least he didn't look like he'd cry.

'That's all over, love,' he sighed. 'And with time, and some professional help, I'm hoping your mum can forgive me.'

'But what about Mum's... problem?'

'Well, obviously we'll be working on that too!' he said. 'Can you drop it now please, Alberta!' Dad put his window up and turned the engine on.

'Fine!' I said, turning back to the house.

Inside, Mum was on the phone to Mayor Pizzey so naturally, I hid in the hallway and listened in.

'Well that's just ridiculous, Julian!' she said. 'Fancy giving young people that kind of hope when you knew all along when you granted that permit that... yes I am aware of the council's position on re-forestation, Julian... yes, I accept that, but can I remind you... I'm just asking that you let them have their concert. They've worked so hard... and one day, Julian... it's all I ask... you do realise that I have... I *am* calm, Julian... I'm just saying... look, I was hoping I wouldn't have to spell this out but... I *do* have a level of influence, you know!'

Mum slammed down the phone. Go, Mum! I thought.

CHAPTER 39

Massimo's parcel arrived at last! Mikki called and said he'd checked it all and everything was there and in working order, not that he had tested it on an actual tree yet.

'We still need speakers,' Mikki said. 'But Dad said he'd get some for us. There's a battery-powered system at the hire shop in town. It's got a microphone too, for when you address the crowd. Which reminds me... how's that speech going, Alberta?'

'I started writing it last night,' I lied. I actually hadn't written a thing, just thought about it, then avoided thinking about it, then felt totally sick about it, then as much as possible tried to imagine the speech going super well. Still, no actual writing of it.

'Don't worry, Mikki. I'll be prepared.'

Mikki had arranged to meet Seth up in the forest that morning. He was super keen to make a video introducing Seth (Mikki's new hero), and how he was going to climb the Memory Tree with his rock-climbing equipment.

I was more interested in whether Seth had any news from his dad, like Paul Cromby changing his mind about cutting down the forest, or maybe needing to postpone.

When Mikki and me and Clementine got to the pine grove Seth was already there. He'd lined up a bunch of climbing ropes neatly on the ground by the Memory Tree along with a helmet, a harness, gloves and ... a spearfishing gun.

'Is that like a legit rock climbing thing?' I asked. I still couldn't believe I was even talking to Seth Cromby. The sight of him still gave me the creeps, even if he was our only chance to hook the plant-music device.

'Not exactly,' said Seth, 'but I was inspired by that comment on YouTube about the crossbow. I need to get a throw line up at least seven metres and over that branch.' Seth pointed to one of the Memory Tree's lowest, but strongest looking branches. 'So I thought Dad's spear gun might be just the thing. I'm going to try shooting the throw line up.'

Mikki looked concerned. I could tell it was the idea of Seth Cromby firing a spear gun at his special tree.

'I may have check in with the Memory Tree about that method,' Mikki said. 'But first I need to pack away my grandfather's offerings.'

'The photos and all that?' Seth asked. 'I was wondering what that was.'

While Mikki was busy with the Memory Tree, I had a couple of questions of my own.

'Seth, how did you even find out about our YouTube channel in the first place?'

Clementine couldn't help butting in. 'Yeah, Seth,' she said. 'When did you decide to become a troll?'

Seth laughed. 'Same as how my dad found out,' he said. 'From Mikki's mum.'

I take back everything I said about Mikki's parents causing less drama than mine. Mum might be annoying but at least she didn't throw me under a bus!

'So you just had to go ruin it?' I joked (not joking).

Seth laughed. 'I guess I was angry... your dad telling my parents about your arm 'n' all.'

'About what *you* did to my arm!'

'Yeah, I know... I guess I was angry with myself, especially about getting grounded. I lost my job at Woolies and everything.'

'Oh, poor you!' I said sarcastically.

'Well anyway, I was mega bored being grounded... and I'd been up here with my dad. So when I saw your video—'

'I get it. You just couldn't help going feral.'

'Birdy!' Clementine protested. 'That's hardly how you speak to someone who's doing us a favour!'

Seth laughed. 'It's okay, Clementine. I did go feral, at first. But then I started getting really into what you guys were saying about trees.'

Mikki had finished with the Memory Tree and all his grandfather's offerings were neatly packed away.

'I checked with the Memory Tree,' Mikki said. 'And it's okay. Whatever it takes to make the forest concert work.'

Then he set all the wires from the plant-music device carefully next to Seth's ropes.

'Are you ready to introduce Seth to our subscribers, Alberta?' Mikki said.

Seth and I stood side by side in front of the Memory Tree and waited for Mikki to get ready with his camera. I still felt like I needed to pinch myself with the weirdness of it all – Seth being not only nice, not only helpful, but... life-saving, or at least that's how Mikki and Clementine felt. Seth was shuffling around on his feet, and I could tell he felt a bit nervous.

'You just need to be yourself,' I said. I knew it wasn't that reassuring for Seth, but it was the best I could do.

'Yeah, nah, I'm good,' he said. 'Let's do it.'

The green light illuminated on Mikki's camera. 'And... action!' he said.

'Hello everyone! It's me, Alberta, and Mikki – here again in our favourite forest and boy, have we got an interesting video for you today. But first you need to meet someone that many of you might already know from our comments feed as "A-non-e-mous". You'd better believe it! Our dreaded troll A-non-e-mous turns out to be this guy, Seth Cromby, and he lives right here in Kingfisher Bay. I know! You want to say hi, Seth?'

'Hey! I'm Seth, pleased to meet you... listen, I'm not proud of it, but yep, I was the troll, that's me... wait! That was the old me!'

'But the good news is,' I continued, 'Seth is going to help us out with the most difficult part of this whole forest concert, which is how to get this here wire and clasp, *all* the way up the Memory Tree where he's going to clamp it onto some of its live, green foliage. So thanks for all your weird and whacky suggestions because they did inspire Seth to come up with a plan. How 'bout you explain what you've got in mind, Seth?' I prompted.

'Sure,' he said. 'But first... if it's okay with you guys, there's something important I need to say.'

'Of course,' I said. Fact was, I knew Mikki would edit out anything we weren't happy with so it didn't really matter what Seth said. I was happy to just play along. But that doesn't mean I wasn't taken by surprise, either, because I was surprised, I tell you, I *was*.

'I just want to say how sorry I am... not just for being an idiot online, but for breaking your arm, Alberta. I still can't believe I actually did that.'

Seth took me completely off guard. There was no way I had planned on telling the world that Seth had broken my arm!

'I really admire what these guys are doing,' Seth said. His voice went all thin. I couldn't handle it if Seth cried, even if we could edit it out later. 'So—'

'So we're going to stay super focussed on our vision,' I interrupted. 'And Seth ... we're just all dying to know ... how are you going to get this clasp onto those pine needles growing all the way up there?'

'Cut,' said Mikki. 'I just need to catch some other small pieces first.'

I joined Clementine by the fireplace, glad to be offscreen. The focus would all be on Seth now, coiling up his throw line so it wouldn't get tangled when he shot it out of his spearfishing gun and sent it hurtling up to the nearest bough of the Memory Tree. I wondered how many attempts Seth would need to shoot it high enough to go over that branch?

'Before we get started,' Mikki said, 'I think you should tell people not to try this at home.'

'No worries,' said Seth. He made everything look so effortless as he tied a figure-eight knot in the throw line and attached it to the end of the rubber cord of his spearfishing gun. Soon they were ready to go. Mikki shooting his film and Seth shooting his spearfishing gun.

CHAPTER 40

Mikki was filming close-ups of Seth tying knots and attaching the throw line to the end of the spearfishing gun. Seth turned to where Clementine and I were still sitting.

'You guys stay there. You gotta make sure you're always behind me okay?' he called.

'Got it!' I yelled back.

'Like, as if we're going to put ourselves in front of Seth Cromby and a spear gun!' Clementine whispered. She had a real knack for talking without moving her lips. There was a time before her obsession with circus skills that she practised a lot of ventriloquism with L'éléphant.

'Yeah, like as if I'm going to risk Seth Cromby taking out my other arm too!' I giggled. Clementine started giggling too and soon we couldn't stop, mostly because we were meant to be totally silent while Mikki filmed Seth doing his *don't try this at home* piece. Mikki gave us an undeniable *shoosh* look.

'And...action,' Mikki said. But at the sound of Mikki's cue Seth froze completely, totally like a rabbit in headlights. It lasted for a good three seconds. Then he spontaneously sprang into life.

'So, guys, we are not recommending this method at all. In fact, you should *never* try this, okay? But time is running out and...we're just going to give it a try.' Seth held the spear gun in clear view of the camera. 'As you can see, I've taken the actual spear part off this spear gun and adjusted the length of this rubber band by knotting in some extra line. This here is a weight that's going to bring it back down. Hopefully, it's going to shoot out like a catapult, high enough to get over the nearest branch...must be seven, eight metres high?'

Seth squatted down and aimed the spear gun straight up the trunk of the Memory Tree. 'Like I said, this is not at all conventional and if my dad found out I've pimped out his spear gun for this particular purpose...oh boy...let's not even go there! Okay, so the main thing is to make sure there is absolutely no way anyone could get hurt. You all safe, guys?' Seth yelled out.

'All safe!' we chimed back in unison.

'All right. Let's see if this thing flies! On the count of three...one, two...three!'

Seth pulled the trigger. I closed my eyes. The gun let off a short hiss, then there was a thud as the weight hit the trunk. Ouch! I thought on behalf of the Memory

Tree. But the line didn't make it over the branch. It reached high enough all right but it just hit the trunk then dropped back down again with a thud.

'I think this might take a few tries,' Clementine whispered.

Clementine was right. There were eight more attempts with exactly the same result – the line went straight up, reached the branch but didn't loop over it. And the poor old Memory Tree took a hit in the trunk each time. I could tell by the pained expression on his face that Mikki was slowly losing his tolerance.

'Once more, guys!' Seth said. 'This time it'll work… I promise!'

I could already imagine watching all the attempts back on video, like the bloopers at the end of movies.

Seth put the spear gun down and rubbed his hands together, like he was trying to warm them up. 'Come on!' he said to himself. He patted the Memory Tree's trunk before squatting down again, ready to fire. We all watched in silence, the line shooting up… up… up… and… *over* it went, right where we needed it, over the branch and dropping back down with the most satisfying thud into the pine needles. We broke into applause, all except Mikki, of course. He kept filming.

'Whoo hoooo!' squealed Clementine. She ran over to Seth and gave him a huge hug. After all the anticipation and failed attempts, I was overflowing with excitement too.

'Seth! I knew you'd do it. I knew it! I knew it!' I shouted.

Seth was super charged-up. He disconnected the spear gun and pulled the two ends of the throw line in towards his chest. 'You little beauty!' he said.

Mikki stopped filming and gave Seth a pat on the back. 'I'm so relieved,' he said. 'I couldn't take the suspense much longer.'

Seth got busy clipping and unclipping and tying and untying his ropes, getting himself ready for the next big part – actually climbing the tree. He turned to Mikki for approval. 'We have to secure one end of the rope around the base of the tree.'

'Okay,' Mikki said.

Seth tied the rope low around the Memory Tree, while Mikki filmed the whole thing. Then Seth checked his climbing belt, making sure everything was clicked in and locked off. It all just looked like a tangle of ropes and pulleys and knots to me, but I guess if you're into rock climbing the 'Rapid Ascent/Descent System' would have made a lot more sense.

The first thing I noticed when Seth finally started his climb was that it didn't seem that rapid at all. It was impressive, but kinda slow. With one foot in the foot loop and the other pushing off the trunk of the Memory Tree, Seth jumped off the ground and, sitting in his harness, hauled himself up, working the pulleys and ropes he'd attached to slowly made his way up the trunk. He was almost halfway.

'It's all working fine,' he called. 'Getting a good view from up here too!'

'Seth! Can you reach any pine needles?' I yelled.

'Not yet!' He kicked off the trunk and pulled himself a little higher, then higher again.

'I'll try now!' he called. Seth had made it to the bough that the throw line had gone over so he couldn't climb any further without setting up another line to a higher branch above. 'If I can just crawl along here a bit...'

'Seth, be careful!' Clementine called out.

'It's okay,' he answered. 'I'm attached to the climbing rope. Don't worry!'

We watched in silence as he lay on the branch and started edging himself along like a caterpillar. He brushed over a thinner branch, which snapped and fell to the ground. Clementine clutched my hand.

Seth wriggled further and further along until he had almost reached a bunch of green pine needles. He unzipped his kit bag on the side of his belt and unravelled the length of wire with the clamp attached. Then he stretched a shaky arm towards the closest bunch of pine needles.

'Did it!' he yelled. 'Now I just need to make sure it's secure so we can leave it clamped on until the night of the concert!'

'What if a bird takes it?' Clementine asked.

'Mmm...good point,' I said. Seth couldn't hear us chatting but Mikki and Clementine and I all agreed that it was too risky to leave the electrical wire and clamp up in the Memory Tree. It was a vital piece of equipment and if anything happened then the forest concert couldn't go ahead. What if a kookaburra stole it?

'But we could leave the throw line in the tree,' I said. 'That way we wouldn't need to do the spear gun part again.'

Mikki and Clementine nodded in agreement.

'Seth!' I called.

'Yeah?' he yelled back.

'We've decided not to leave the electrode up there. Sorry, Seth, but you'll have to climb the tree again for the actual concert!'

'Serious?' said Seth.

'Serious!' Mikki yelled. 'Sorry, Seth!'

Seth unclamped the wire and let it float back down to the ground. Then he set about squirming backwards along the branch again before starting his descent, which was a whole lot quicker compared to the climb up. By then I was *full* of appreciation for Seth Cromby. There was definitely no one else in the universe who could have scaled that tree, and all without us having to alert any parents. But I wasn't sure if Seth would be annoyed about having to make the climb again for the concert. He bounced himself carefully off the trunk with his feet as he made his way back down. Finally he landed with a firm thud, smiling from ear to ear.

'That was fun!' he said.

'So you don't mind having to do it again on the day of the concert?' I asked.

'Are you kidding?' Seth said, unclipping his harness from the climbing rope. 'I can't wait to climb this old guy again!' He packed up his things as fast as he could, apart from the climbing rope which he left tied to the Memory Tree, ready for the concert.

'I gotta go,' he said. 'Dad will seriously kill me if he finds out I've stolen his spearfishing gun.'

Mikki looked at his watch. 'We have to go too, Alberta. Dad said he'd take me to the hire shop to pick up the speakers.'

CHAPTER 41

I woke in the night at 4:44 a.m. I knew it would be 4:44 even before I checked the time because it's *always* 4:44 a.m. if I wake in the night with my mind abuzz. I checked the clock. Sure enough – 4:44 a.m.! There was still so much to do for the forest concert and as much as I'd been focussing for days on the best possible forest concert scenarios, in the deep silence of night my mind had flipped over. Now, like the worst kind of waking dream, all I could think about was what might go wrong. The worst-case scenario, of course, was the horrific notion that the trees would already be gone before the forest concert had even begun. That's if Mayor Pizzey really did give permission for Seth's dad to do the job earlier that day. Our only hope with that one was that Seth promised to mess with Paul Cromby by letting down his car tyres, if things got really desperate. Then there were all the other worst possible scenarios, like the one where we were all set up in the forest in front of a real live audience and who knows how many people online. I had just given my big speech, kept it short and sweet, like Mikki and I had planned, but when it was time for the Memory Tree to burst into song...nothing happened. There I was, standing in front of the Memory Tree, while the murmur of chatter grew louder and louder in the audience. People were laughing and jeering, mean people like the Kingfisher Krew, who'd really only turned up to see us fail in the first place. Even Sylvie and Georgette and Bella were sniggering and laughing while Clementine was crying on account of the mean comments flooding in online. I had painted the scene in my mind in so much detail I could almost smell the forest as I lay tossing and turning in my bed. And then there was my speech. I had told Mikki that I had it under control...but I still hadn't written one word.

I needed to get out of that forest (and my bed) and get started. As I switched on my light I heard Mum's footsteps coming down the hall. Then, she was in my actual room.

'Alberta!' Mum whispered, 'Please tell me you haven't stayed up all night?'

'I just woke up,' I said. 'I have to work on my speech. Anyway, why are you up?'

'Just not sleeping well these days,' she said. 'But I do have some good news. Come on. I'll make us both a cup of herbal tea.'

I followed Mum to the kitchen with my notebook and sat at the table while she put the kettle on. Fact was, Mum's idea of good news could mean anything. Her last good news announcement was Netflix wanting to make her book into a TV series. Was it possible *Tammy Bracken's Guide to Modern Manners* might also become a musical? I was already deep into imagining a chorus line of actors in cutlery outfits when finally, Mum joined me at the table with two mugs of chamomile tea. I looked at her expectedly.

'Well, after you'd gone to bed, I spoke to Mayor Pizzey again,' Mum said, 'and it turns he's agreed to postpone Paul Cromby and his men until the day *after* your forest concert.'

'For real? Oh my God!' I said. 'I can't wait to tell Mikki! How did you manage to turn him around?'

'Well... let's just say I reminded him of the upcoming council elections and how after the dreadful situation he caused with the *excrement* in the front beach car park—'

'The poo incident,' I interrupted.

Mum took a sip of tea. 'I simply pointed out to Mayor Pizzey that, under the *circumstances,* he needed all the community support he could muster right now. It certainly wasn't going to help him in the popularity stakes if he was *seen* to be cancelling an event that would bring together nearly the entire voting community of Kingfisher Bay.'

'Nice one, Mum!'

'Now, of course, he's organised for a journalist from the *Kingfisher Gazette* to be at the forest concert, as if the whole thing was his idea. I'm telling you that man hasn't got a bone of originality in his body!' Mum chuckled. 'But I can't take all the credit. Apparently Harriet had given him a good push too.'

I leaned over and gave Mum a kiss. 'Thanks so much, Mum!' I said, feeling the weight of my biggest worst-case scenario literally disappear. Throughout the conversation I felt there was a bigger conversation that needed to happen too. I had a question for Mum, though I knew she probably wouldn't answer it. In the end I just blurted it out anyway.

'Mum, are you going to let Dad come back home?'

'Alberta, it's not that simple, darling. There are things you don't understand.'

Boy did she have a point there! It took all my self-restraint not to blurt something out about the shoplifting issue.

'Well, are you?' I asked. 'People can change, Mum. Just look at Seth Cromby!'

'Don't get me started on that Seth Cromby!' she said, clunking her mug down on the table.

'Anyway, I've forgiven Seth for what he did and maybe you should forgive Dad too?' I suggested.

Mum got all jittery and couldn't look me in the eye.

'I mean, it's not just about you, Mum. There's me and Clementine too.'

Mum was quick to change the topic. 'The other thing I need to mention is that I'll be going to the city on the day of the concert. It's the only day I can shop for an outfit for my TED Talk and I've seen the perfect dress at David Jones. I need to try it on, but they said they'd only hold it for one day.'

I wondered why Mum couldn't find a dress here in Kingfisher Bay. I remembered the haul of clothing I'd found from Penelope's by the Sea. And all the other stores. Clearly, she hadn't shoplifted anything she liked enough yet! Or, maybe after talking with Dad she needed to avoid all the shops in town?

'You'll be back in time for the concert though, won't you?'

> **Tammy's Tips**
> #16 GOOD MANNERS MEANS
> ARRIVING ON TIME
> *Being late to a special event such as a ceremony, show or performance displays terrible manners and is disruptive to others. Always arrive fifteen minutes early to get settled before the event begins.*

'Of course, darling. It will just be a quick dash. I wouldn't miss your forest concert for the world. Especially after my conversation with Mayor Pizzey. I'm so proud of you kids for fighting for what you believe in. God knows us adults don't always set the best example.'

You can say that again, I thought.

'Oh, I gave the forest concert a plug on my Instagram too, not that it has much to do with good manners!' Mum laughed.

As it grew light outside I visited the fig tree in our yard. I was hoping it might help me find just the right words for my speech. I sat cross-legged at the base of the tree with my back against its trunk, my notebook, open to a blank page, nestled between my knees. As I breathed in and out I felt my mind clear. Slowly my thoughts turned to the best possible version of a speech. That's when a ripe purple fig fell right onto the middle of my page. I knew I was on the right track.

CHAPTER 42

Mikki's dad opened the door, which made me feel instantly awkward even though it was his house, so why shouldn't he open his own front door when somebody rang the bell? I guess I'd just assumed I'd get Mikki because he knew I was on my way over. But mostly I felt awkward because Mikki's dad was still in his pyjamas. For some reason, I didn't know where to look.

'You're up bright and early, Alberta,' he said cheerily.

'Oh, hi, Mr Watanabe,' I said. 'I hope I didn't wake you?'

'No, no,' he said. 'We're all up early around here.'

I started to kick off my shoes but Mikki's dad stopped me. 'Mikki's outside in the garage. Come, I'll show you,' he said.

I followed Mikki's dad back out the front door and down the path around the side of the house. 'Thanks for hiring the speakers for us, Mr Watanabe,' I said.

'My pleasure, Alberta. Let's just hope it all works. It's quite an ambitious event you two have planned.'

'Yes, quite,' I agreed. In the Watanabe's garage Mikki had all the components of the plant-music device spread over the ping pong table.

'Hey, Berts!' Mikki said. I could tell by the look he gave his dad that Mikki was embarrassed about the pyjamas too. 'So glad you're here. I'm busting to test the plant-music device.'

All I could see was a tangle of wires and leads and the event speakers that Mikki's dad had hired for us. Mikki's dad looked slightly concerned.

'All going okay, Mikki?' he asked.

'Great!' Mikki said. 'The device lets you choose from a bunch of sound settings. There's one hundred and twenty-eight instruments and a choice of scales too. Take a look.' Mikki scrolled through the instruments list on the plant-music device... *piano, harpsichord, glockenspiel, vibraphone, marimba, xylophone, tubular bells, church organ, accordion, harmonica, guitar, violin, viola, cello...*

'I don't get it,' I said. 'I thought the Memory Tree was going to play its own music?'

'It will,' Mikki said. 'Like Massimo said – the vibrational pulse is alive in the tree and the device detects that and feeds it through a synthesiser. It turns vibrations into musical sound.'

'Oh,' I said. I must have looked disappointed.

'So now we need to choose the type of instrument sound best suited to the Memory Tree... Let's just try a few and see, huh?'

'One hundred and twenty-eight instrument sounds?' Mikki's dad said. 'I might leave you to it.'

'Okay, Dad,' Mikki said.

'Thanks again for all your help, Mr Watanabe,' I said.

'My pleasure,' he said. 'I can't wait to see how it all goes on the night.'

'Sorry about my dad's PJs,' Mikki whispered once his dad was out of earshot.

Mikki and I took the device out to the back garden to find a suitable tree to test it with. There were so many trees to choose from, and not just Australian natives either. I immediately recognised an oak, an elm, a sycamore and a birch and there were more that I didn't know the names of too. Together the trees created a magical, shade-filled glade. All completely still. While Mikki was busy connecting all the wires to the plant-music device, I looked for a tree with low enough branches, one where we could reach some leaves without needing to climb.

'How 'bout this one?' I asked. 'I love the leaves. Each one is a red star.'

'It's called a liquidambar,' Mikki said. 'My mum's favourite tree too, but she said it shouldn't be turning red so early. It's not even autumn yet.'

'Same thing happened last year,' I said.

Mikki singled out the wire with the metal probe at the end and pushed the spike into the soil close to the base of the tree. Then he took the wire with the clamp on the end and attached it to one of the liquidambar's leaves. He turned on the plant-music device and... just like in my worst case scenario... *nothing happened!*

'Total nightmare,' I whispered.

'Have patience, Alberta!' Mikki said. 'This is what rehearsals are all about.'

Mikki checked the digital display on the plant-music device. 'Mmm... *Bad Contact,*' he read out loud. Mikki unclipped the wire and tried it with a different leaf, firstly wetting the leaf with a little saliva.

'What if the device says "bad contact" on the night?' I asked. 'We won't be able to do anything about it.'

But Mikki didn't respond, it was like he hadn't even heard me. I felt completely useless, especially as there were still so many other things to do. Not only that, I felt like all the questions I was asking would have been annoying. I felt like I'd become Clementine!

'Mikki, I'm not much help with the technical stuff. Maybe I'll keep working on my speech?' I asked. 'I've nearly nailed it but I need to get a print-out at the library. I could come back later, okay?'

'I think that's a good idea,' Mikki agreed, a little too enthusiastically.

Just then Seth appeared and Mikki explained the bad contact issue.

'It's no big deal,' Seth said. 'If it happens on the night I can be up that tree in no time at all.'

CHAPTER 43

Through the glass doors at the library I saw Clementine behind the front desk, busy covering a stack of books. Mrs Jefferson, the librarian, was in one of the aisles, helping someone find a book. Clementine looked surprised to see me. 'I thought you'd be at Mikki's?' she said. 'Did you get the plant-music device to work?'

'Not quite,' I said. Clementine looked concerned.

'Don't worry, Clemmy. Mikki will get it working soon enough.' I was trying to convince myself more than Clementine. I hoped like anything Mikki and Seth had it sorted.

'I have to finish these books,' she said. 'But Dad called before you left for Mikki's. He asked us to leave all the things we need for the forest concert in the front room. He wants to pack everything in the car after work tonight, so we're all set for tomorrow.'

It was hearing Clementine say 'tomorrow' that caused my nerves to amp up to the next level. I swallowed hard.

'Alberta, what's wrong? You look pale,' Clementine said.

'Just a bit of stage fright, I guess... I'll feel better once I've printed out my speech and rehearsed.'

Mrs Jefferson appeared at the desk. 'Hello, Alberta,' she said. 'We're all really looking forward to your little musical event tomorrow. A twilight concert. What a lovely idea.'

'Thanks, Mrs Jefferson,' I said. 'So glad you can come.'

'I'm not the only one,' she said. 'It seems like the whole town is coming... will your parents be there?'

'Sure will,' I said. 'Just wondering if there's a computer free. I still need to print my speech?'

'Oh, I can't *wait* to hear it,' Mrs Jefferson said. 'Take number five, Alberta.'

After I'd finished with the printing I logged onto YouTube to check on the registrations for the forest concert livestream. I sure didn't expect what I found. I almost fell off my chair when I saw there were eight thousand and twenty-three registrations! 'What!' I exclaimed out loud. Mrs Jefferson gave me a look. Ever since our last video where Seth had climbed the Memory Tree, subscriptions to our channel had definitely increased, but eight thousand and twenty-three registrations for the forest concert was next level nuts. Then I remembered how Mum had promoted the concert to all her good manners followers on Instagram. *Jeez, Mum*, I whispered to myself, scrolling through some of the comments.

Miss Prim 2 seconds ago
What a delightful idea! ♥

Astrofig 24 seconds ago
Simply cannot wait for this! I've set my alarm.

Yolanda 1 hour ago
See you in the forest guys!!! Love you, A-non-e-mous! ♥ 🌰

Van Van 1 hour ago
Seen all your vids so far. Wouldn't miss it for the world! 🌍 🌲 👏

Kamii Kaze 1 hour ago
A-non-e-mous for President!

My heart started pounding. Tomorrow. The forest concert really was tomorrow!

I decided to use my time at the library to write a new list. The one I'd started a couple of days ago had so much crossing out on it, and notes scrawled in between the lines, that it was no longer reliable as a list. I needed to have everything absolutely crystal-clear in my mind. Clementine would be set up on our camping table in the forest with the laptop. She would be in charge of the YouTube channel and video streaming while I hosted, the Memory Tree played its music and Mikki filmed.

I quickly scrawled, 'charge laptop' at the top of the list. Seth would be in charge of damage control if anything from the list of possible worst-case scenarios played out. He'd bring his climbing gear just in case he needed to scale the Memory Tree again. I figured that if we all just stuck to the tasks on our list surely everything would turn out right? From then on, I had only one thing in sight. We were going to save the forest, and of course, Mikki's sacred Memory Tree. It was at that exact moment I felt my phone vibrating in my pocket. It was Mikki. I ran out the front of the library to answer.

'Mikki?' I said. 'Hello?' But Mikki didn't answer. I was just about to end the call, thinking Mikki had accidentally made a pocket call. But I finally heard something on the other end. It was the deep chimes of ... music! Mikki had obviously got the plant-music device working!

'Mikki!' I screamed down the phone.

'It's the liquidambar tree, Alberta!'

'Aagh!' I squealed. 'I can't believe it!'

Later at home, when Dad pulled into the drive, both Clementine and I were still adding bits and pieces to the pile in the front room. We'd expected Mum to stay in her den like she usually did when Dad came around but this time she made a point of coming to the front door to greet him, although I can't say she was all that friendly. Mum told him about her trip to the city to shop for her TED Talk outfit.

'I'm sure you'll find something nice, love,' Dad said. 'And we'll all look forward to meeting you up in the forest when you get back.'

Clementine brought in some fold-up camping chairs from the garage. Then she ran and got her stilts and added them to the pile.

'Seriously?' I asked.

'Shut up, Birdy!' she answered. 'I need to practise on pine needles too.'

'Clementine!' I said. 'This isn't all about you!'

'Aw, come on, love,' Dad said. 'Let's just get this all packed in the car.'

'Be nice to your sister, Alberta,' Mum added. 'Remember what we said about kindness?'

I spent the rest of the night refining my speech and when I felt it was just right I called Mikki and read it to him.

'You've nailed it,' he said. 'It's so good. Will you be learning it off by heart?'

'No way, Mikki!' I said. 'I'll definitely be using my notes. I don't want to leave a single thing out.'

'Fair enough. Well... I'm still responding to all the comments on YouTube, so...'

'I guess I'll see you in the morning,' I said. 'Make sure you get some sleep too, Mikki!' I added.

'You too, Bertie,' Mikki said. 'We both need to be fresh like a forest!'

CHAPTER 44

Tomorrow came at last and Dad picked us up on his lunch break to take everything up to the forest. All the op shop blankets and cushions Dad and Clementine had bought were stacked neatly onto the front seat. The rest were in the boot. When we got to the Watanabe's, Mikki had everything neatly packed into four milk crates, apart from the two speaker boxes. Dad helped Mikki pack everything in the car.

'Are your parents home, Mikki?' Dad asked.

'No, Mr Bracken. They'll be back later,' Mikki replied. 'They're both looking forward to the concert more than anything.'

'That's great,' Dad said. 'We'll be sure to save your parents a picnic blanket right next to ours.'

On the way to the forest Dad asked about a million questions.

'So how many do you think will come?' he asked.

'According to the email RSVPs we have sixty-five people attending. Our Facebook page has seventy-seven with another one hundred and twenty-two people interested,' said Clementine.

'That's a huge response,' said Dad. 'You've got to be happy with that, huh?'

'Plus there's our YouTube live stream,' said Mikki. 'We've got nearly nine thousand registrations worldwide.'

'You don't say!' said Dad.

We had to make three trips from the car park and up to the pine forest and back in the heat, with all the gear. When Dad closed the boot of the car he had underarm sweat marks on his shirt.

'You kids got all you need?' he puffed. 'I've got an inspection in half an hour and I'm going to need a change of clothes!' Clementine and I nodded in agreement. Dad sure didn't look like someone you'd want to have showing you through a house.

'Thanks for your help, Mr Bracken,' Mikki said. 'We definitely couldn't have done this without you.'

Dad patted Mikki on the back. 'All in a day's work. Now you kids make sure you drink lots of water. It's sure looking like a hot one up here today.'

'We will,' I said. 'And thanks a bunch, Dad. We'll see you tonight!'

Clementine ran and wrapped herself around Dad's waist. 'You're the best, Dad!' she squeaked. 'Promise not to be late!'

'I won't,' he said, clicking himself into his seat.

'Oh...Dad!' Clementine shouted. 'Since you're all friendly with Mum again can you do some convincing about my party? Please?'

Dad laughed. 'I'll see what I can do, Clementine, but let's just enjoy tonight first, shall we?'

'And the fish finger hedgehog?' Clementine yelled after him.

The sun was directly overhead, flicking in and out with any small movements of the forest canopy. Soon there would be the long shadows of trees. The three of us got to work. It was like we all knew exactly what to do without even needing so speak. Clementine set up the camp table for a makeshift reception area, with the laptop down one end. She stacked all the rugs and cushions in neat piles ready to give to people when they arrived. We were all so focussed we didn't notice when Seth arrived.

'How many are you expecting?' He looked all fresh, like he'd just had a swim.

'Oh, hey, Seth,' said Clementine. 'We've had sixty-five actual RSVPs. But you never can tell with people.'

Mikki was over by the Memory Tree with the speakers and a crate full of wires. 'Hey, Seth!' he yelled.

'Hey, Mikki! Berts!' Seth said.

Berts now? I thought. Really?

'Seth, it's probably best to get the electrical wire up there straight away so we can clamp it on and make sure we get a good connection. Then we can do a proper sound check,' said Mikki.

Seth gave Mikki two thumbs up. I was looking everywhere for the print-out of my speech. I was sure it was in my pack, but I emptied it out and it wasn't there. Meanwhile, Clementine was trying to walk on her stilts, taking ridiculously high steps due to the thickness of the pine needles and tripping on the uneven ground. We were both growing more and more frustrated.

'Clemmy, did you see my speech anywhere?' I asked.

'How should I know where it is?' she yelled.

'Could it still be in your dad's car?' Mikki asked. That's when I remembered being squashed into the back seat with Mikki and Clementine. I had put the pages safely into the pocket behind Dad's seat. With all the trips between the car and the pine grove with our gear, I'd forgotten to take the speech back out again.

'Oh no!' I cried. 'You're right, Mikki. I left it in Dad's car!'

I tried calling Dad but his phone went to voicemail. By then, it was almost four o'clock. In just over two short hours everyone would be arriving.

'It's no big deal,' Clementine said. 'You know where it is and you can get it when Mum and Dad arrive. They said they'd come early, remember?'

She was right, of course.

Until Mum called. And as soon as she started speaking I could tell something was wrong. Her voice sounded so small and muffled that I could hardly hear her. At first I thought it was a bad connection but it wasn't that. It was because she was crying.

'Birdy,' she said. 'Birdy, promise me you'll keep this to yourself?'

I moved away from the others and literally hid behind a tree. 'What is it, Mum?'

'Shh!' she said. 'I don't want Clementine to hear.'

'Mum, where are you? What's wrong?'

'I need you to assure me that Clementine isn't listening. Please, Alberta.'

I moved even further away, right to the edge of the pines.

'I'm nowhere near Clementine. Mum, what's going on?'

Mum's voice dropped to an even lower hush. 'Birdy, I'm still in the city... I'm with the... I've been *apprehended*... by the... police.'

Now Mum was sobbing. I felt my stomach dropping like a stone, my heart pounding, my whole body prickling cold.

'I'm so sorry, Birdy.' Mum sobbed. 'I'm so ashamed... but you have to promise me you'll cover for me... make up a story for Clementine.'

For a moment I didn't understand. I hadn't said anything about Mum's shoplifting so far, so why would I start now? But more importantly, Mum was still a two-and-a-half hour drive away. She wasn't going to make it to the forest concert! My eyes filled with tears. Everything became real. Mum had finally been caught shoplifting, like I'd always feared she would. I just hadn't dreamed it would happen today.

'Mum!' I cried. 'Are they going to put you in jail?'

'No!' Mum sobbed.

'Why do you do this? You have to get help, Mum! You have to promise!'

'I will... I promise. Your father's on his way now.' Dad was hardly the help I had in mind!

'What? No! My speech... I left it in his car... I need Dad back here in time for the concert.'

'I'm sorry, Birdy,' Mum sobbed. 'I didn't know who else to call. He's the only one who knows, apart from you. And I would have called Aunt Robina but... oh God... she doesn't know either—'

'Why not?' I cried. 'You tell her absolutely everything else!'

'She's in Darwin anyway, Birdy! At her conference, remember?' Mum's voice was muffled. She must have put her hand over the phone, but I could still hear that she was crying. 'Birdy, please forgive me. I know I'm a terrible person. I'm the worst mother in the world... but promise me you won't say anything to Clementine!'

'I have to go, Mum,' I said and ended the call.

> ## 🌿 Tammy's Tips 🌿
> #17 CANCELLING A PLAN
> *If you need to cancel a plan, always give the person as much notice as possible. Be straightforward and honest. Don't over explain and, ideally, organise something in its place so that the person you are cancelling on understands that you really do value their company.*

I was so angry I had to stop myself from actually kicking a tree. Then I wanted to kick myself for even thinking that! All Mum cared about was protecting Clementine. What about me? In less than two hours I'd be going live with the forest concert to half of Kingfisher Bay and literally thousands of people on the live stream from all over the world. As if this wasn't enough pressure without losing my notes. Now I had to make up some lie for Clementine too. How was I meant to explain why *neither* of our flaky parents would be showing up to support us? A flock of raucous lorikeets burst from the foliage of a eucalypt at the edge of the pine grove. I watched as they clamoured above the treetops and faded into the sky. How easily they disappeared. If only I could too. Away from Clementine and Mikki and Seth, away from the forest concert and Kingfisher Bay and all the people who were about to show up, and away from the killers of beautiful trees, away from my mother's obsession with manners *and* shoplifting, away from the lies she expected me to tell.

'Alberta! Where *are* you?' It was Clementine. She had found me.

I raised my broken arm and wiped my tears on the fabric of my sling.

'Who were you talking to?' she asked.

'Just trying to find Dad,' I said. I knew I had to shape up fast... accept it, and ride it out. I had already made all those videos with Mikki, where I'd surprised myself with how much I'd learnt from all my reading about trees, and I hadn't needed any notes. Surely it would be the same for the forest concert?

'Forget about your dumb notes,' Clementine said. 'Anyway, Dad's gonna be here soon, so what's the problem?'

'You're right, Clementine,' I said, almost believing the lie myself. 'Let's go save a forest!'

CHAPTER 45

As twilight fell the pine forest filled with people. And even though there were so many more than expected there was a respectful hush in the air, kind of like at the library. Apart from Clementine, of course, who's voice could be heard across the forest as she insisted on greeting everyone from her stilts. People were nestled between the pines on colourful cushions and rugs and the whole scene was aglow with the light of paper solar lanterns that Seth had strung between the trees.

Bella and Sylvie arrived with Bella's mum. Sylvie gave me a huge hug. 'I can't believe it. It all looks so pretty!' she exclaimed.

'Thanks, Sylvie,' I said. 'I saved you a spot!' I pointed to a tartan blanket next to our green one up close to the Memory Tree. Bella's mum set down an esky filled with cool drinks and unpacked their picnic food. But I didn't have time to hang with them. I had to tell Clementine to get off her stilts and make sure the laptop was ready for the live stream. I also wanted to avoid anyone asking about Mum and Dad. Mikki was setting up his tripod in front of the Memory Tree, lining up the camera's viewfinder to where I'd soon be delivering my speech (gulp). That's when I saw Georgette in the audience, sitting with her parents, eating crackers and cheese. Pip and Harrison were there too, on a rug right next to Mayor Pizzey and family. Seth had already clasped the electrical wire from the plant-music device to the pine needles above, but was hovering close by, just in case he had to scoot up the tree to fix any connection issues.

'Hey, Birdy!' Clementine stomped towards me on her stilts. 'I've counted one hundred and thirty-seven people already... but where's Mum and Dad? They said they'd come early!'

'Clemmy, enough with the stilts already!' Clementine stepped down from her stilts and leant them against a tree. I woke the laptop and opened our page on YouTube. The live stream was scheduled to start in five minutes! But Clementine was more interested in our family's vacant picnic rug. 'You need to call them, Bertie!' she urged. I acted vague.

'They're probably here somewhere. Maybe just behind a tree.'

'That's rubbish, Alberta!' Clementine squealed. 'As if they wouldn't say hello!' I'd be upset if I were her too. At least I knew what was going on. Apart from telling her the truth, which was out of the question, or telling her an outright lie, which also didn't feel right, the only tactic I could think of was to distract her.

'Clemmy, look!' I said, pointing to YouTube on the laptop screen. 'Massimo's already here. Send him a wave!'

'I know what you're doing,' Clementine said. 'It's called gaslighting and it's very manipulative, Alberta!'

'Come on, now you've got yourself all worked up,' I said.

'See what I mean!' Clementine screamed.

Mikki gave me a signal to come over to the Memory Tree, where he was chatting with his parents. My cue to escape.

'Got to go now, Clementine,' I said. 'Wish me luck!'

'Fine!' Clementine said, grumpily.

Mikki's dad patted the Memory Tree. 'Oh yes,' he said. 'This one's a real beauty, Mikki. I can see how it makes you feel close to your grandfather.'

'Yes,' said Mikki. But he was distracted, and time was running out.

Soon Mikki's parents had set themselves up on the rug next to the empty one meant for Mum and Dad. Junko arranged delicious-looking snacks onto share plates.

'We thought your parents might be here by now?' Mikki's dad said. Junko must have read my embarrassed expression.

'We could really do with some help sharing our picnic,' she said cheerfully. 'There's enough here to feed an army!'

'Should be arriving any minute, Mr Watanabe,' I lied. Mikki's parents seemed to buy it.

※

It was time for the forest concert to formally begin. I stood in position in front of the Memory Tree, being careful not to step on any of the plant-music wires. Mikki handed me the microphone and turned on the speakers, ready to broadcast my words to the audience … and the world.

'Just switch it on here when you're ready,' Mikki whispered. 'Go for it, Alberta! You'll be great!'

I took one more desperate look in my sling for my speech notes, even though I knew the pages weren't there. When I took the microphone from Mikki I noticed my hand was shaking. I pulled a long slow breath in, inviting all the goodness of the forest into my being. I could feel the strong presence of the Memory Tree supporting me from behind. This would be no different from all the other times Mikki had filmed me speaking in front of the Memory Tree, I told myself. Just that I was in front of hundreds of eyes. I looked up to the forest canopy, at all the pines leaning in as if they were anticipating what I might say. Soon, I'd be speaking on behalf of every one of the pines, and for all trees. And in the history of my young life, I knew it was the most important conversation I'd would ever have. And when the Memory Tree took over, words wouldn't matter at all. I released a long breath. *Here we go,* I said, switching on the microphone.

The audience suddenly fell into silent anticipation. Mikki stepped aside from the tripod, his cue that he was all framed up and ready to go.

'And ... go,' he whispered.

A big breath, heart pounding ...

'Well, hello everyone, and for those who don't know me, I'm Alberta Bracken, one of the creators of this very special forest concert, along with Mikki Watanabe, behind the camera, Seth Cromby and my sister, Clementine Bracken.' Clementine was sitting with Harriet on the Pizzey's rug. When I looked at her, she gave me stink-eyes.

'So ... welcome to our concert and thank you so much for supporting us and, more importantly, these beautiful old trees. We'd like to acknowledge the traditional owners of this land. There were three groups living in this country and when miners from the Californian gold rushes in the early 1850s came to Australia in search of gold it was the kindness of these first people that guided them into this valley from the north. One of those gold prospectors was a man called Clive Fullerton. You can see what's left of old Clive's house over here. It's believed Clive brought with him seeds from the Monterey pine and created his own plantation in what has since become the Kingfisher National Park. These beautiful trees are now over one hundred and seventy years old.

'Over the summer, and especially since Mikki's grandfather passed away, we have learnt a lot about trees. Mikki's grandfather was a scientist in Japan and was involved in research about how trees can influence human wellbeing. In fact, throughout the entire history of human civilisation trees have played a significant role. Humans of all cultures have chosen trees to bear witness to births, deaths, wars, weddings, and all sorts of sacred rituals. This makes trees just as much a part of our ancestry as the humans that existed alongside them.

'Mikki calls this tree his "Memory Tree" because it reminds him of his beloved grandfather, all the special times they shared, and all the valuable things his grandfather taught him. Visiting this old tree has been a way for Mikki to continue his relationship with his grandfather, to honour him and now…to say goodbye.' I looked to Mikki and his family in front of me on their rug. Mikki had tears in his eyes. His mum and dad each gave me a subtle nod in approval of what I was saying.

'When Mikki's with the Memory Tree he feels the spirit of his grandfather living on. Not everyone has experienced the living essence of trees and I feel so fortunate that Mikki has passed on his grandfather's knowledge to me, the same knowledge we share with the world through our YouTube channel, *Mikki and Me and the Memory Tree*.' I noticed Mr Watanabe wiping tears from his face. But I kept on going.

'What I have learnt is that trees are a lot like humans. Trees live in communities, communicate with one another and defend one another's survival. What science now tells us is that humans, trees, animals, plants, insects, all living things, exist in the same unified field of electromagnetic vibration. Everything has its own unique life force, no matter what the species, or country of origin. Just like humans, every tree has the right to live its life... which reminds me of one of my favourite quotes. It's by an Irish botanist called Diana Beresford-Kroeger, from her book *The Global Forest*. Luckily, even though I've lost my notes, I know it off-by-heart. It goes like this...

'"No one species is better or worse than the other. They are equal to one another in a chain of connectivity. Each bee, each wolf has the right to dream or die, has the right to live a life, its own particular life, of wonder. And it has a right to that home until the end of time."' I felt my words gently land across the silence of the audience.

'As you know, this forest has been earmarked for removal by the council as these trees are not native to Australia. But they are a part of our history, they have existed for well over a century and we believe they have a right to live out their lives. We have spent a lot of time up here in this forest and we've grown to love it. To us, this is not just a bunch of trees but a community of beings.

'Tonight, this tree, the wise elder of this forest, the one we call the Memory Tree, will make its voice heard for the very first time. We hope you enjoy our forest concert – on behalf of all the pines in this forest, and for all trees.

'Thank you.'

Mikki disconnected my microphone from the speakers and plugged in the plant-music device. The display scene lit up saying... *Wait For Signal.* If the electrodes didn't pick up a signal from the pine needles then Seth would have to climb back up the tree. Mikki and I were glued to the display screen. Every second the display still read, *Wait For Signal* felt like an eternity.

Finally, it changed to, *Play Music*!

'Phew!' whispered Mikki.

'Phew!' whispered Seth. And we waited...

Suddenly, the silence of the forest was broken by a single deep tone, the unmistakable, breathy pipe sound of a church organ! There were actual gasps from the audience as The Memory Tree said, loud and clear... *I AM HERE!*

Then, silence. Terrible, deafening silence.

Mikki checked the plant-music display. 'Mikki, do you think that could be it?' I whispered, even though the screen still said, *Play Music.*

'Wait,' Mikki whispered. 'I read about this. There's a moment when the tree recognises itself making music. When it does, it apparently becomes more enthusiastic.'

'Come on, Memory Tree!' I whispered. 'Be enthusiastic!'

The Memory Tree answered with a cascade of sound, as loud and as grand as the old tree itself. Church organ tones hurtled down like water running off a cliff, then there were chimes, heavy and pounding like hammers. The forest boomed with sound, without any organised tune or melody, but with the might and force of thunder. Then, another silence before the tones could be heard again, this time floating and delicate like butterflies. In the audience I saw Mayor Pizzey, his face lit up in awe. Mrs Pizzey was in tears. I wished so much for Mum and Dad to be there.

People were lying on their backs, gazing to the tall tips of the trees swaying gently above. As if responding to the calmness of the night the Memory Tree had slowed itself down, now just emitting a series of sparse, low tones. The silence between the notes gradually grew longer as the forest sky became a dark inky blue. And then, in the midst of the silence, it was over. The plant-music display flashed, *Low Battery*. It was the perfect time to close.

The whole audience burst into applause. Mikki, Seth, Clementine and I formed a line in front of the Memory Tree and held hands. Everybody stood up, clapping and cheering as we prepared to take a bow, just like actors in a theatre. That's when I saw Seth's parents in the midst of the audience too, and Seth's dad making the loudest whistling noise of all with his fingers. We raised our arms to the real musician, the Memory Tree. I could feel all the trees in the forest cheering along. Bravo, Memory Tree. Bravo!

CHAPTER 46

Afterwards, the forest was alive with chatter and excitement as people packed up and got ready to leave before nightfall. Mayor Pizzey was the most excited of all, as he gathered us together for a photograph in front of the Memory Tree. Afterwards we saw him talking to the woman from the *Kingfisher Gazette*.

'I'd like to interview you two straight after,' she said to Mikki and me.

'Sure!' we both said in unison.

Meanwhile, without Mum and Dad to help, we had a lot of packing up to do. Clementine and I gathered all the blankets and cushions and folded them into neat piles. She definitely knew that I knew something she didn't know about Mum and Dad, but she'd given up asking and at least had the good sense not to cause a scene in front of Mikki's parents. Even Clementine seemed to appreciate the events in the forest that night were sacred to Mikki's family. After we'd finished with the rugs we gave Mikki and Seth a hand taking down the lanterns.

Then we sorted out all the sound equipment at the base of the Memory Tree. Mikki's parents helped too and kindly offered to drive us home – all while avoiding talk about our parents.

'Your grandfather would have been so proud,' Mikki's dad said.

'He is,' Mikki replied. 'The Memory Tree keeps telling me.'

Junko gave Mikki a long hug. 'It was the most perfect farewell,' she said.

Mikki's eyes welled with tears as he looked high into the branches of the Memory Tree to the darkness.

'Goodbye, dear Grandfather,' he whispered. And I almost cried myself. We both knew that next time we visited the forest there might be no pines here at all. It was a haunting, horrible reality.

That's until we saw Mayor Pizzey and Seth's dad having a discussion by the old fireplace. The journalist from the *Kingfisher Gazette* was hovering around them too. We needed Seth to go spy and find out what they were saying. But Mikki had another one of his ideas, and like all the others it involved me being centre stage. He picked up his camera and turned it on. Luckily for Mikki, this time I didn't argue. I was still buzzing with a sense of achievement, which made me feel extra brave.

'Go over and talk to them, Alberta,' Mikki said. 'Our subscribers are going to be wanting an answer!'

Before I knew it, I was interrupting Mayor Pizzey's conversation.

'Mayor Pizzey, Mr Cromby, you have to admit tonight's forest concert was a huge success. Do you really still plan to destroy all these beautiful trees? It's not every day a forest gets a standing ovation.'

'Well, Alberta,' Mayor Pizzey said, 'tonight certainly was a powerful display. I haven't seen the town so united since Kingfisher Bay beat the North Coast Wallabies in the 2012 Grand Final. There's a few people I need to consult, but for now... let's just say I'm now seriously reconsidering the whole thing.'

I almost screamed with excitement but Clementine beat me to it. Not because of what Mayor Pizzey had said – she wasn't even listening in to the conversation. But from out of the shadows, Clementine's voice was unmistakable.

'Oh my God!' she hollered.

It was Mum and Dad. They were walking towards us... holding hands!

'Where were you?' Clementine cried. 'You guys missed an actual miracle.'

Mum and Dad both looked to me as if I should be the one to come up with an answer. But I just bounced the look straight back at them.

'Yeah, guys... where were you?' I asked.

Mum's eyes were swollen and red. She sure looked like she'd been through an ordeal.

'It's a long story, girls,' Dad said. 'But let's just get packed up here first, huh? We can't wait to see the video back at home.'

'But where were you?' insisted Clementine. Surprise, surprise, she just wasn't going to let up.

'We're so sorry to have missed the show,' Mum said. 'How 'bout we pick up some ice cream on the way home?' Mum knew Clementine well enough to know a food bribe was her only ally right then.

'Yes! Can we get rocky road? Pleeeeeaaaaaase!' Clementine whined.

'Calm down, Clementine,' Mum said. 'If it means that much to you we can get rocky road.'

※

It was amazing to watch the video on TV later at home, even though I'd just lived through it all in real life. This time I didn't have anything to worry about, like nerves or potential worst-case scenarios. I was just one of the audience like everyone else. At the end, the part where Mikki and me and Clementine and Seth took a bow... I even cried. And there were more tears with the standing ovation.

Mum and Dad had tears in their eyes too.

'So proud of you, love,' Dad said.

'What about me?' Clementine protested.

'Clementine, don't be silly,' Mum said. 'We're proud of both of you.'

'Anyway, Mum,' Clementine said. 'You still haven't told us why you and Dad missed the concert!' Dad turned the TV off and I could tell that things were about to get serious. There were so many questions left unanswered, like what had happened with the police. Would Mum have to go to court? Would she still be doing her TED Talk? Did she have to give the outfit back? But I knew they wouldn't be revealing any of these things to Clementine. So I just had to play along.

'There's no point beating around the bush,' Dad said. 'You girls are more than aware of the...problems your mother and I have been dealing with.'

'You mean because of that Ursula Hoffman?' Clementine asked. Dad rolled his eyes.

'As I have already explained, Clementine, I made a terrible mistake, and I would appreciate you not bringing up the topic of Ursula Hoffman ever again!'

'Sor-ree!' Clementine said. 'No need to bite my head off!'

Mum took a deep breath. 'Look, it's not all Dad's fault. There's been a lot going on for me too and we're both sorry for the disruption that it's caused...you girls shouldn't have to worry yourselves about the chaotic lives of your parents.'

'We'd like to make things right,' Dad said. 'And, despite the mess we've made of late, your mother and I care very much how you girls feel...so we're asking you now, how do you feel about us trying to be a family again?'

'Like, you coming back home?' I asked.

'Exactly,' Dad said. 'Your mother has found it in her heart to forgive me—'

'I said I'd *try* to forgive you, Roger,' Mum corrected. 'I said I would *try*.'

Dad patted Mum's knee. 'That's good enough for me, love,' he said.

'Yay!' Clementine squealed. 'Does that mean I can have my slumber party? With a mashed potato and fish finger hedgehog?'

Oh, Clementine! I thought. When will you *ever* learn about timing?

I had lots of my own questions too. Mostly about Mum. But I had to accept that maybe I'd never get the answers. All I did know was it had been a huge day. I was so tired, and I couldn't wait to collapse in bed... but not before I logged onto YouTube. Can you believe Mikki had already posted the video of me talking with Mayor Pizzey? And there were literally thousands of comments. I almost fell asleep reading them!

GingerBiscuit 24 seconds ago
Can't believe you guys pulled this off!! 👏 🖤 🌲

TreeSong 26 seconds ago
What a feat! I cried when I heard Memory Tree sing. Can't stop watching the video. Love you guys soooo much!!! 🏠 🖤 🎵

Massimo Paolini 26 seconds ago
Tonight you make my heart break in two!! Please, you can keep the plant-music device. It makes me so happy to give this gift to you. Trees all over the world breathed a sigh of relief.

SunsetDaze 28 seconds ago
I can't believe the concert worked and you saved the trees. I want to make a forest concert too.

A-non-e-mous 30 seconds ago
It was such an awesome night in the forest but the best thing of all... looks like ol Mayor Pizzey completely caved!! Even Dad's changed his tune!! 'Scuse the pun, ha ha. LOL! 🏆 🍸 👋 👍 🌲 🎵

PeppermintGum 35 seconds ago
This is so awesome. Congratulations to all who helped out. Loved the stilt walking too!!!

CHAPTER 47

A text from Mikki woke me early the next morning.

 Have you seen the newspaper? It's official. We saved the forest, Alberta! Call me!

I jumped straight out of bed, ran to the letterbox in my pyjamas and brought the paper back inside. Mikki was right. There we were on the front page of the *Kingfisher Gazette*!

Twilight Forest Concert Leaves Audience Spellbound

Kingfisher Shire has revoked its decision to remove a historic grove of pine trees after a captivating live concert performance in the forest last night. The Twilight Forest Concert was the mastermind of eleven-year-old eco-activists Mikki Watanabe and Alberta Bracken.

'We wanted a peaceful protest,' Mr Watanabe said, 'where people could appreciate the true essence

of trees through a language we can all understand. Music.'

And understand they did. In front of over one hundred and thirty people and to an online live stream reaching thousands worldwide, the largest tree in the pine forest could be heard across the night, pulsing out its musical signals like an orchestral church organ... even if the pine's cultural heritage is slightly out of tune with the other native tree species in the Kingfisher National Park!

'We had so much support online,' Ms Bracken said. 'Including technological support from leading thinkers, scientists and musicians from across the globe...'

Mayor Pizzey from the Kingfisher Shire, who had given approval for the trees to be removed, said he was sceptical about the concert at first but promised his daughter he'd attend, just one day before the trees were to be cut down.

'I was completely blown away,' he said. 'To be honest I'd never thought that trees were... well, they're no different to people in the end, are they? Doesn't matter what country they're from. What I learnt from these kids is that trees are beings, and have a right to live.'

Mayor Pizzey said the decision to revoke the removal of the pine forest was a 'no brainer' after the concert. 'Not only that, we're hoping young Alberta and Mikki will assist the council in promoting forest bathing in the Kingfisher National Park and that the Twilight Forest

Concert can be a regular summer event. After the disappointing tourist season we've all had it could be just what we need to put Kingfisher Bay back on the map,' he said.

I called Mikki. He'd been on YouTube all morning.

'We need to go to the forest again to make a celebration video,' he said. 'The channel has gone completely nuts. Should we ask Clementine and Seth to come too?'

But Clementine didn't want to come to the forest. She had something of her own to celebrate. Dad was officially moving back in and she'd have him all to herself while Mum went to Sydney for her TED Talk. Don't get me wrong, I was feeling happy about being a family again too but... well... just not as excited as Clementine. I guess I was still worried about Mum and whether there'd be another phone call from the police. Before I left for the forest, when Mum was packing her bag for Sydney, I couldn't help bringing the whole shoplifting thing back up.

'Oh, Alberta, I don't know what got into me,' she said. 'Your father and I have been speaking to professionals and apparently it's not an uncommon reaction to grief... people do all sorts of irrational things... all that hoo-ha with your father... It's been a very stressful time, darling.'

'So does that mean you won't do it again? Is it something you can actually control?' I asked.

'Oh no, I've learnt a harsh lesson,' Mum reassured me. 'And I'm getting expert help too. I'm sure it's—'

''Cause I really don't want to have to visit you in jail.'

'God no!' Mum said, zipping up her carry-on. 'Oh, Alberta, I'm so ashamed. The whole thing is just a blur.'

'You should be ashamed, Mum,' I said with a deadpan face. 'Milky Bar is not even actual chocolate!'

We both laughed and Mum gave me big hug.

'So proud of you, my girl,' she said. 'Thank you for being so understanding and keeping it a secret from you know who,' she whispered.

'You mean the almost nine-year-old who's still carrying on about that slumber party?'

Mum laughed. 'Oh, Clementine can have her hideous slumber party if she must! And that dreadful fish finger hog of hers too!'

A car horn sounded outside.

'Got to fly, lovely!' Mum said. 'That'll be my cab.'

CHAPTER 48

At the end of the holidays Mikki and his family had to return to the city. On his last day in Kingfisher Bay I dropped all Mikki's books back and we went up to the forest on Mikki's electric bike, one last time. Saying goodbye to Mikki was harder than I'd thought it would be. Considering we hadn't even really been friends before the summer we'd done so much together. We were a team. We not only saved the pine trees but we now shared a thriving YouTube channel as well. It felt like such a harsh ending but I just couldn't see how we could keep it all going with Mikki at school in the city. How would we ever be able to make videos?

'We can still shoot on weekends,' Mikki said. 'And school holidays. Maybe in the winter we could even try our luck on the whale boat?' That idea sure made me feel a lot better.

'Whale videos would be super cool!' I said.

'Sure would,' Mikki said.

When we got home from the forest I said goodbye to Mikki's mum too. She was in the kitchen clearing out their fridge. 'It must almost be time for that plaster to come off, Alberta?' she asked.

'It is. Actually, Mum's taking me to the hospital later today,' I said.

'You won't know yourself with your two arms back in action!' Junko said. 'But look at all you've achieved with just one!'

'Thanks, Junko,' I said. 'I guess I'll see you when you're back down.'

She laughed. 'Next weekend then!'

When Mikki walked me to the front door I noticed the cabinet in the lounge room, the one with the photos and the offerings and I wondered how Mikki was feeling about his grandfather. He must have noticed me looking.

'You know, Alberta, saving the Memory Tree really did help me say goodbye,' he said.

'So glad it worked out,' I said.

'Wanna borrow my bike now that you're getting your plaster off? I can give you a key to the garage.'

'Oh my God, Mikki. That would be the best thing ever!' I gave Mikki a big hug.

'As long as I can use it on weekends!' Mikki laughed.

※

Driving to the Regional Base Hospital with Mum was so much better the second time around. For a start I didn't have a freshly broken arm and Mum wasn't acting all weird and not taking Dad's calls and not telling me why. Nurse Margaret was still there on the desk though and she hadn't gotten any friendlier either. I was so excited to get my cast off. I couldn't believe I'd be able to go boogie boarding again. Not only that, I'd be riding to the beach on Mikki's electric bike!

Dr Melendez cut off my plaster with a tiny power saw. At first I was worried he would cut into my skin but the whole thing was finished in no time. Dr Melendez prised the cast open.

'There we go!' he said. 'It's as good as new!' But I wasn't so sure. My skin had turned white and was super hairy. Not only that... my arm smelt like some kind of cheese. Dr Melendez must have seen the total *yuck* look on my face. Or maybe he could smell my arm too. Even Mum winced.

'Nothing that a bit of a wash and some sunshine won't fix,' he said. 'Now off you go and enjoy the rest of the summer!'

CHAPTER 49

Clementine really pushed the envelope with her party plans. It must have been the burst of confidence she'd found after the success of the forest concert. And suddenly everyone wanted to be her friend again. Mine too. It's amazing how popular you become when you get your photo in the paper with an out-of-tune tree!

When Clementine showed me the invitations for her Bad Manners Slumber Party I really thought they would push Mum over the edge. But I was wrong. Ever since getting back from her TED Talk in Sydney, Mum was a different person. Or maybe it was the couples therapy? Or Dad coming back? Or *Tammy Bracken's Guide to Modern Manners* being made into a TV series? Or maybe it was all these things happening at once?

Fact was, on the day of Clementine's Bad Manners Slumber Party, Mum just let it all flow...just like tomato sauce down a mashed potato hedgehog's back!

Dad had scooped hot mash onto a huge white platter and put it on the middle of the table. He used a spatula to sculpt the mash into the shape of a large round hedgehog's body. Then he splodged on a smaller pile of mash for the head while Clementine and her friends watched on in awe.

'Now for his eyes!' Clementine said. Mum passed her the bowl of green peas she'd prepared and Clementine poked two of the largest ones onto each side of the hedgehog's face.

'The nose!' everyone said at once. 'Dad? What did you do with the burnt toast?' Clementine asked. 'Something I prepared earlier,' she explained to her captive audience.

'Right here,' said Dad. Dad used the spatula to make the hedgehog's nose area slightly more pointed, then Harriet pressed a round of burnt toast onto the end for a nose. Clementine squealed with delight.

Mum opened the oven where a forty-pack of fish fingers were heating on a tray. She prodded one with a fork. 'These are done,' she said.

'Ooooh!' Clementine's friends gasped as Mum put the oven tray onto a wooden board on the table in front of them.

'Now we can all help make spikes!' Clementine cried gleefully. 'Like this!'

She picked up one of the fish fingers and pushed it half into the mash, angling it carefully toward the back. Daisy put hers in next, close to Clementine's.

'Everyone can have a turn!' Clementine said, poking in another, and another. Soon all the girls were reaching and poking and licking their fingers, covering the hedgehog's back with fish finger spines in no time.

'Who wants to do the sauce?' Clementine asked.

'Me!' I said. Clementine looked slightly annoyed, like I wasn't an actual friend so I shouldn't be snapping up her party jobs. Really? After making her local marketing coordinator for a whole forest concert? She and I both knew that I had *earned* Queen of Sauce.

'Here, love,' Dad said, passing me a new squeezy bottle of tomato sauce.

I oozed the tomato sauce all over the hedgehog's back, trying to distribute it as evenly as I could.

'That'll do, Berts,' said Clementine. She stood back to assess the scene.

'He's perfect!' Clementine whispered.

The fish finger hedgehog really looked a treat, even though it was also quite disgusting.

'Quick, someone get a photo!' Harriet shrieked.

'He is quite cute,' Mum said, sparking up her phone.

'Ready, guys?' Clementine said, clapping her hands. 'Tuck in!'

Watching Clementine's friends devour a mashed potato hedgehog with fish fingers for spikes, peas for eyes, a burnt toast nose and all smothered in tomato sauce was quite something. They took to it like vultures, scooping up the mash with the fish fingers, stuffing it in their mouths, licking the sauce off their hands.

And nothing made Clementine happier than when they all sang happy birthday with their mouths full, spitting morsels of fish fingers across the table. They were in bad-manners heaven!

Mum got an absolute winner photo of Clementine, grinning from ear to ear with her mouth full, a saucy fish finger in one hand, in the other, a greasy-fingered glass of lemonade. It was literally only a matter of minutes before it turned up on Mum's Instagram, right next to all her photos from Sydney. And then there was the caption... *When it comes to modern manners, it's important to have the odd exception to the rules!*

Tammy's Tips
#18 MANNERS ARE NOT EVERYTHING
While good manners are necessary and desirable, they are not the be-all and end-all of social interactions. Always judge a person by the love they have in their hearts, and not by the manners they may or may not have had the privilege to learn.

All those days riding to the forest on the back of Mikki's electric bike, I'd also imagined myself gliding to the beach with my boogie board. And suddenly, there I was, with my newly-healed (still pale and hairy) arm doing just that.

To the sound of the familiar hum of the motor, I literally buzzed straight past the place where I had fallen all those weeks ago. But seeing Sylvie and Georgette's bikes locked to each other in the bike shed (and Seth's bike thrown on the ground), it felt like no time had passed at all. I stood at the top of the stairs with my boogie board and everything I'd need for a bumper day at the beach with my friends. The salty north wind whipped hair across my face. I could see Bella in the water, out the back, waiting for the perfect set to roll in. Harrison and Seth were there too. The sun, visibly climbing a cloudless sky promised a scorching day ahead. I thought about the forest and the remembered cool shade of the pine grove. But not for too long. It was time for me to take a break in my conversation with trees. I was ready for a long overdue talk...with the ocean.

ACKNOWLEDGEMENTS

Thank you to all at Allen & Unwin – to Jodie Webster for believing in this story, Sophie Splatt for her expert editorial support, Debra Billson for her dreamy cover design and Mika Tabata for her helpful feedback. I'd also like to acknowledge my dear friend Simeon Ayres, who recommended Stephen Harrod Buhner's compelling work, *Plant Intelligence and the Imaginal Realm*. This book inspired many conversations with trees and was an early spark to creating this story. I further acknowledge the work of Professor Yoshifumi Miyazaki, Suzanne Simard, Diana Beresford-Kroeger and the Damanhur Foundation for their collective influence and contribution to this work of fiction.

ABOUT THE AUTHOR

Marion Roberts always wanted to be a fashion designer, but she studied science, alternative medicine and psychotherapy instead. She worked as a naturopath and also a chef, as well as teaching people to cook. Marion started writing because she wanted a job she could do in her pyjamas. Also, her friends kept saying her emails were too long, and she needed to find another place to put her stories. She was born in Melbourne, which has always been her home town.